dangerous conversation

PAUL BOLAND

Pittsburgh, PA

ISBN 1-56315-226-6

Paperback Fiction
©Copyright 2001 Paul Shandlay
All rights reserved
First Printing—2001
Library of Congress #00-106123

Request for information should be addressed to:

SterlingHouse Publisher, Inc.
The Sterling Building
440 Friday Road
Pittsburgh, PA 15209
www.sterlinghousepublisher.com

Cover design: Michelle S. Lenkner—SterlingHouse Publisher
Page Design: Bernadette Kazmarski

All rights reserved. No part of this publication may be reproduced, stored in a retrieval system, or transmitted in any form or by any means—electronic, mechanical, photocopy, recording or any other, except for brief quotations in printed reviews—without prior permission of the publisher.

This is a work of fiction. Names, characters, places and incidents either are the product of the author's imagination or are used fictitiously. Any resemblance to actual events or persons, living or dead, is entirely coincidental.

Printed in the United States of America

For Sergeant Joe

acknowledgements

Special Thanks to:

My wife and sons for their patience.

Keith E., Dave, Steve, Howie, Eddie, Ira, Steph, and Andrea for their editorial and legal advice.

chapter 1

Some said he specialized in death. Others said he was a patriot. But Danny Sullivan didn't care much what people said. His time on the earth was limited.

Sullivan sat on the business end of the convict/visitor plexi-glass divider, playing with a lit cigarette with his nimble, bony fingers. The once burly Irishman had been reduced by his incarceration. Now thin and skeletal, his sunken eyes and dirty, matted shoulder-length hair gave him the appearance of something not quite alive. But to stare into those eyes, into the blue of insanity, was unnerving even for the most experienced death row guard.

The cigarette danced between his fingers like a twirler's baton. Cuffed, bound at the hands and ankles, he was far from home, far from Ireland. Convicted of something he had done dozens of times. Only this time he had been caught.

Youngman, his lawyer, entered the room abruptly and threw his briefcase on the table on the good-guy side of the glass.

"You look like someone pissed in your coffee," Danny said from behind the divider.

"You sure can turn a phrase, Sullivan," Youngman said.

"Comes from all the time on my hands."

"Well, in case you were too busy thinking up new witty retorts, you may have missed this." Youngman pulled a copy of the *Philadelphia Inquirer* out of his briefcase and pressed it up against the glass. "Your friends are up to their old tricks again."

The headline read: "IRA BLAST KILLS 4 IN LONDON". The Irish republican Army had renewed aggressions.

"I read the paper," Sullivan responded matter of factly.

"This won't help us, Danny."

"Like anything would!" he said, raising his voice and slamming his fist against the plastic.

Youngman walked away from his side of the table and began to pace the gray cinder block room. Sullivan's antics, playing the tough guy.

The tension between the two men had come to a head over the last few days. After ten years on death row, convicted cop killer Danny Sullivan had days to live.

Youngman sat back down and stared at Sullivan. The blue prison shirt hung off him. Sullivan weighed thirty pounds less than when Youngman first met him, the same thirty that Youngman himself had gained. But the eyes were still there. The eyes of a madman. A mad dog, as the British had called him: "Mad Dog" Sullivan.

"Listen Danny, we still have over a week. It doesn't look good, but stranger things have happened."

"Name one," the convict asked.

"How about a wrestler being elected governor?"

That seemed to break the mood. Danny smiled slightly, enough to expose some of his tar stained, jack-o'-lantern dental work. He smoked way too much. No matter.

"All I was saying is that this attack could not have come at a worse time for you. Any sympathy we had has gone right out the window," Youngman reasoned.

Danny sat silently, mulling over the actions of his former compatriots and the impact of those actions on his attempt to cheat Pennsylvania's electric chair. He still believed that they would get him out. He knew too much. He knew where the bodies were buried.

Youngman took his suit jacket off, showing off his starched white shirt and colorful suspenders. The first real spring day of May and the room was warm. He ran his fingers through what was left of his hair and slumped back into his chair. He didn't like what Danny had done, but it wasn't his job to like it. It was his job to keep his client alive.

He stared across the room at Danny who had become pre-occupied with a spot on his shirt. Their lives had been intertwined for so long now, but he still had no idea what made "Mad Dog" tick. Or more importantly what ticked him off.

The two sat in silence for a few minutes. Their time together was filled with long pauses, each man contemplating how to get out.

"I knew it wouldn't last, ya know, that sham of a cease-fire. Wouldn't last I said," Danny answered no one in particular.

"That aside, we need a way to diffuse this somehow. We have to do something, maybe a statement from you condemning the bombing? Could show you're a changed man, softened just a bit."

Danny's face turned red for an instant and Youngman wished he hadn't used the word "soft," but this was not a court of law and he could not withdraw the statement. Danny had had his chance to sell out his friends years ago to the American Justice Department, but refused. For the right information he could skip the shock therapy and live out his days in a 4 x 4 cell. But now, so many years later, could that information save him?

Sullivan leaned forward in his chair and Youngman expected him to ooze through the glass and grab him around the neck for having made such a suggestion.

"Let me think about it." Danny's words were cool and calm.

"Good. At least give it some thought. But do me a favor, make up your mind quickly. Any reaction from you should come right away so it doesn't look calculated."

"Even though it is?" he shook his head. He didn't understand lawyers.

Youngman smiled as he put his jacket back on. He admired Danny in a strange way, giving his life to a cause while he himself was a mercenary. Such passion. And a temper.

"I've got to run. I'll be back. Think about it, okay?" Youngman said as he picked up his briefcase. Then he noticed Danny was looking down at his shirt, mumbling.

"What was that, Danny?"

"Oh, uh, Theresa. Today's her birthday. I was just singing 'Happy Birthday' to her. She would have been twenty-eight, or is it twenty-nine. Lost count. Imagine that, my little sister almost thirty."

Youngman stood motionless.

"Maybe that's what I get. That's my punishment."

Danny lifted his head, "What would you have done if your sister was killed by a drunk driver?" Danny said in an even tone.

Youngman paused. Technically, Danny hadn't known that the driver of the car that had killed his sister was drunk. He hadn't known he was drunk or a cop when he snuck into the country, tracked the man down, and beat him to death with a baseball bat.

"I have to go, Danny. I'll be back this afternoon." Youngman turned and left.

chapter 2

The trick was to not let on that you were listening. Keith folded the newspaper onto his lap and closed his eyes. He felt the breast pocket of his suit for the tape recorder.

The PATH train was crowded and noisy. Friday rush hour home, underground from downtown New York City to Hoboken, New Jersey. It was the main transport for Wall Street types who lived on the other side of the river.

The two young men in front of Keith kept their voices low, but just loud enough for him and the tape recorder to pick up every word.

"I could never work for a woman, I'll tell you that much," the blonde haired man said to his traveling partner.

"I know what you mean, man. They're impossible to deal with. Hormones raging all the time," replied the dark haired man, to the knowing nod of his friend.

"Oh, and they're all victims. Always quick to point out how hard it is for them to get ahead. Glass ceilings and all. Like it's easier because we're men."

"I am with you, my friend. I interned over at Swanson my senior year and worked for this dragon lady. She must have been jealous of me or something because she was always on me."

"I know. Now take my sister. She gets married, stops working, has three kids. Like that isn't enough, right? She isn't itching to get back to work. What a life, huh?"

"Enough said."

"Enough said is right. I don't know what some women are thinking."

Keith zoned out as the two went on and on. One thought went through his head: as bad as these guys sounded, they were the type of guys who always got the girl, always dated the cheerleader. These were the guys he lost to. These were the type of guys he had lost Shannon to.

The subway train slowed as it entered the Hoboken station, pitching and screeching as it turned the last corner. Keith opened his eyes as the bustle of commuters standing and jockeying for position at the doors drowned out the end of the "enlightened" male workshop. He sat while others rushed. The train stopped and emptied. The race was back on.

Keith left last, walking slowly. The car doors closed behind him and the bell went off and the train went on its way to Jersey City. He walked up the station stairs to a landing and then up another set to street level where he found the bustle.

Hoboken was a party town, a stop between college and adulthood. The bars near the PATH station all had lines outside them; the sidewalks were teeming with commuters heading home. There was a buzz. Spring was breaking through. All this in one square mile. If New York was the city that didn't sleep, Hoboken only took short naps.

Keith made his way up Washington Street, the main drag that ran the length of Hoboken. He passed storefront after storefront: pizza place, dry cleaner, bar, then repeat. Cars were double-parked without regard to consequences. The sidewalk was packed with pedestrians. Joggers weaved through it all.

And there Keith was, just another fish in a sea of spiffy business attire.

Six blocks later he was in his apartment. The one bedroom dwelling above the frozen yogurt shop wasn't very big; small bedroom, small kitchen, small bathroom. Large rent. But that is what you paid for the convenience of Washington Street.

He undressed quickly, shedding his three-piece suit onto the old, worn hardwood floor. He stood in front of the full-length mirror that was crudely nailed to the back of his bedroom door. The beer gut had vanished from his six-foot frame. The workouts had paid off. He was starting to get the muscle tone that he had only read about or seen on TV.

He looked over his dark brown hair that was getting a little long and ratty for an accountant. "So what?" he said to the reflection. He flexed his bicep and laughed at the result. He dropped to the floor and did fifty, clap in the middle, pushups.

He changed into shorts and a Penn State sweatshirt, then took two short steps out the bedroom door and into the kitchen. He grabbed a beer out of his refrigerator that contained little else. His reward for a long week.

Four more short steps and he was in the living room. He popped a Counting Crows CD into his boom box and was careful to play it at a reasonable level. The walls were thin and the neighbors were cranky.

Keith sat at his desk, which also served as a dining room table, and turned his computer on. The desk and small bookcase were flush against the far wall and were blonde wood, "assemble it yourself," Scandinavian specials. The desk was cluttered with mail, framed pictures, and assorted yet-to-be-filed papers. In contrast, the bookcase was neat and organized, the only clutter a Penn State baseball cap on the bottom shelf with several years of beach tags pinned to it.

He picked up the tape recorder and pressed *rewind* as he logged onto his e-mail. The mini-recorder rested on top of his unfinished résumé. Keith had mail, so said the cheerful voice. Two items, he recognized both senders. He clicked on the first one:

> *Keith, it's your mom. Wanted to check on your progress with the job search. You only have a few weeks left. I think you may want to reconsider*

the move to Dallas. It's such a good company and I am very nervous about this writing thing. Love you.

Keith smiled. She would not give up. But there was no way he was moving with his company to Dallas. And he was going to give his writing thing a try.

Keith had joked with friends that his life had become a country and western song: lost his job, lost his girl, car got stolen, dog died. A year-long parade of silver lining-less clouds. Sometimes you had to make your own silver linings. He had always done the safe thing. Went to a good solid, state school, chose a safe business major, took a stuffy, safe job out of college, paid off his loans and helped his brother and sister through college. None of it was what he had wanted. So, he would do the "writing thing." And the first step was not relocating with his firm to Dallas.

He clicked on the second message. It simply read: "7 days to go." The message had been the same from Dave for the last 231 days. It was seven days until he and his friends from Philadelphia took possession of their summer house in South Jersey. Seven days to Memorial Day weekend. That was something to look forward to.

There was no third message to click on, though he had hoped there would be one. He had hoped everyday for the last year that there would be something. He had not heard from Shannon since the night he had walked in on her and another man doing naked gymnastics. He had hoped for an apology, an explanation, a promise that it would never happen again, a reconciliation. None of them ever came.

He sipped his beer and realized how pathetic he had become when it came to her. *Enough*, he thought.

He clicked off-line and opened a word processing program. He took the recorder, set it upright, and hit *play*. He slowly and methodically transcribed the conversation of the young, closed-minded yuppies. It was a sometimes painful process as Keith's typing was of the "hunt and peck" school of training. He hit *stop, rewind,* and *play* on the recorder over and over again to catch up with the dialogue. The CD repeated as he tap-tapped the ten minute conversation. It took him well over an hour.

Now for the fun part. At the top of the page he typed:

> *I was riding the train home the other day contemplating my inability to find a soul mate, a person to be one with. It's tough because I really like women. I was raised by one and have the utmost respect for them. And they smell nice. But somehow my appreciation for the opposite sex does not translate, something is lost. This is then compounded by the lack of respect for women that members of my gender exhibit. And the kicker is the attraction that women seem to have toward men who do not respect them. I heard this conversation on the way home tonight. I am sure these guys will get the girl.*

Keith read it over. It was not perfect, it never was the first time and he would give it some more thought. He would add a closing later. A nice little package. He had a drawer full of them; statement, conversation, closing.

He saved the file and turned the computer off. He went to the kitchen and got another beer. Keith came back to the window in the living room that looked out over Washington Street. The sun was gone, but that only seemed to increase the activity down on the street.

Keith watched a group of four bar-goers across the street in front of Ray's Pizza Parlor. The two girls were both blonde, one in jeans and the other in a skirt. They had no distinguishable flaws. They were talking to two guys, both in suits. Keith recognized one of the girls from his gym. She was not hard to pick out of a crowd even three stories up. Keith had smiled politely at her on a few occasions at the check-in desk, but had never gotten the nerve up to talk to her. He didn't recognize the other girl, but from a distance she looked to be as beautiful as her friend.

The four talked and then seemed to agree on something or someplace to go. As they crossed the street toward him he caught the faces of the two guys in suits. He recognized them from the train. He couldn't believe it.

"Figures," he muttered.

chapter 3

Mr. Jones had held almost every major position in a retail organization over his thirty years in the business, with the exception of Human Resources.

"Jerry, you're fired. Now, get out of my office," Jones said coldly.

The mail room worker sat in a stunned silence. He had thought the chairman, for whom he had worked twenty years for, had called him into his office to thank him for sending out the form letters without being asked.

Jones got up from his chair and stood behind his desk. Tall and thin, well dressed, the only sign of the stress of running a $20 billion dollar retail empire were the wrinkles that dominated the sixty-year-old's eyes. Those stress scars added ten years to his appearance. "Well, get out."

The man skulked out of the office not knowing what else to do.

Jones punched a button on his huge phone pad. "Send Tarman in."

Seconds later Rick Tarman, Jones' director of special projects, was standing at attention in front of the large desk. Tarman's stance and posture, coupled with his high and tight hairstyle, betrayed his military background.

"Do you think I was too hard on him?" asked Jones.

"Well, every time this issue comes up we send out the form letter to the buyer level and above in all divisions asking them to support the company. Jerry realized that the Senate vote was coming up and sent the letter out. He was being pro-active. Yes, I think it may have been too harsh, to answer your question," Tarman said.

"Well, I don't care what you think on this one. I am too damn smart to have people anticipate what I want them to do," Jones replied, eyeing his subordinate.

"Yes, sir." Tarman stood even straighter, if that was possible. He faced the CEO, and despite the fact that the two men were roughly the same height and weight, Jones seemed to be bigger.

"This is a much too important time to have these kinds of things happen," he said.

"Yes, sir."

"How many letters actually got out?"

Tarman took a breath. This type of form letter was sent out by the management of many major companies that did business with China. A simple form letter for employees to sign and address to their senator asking their representative to vote for renewing China's Most Favored Nation status. "Only the Pittsburgh division received them, but the mail room did not distribute them."

"Good. It could have been worse." National Merchandising had fourteen divisions that operated in 42 states. It was the largest department store chain in the world with over 500 stores. Jones had fought internal and external threats for the better part of his twenty years as CEO. But his toughest challenge was ahead.

Jones opened a desk drawer and pulled out a manila folder. "How are things going with 'Irish Stew?'" Jones liked code names for his special projects.

"As planned. It will be taken care of this week. The final resources hit the country today," Tarman said.

"Good. It better go smooth. Not like the Jorgensen fiasco," Jones warned.

Tarman had a flash of Stanley Jorgensen, the man that held that very office before Jones. He had been killed in a botched robbery attempt years ago. "I will see to it."

"I expect you will. I have worked too damn hard to make this business profitable to have some tree huggers tear it down."

"Yes, sir." Tarman sensed the conversation was over and left the room.

Jones had worked hard and had done many things that weren't published in the annual report. He was embarking on another.

… # chapter 4

He was a ghost, a name after all these years, just a name. Fifteen years of stories told and re-told, exaggerated to the point where they did not come close to reflecting reality. He was a legend, a faceless figment of street myth. Tommy Fortune of Hell's Kitchen.

But this myth was making a comeback.

A nondescript rental car pulled up in front of O'Donnell's on 40th. It was 3:00 A.M. and the bar had been closed for the night, as he had instructed. It was as dark as Manhattan gets, even the street lights were out.

Two men emerged from the car and casually walked to the front door of the bar. The driver walked with a slight limp, his red hair bobbing up and down with each step. He carried a duffel bag. The passenger adjusted the bill of his baseball cap further down over his eyes, as if anyone could see his face in the darkness.

The man with red hair unlocked the door, and the men entered. He locked it behind them. He walked directly toward a door to the back of the room while the man with the cap foraged behind the bar, looking for a beer.

"We got plenty in the back, Sean," the red haired man quipped.

"Sure, Tommy."

The two entered the room and Tommy flipped the light switch. Sean settled into a wooden chair, leaned back and put his feet up on the large, round oak table that dominated the space. The room had a 1970's finished basement feel with dark paneling, shag carpet, acoustic tile ceiling and fluorescent lights.

"Nice place you got here, mate," Sean announced. Traces of his Gaelic accent came through in his speech, despite his best efforts.

Tommy looked around the room. It had changed since the last time he had used it years ago. There now was a small refrigerator, a sink, and some cabinets that passed for a small kitchen. The carpet had been replaced but was dirty and worn nonetheless. The table and chairs almost matched.

Tommy pulled two beers from the fridge and went to the table. He handed Sean a beer and put the duffel bag down on the table.

"So, how did you end up owning a bar?" Sean asked as the bottle top came off.

"I own several business like this. Some not like this one at all. All legitimate," Tommy responded.

"No shit. How did a skinny punk from Belfast become Donald Trump?"

Tommy sat down across the table from Sean and opened his beer. "Well I was in this gang, I guess you would call it. We were called the Westies."

"I heard of them. Didn't they used to cut up the people they killed? That's sick," Sean added.

As opposed to blowing them to bits, Tommy thought, and he let that slide. "That was our trademark, unfortunately. Anyway, we were into everything in this part of New York. The unions, numbers, you name it. We brought in money hand over fist. Then things fell apart."

"What happened?" Sean was curious.

"What always happens with crooks. People get too much of everything; booze, women, money. Plus, the FBI got curious when torsos started washing up from the East River. That started the downfall, but I guess everyone had their own story."

"What was yours?"

"I saved every penny, stayed off the drugs, and tried to build connections. I knew it wouldn't last forever."

"You were always the smart one," Sean admitted.

Tommy stared across the table at his old friend. Was *friend* the right word?

"Enough about me. Let's drink to Danny Sullivan. The nastiest man alive," Tommy raised his bottle. Sean did the same.

"To Mad Dog!" Sean shouted.

After the toast, the two men sat silently, reflecting on the fate of their countrymen.

Tommy broke the silence. "So, I guess you're wondering why I went to all this trouble to get you into the States?"

"Well, actually, I was interested in why you changed your name. Tommy Fortune is a long way from Patty O'Brien."

Tommy smiled and rubbed his bad leg. "Well, when I came to the States I wanted to stand out, make a name for myself. Things didn't work out at home with the army, but that was Patty O'Brien. I wanted a new start, new name, new everything. I needed to put Ireland behind me. So, I changed my name." Tommy paused, "Plus, in Hell's Kitchen you can't swing a dead cat without hitting a Patrick O'Brien."

Sean let out a hearty laugh, spitting some beer out his nose and mouth as he did. He took his baseball cap off, releasing his thick, blonde hair. He used the hat to clean up the spill, then put it back on.

"So, you just became Tommy Fortune, just like that?"

"Just like that," Tommy said with a grin.

"What a country."

Tommy got up and went to the fridge. He got another beer and walked it over to Sean.

"Well, now that you mention it, what am I doing here?" Sean asked.

Tommy considered the question carefully.

At fifteen, Patrick O'Brien was an IRA gopher. He was young and was a true believer in the cause: freeing Northern Ireland by any means necessary.

Tommy did odd jobs for the real IRA members, like an apprenticeship. But that was not enough action for the young wanna-be. Tommy filled his vacant hours with petty theft and late night drinking. After stealing and damaging a car that happened to belong to an IRA soldier, Tommy and his friends were about to learn a hard life lesson.

In the dead of night they were taken from their beds by masked men, driven to an abandoned warehouse and shot in the leg. The other two boys got away with clean wounds. The bullet in Tommy's leg struck bone and shattered his leg above the knee.

Six months of rehabilitation later, his parents made arrangements to get him out of Ireland, get him to the United States, away from the trouble he had gotten into. Patrick left on a freighter, bad leg and vengeful heart, never to return.

His vengeance would not have to wait much longer.

Tommy took a deep breath. He had to sell this. "Well, the word is that our old friend Danny Sullivan is going to spill his guts to save his worthless life."

Sean squinted as if that would help him hear the words better. "What are you talking about?"

"Danny is in the process of cutting a deal with the government. They're going to spare his life for information on IRA operations. Contacts, arms dealers, the whole deal," Tommy said in a grave tone.

Sean paused. He had "retired" years ago. If he was ever found, the British had enough on him for several life sentences. "That doesn't sound like Mad Dog to me."

"Neither does this." Tommy slid a copy of the *Philadelphia Inquirer* across the table to Sean. "Page nine."

Sean glanced over a time line, the picture of Sullivan, then his eyes dropped down to the circled headline halfway down the page. "DOG DENOUNCES IRA BLAST."

Sean read in disbelief. In all of Danny's years in American jails there had been no comment about anything to do with the IRA. Not a word. This was a break. This was a desperate man. And he needed to be dealt with.

"It doesn't say anything about a deal," Sean pointed out.

"Why would it? Read between the lines. They wouldn't make something like that public. My sources tell me he's going to get a last minute stay. He's not getting something for nothing."

Sean stood and stalked around the table, then went to the fridge and grabbed a six pack. Sean had a drinking problem, and it was the mistakes he made under the influence of alcohol that forced him into retirement. "It doesn't make sense."

"Sure it does. If you were about to get fried, wouldn't you turn? Would you be so proud you wouldn't want to save your own life? Plus, the word is that Danny is pissed that the army hasn't even tried to get him out. Even Sein Finn doesn't take his calls."

Sean nearly exploded. "Well, what the hell did he expect? He goes off half-cocked and kills an American and then wants us to bail him out? IRA missions in America only happen in Tom Clancy books."

"Bottom line is that there is a leak. A ten-year-old leak, but one nonetheless. It needs to be plugged."

"How are you so sure of all of this?"

"I've got a guy at the FBI. He says that Sullivan's lawyer came to them two weeks ago and that they have been working a deal ever since. Says Danny is ready to name names and tell it all. He'll probably tell them that you're not dead." Tommy waited for the reaction.

Sean slammed his fist on the table. "Can't have that!"

"Yeah, and my name will come up. I've been running guns for years," Tommy added.

Sean looked surprised. "Thought you were done with us?"

"Where there's money to be made, you'll find me. Remember that." Tommy had him going.

"So who knows about this?" Sean sat up straight.

"I've been in touch with the right people, like your brothers. They didn't believe me at first."

"What changed their minds?"

Tommy reached into the duffel bag and produced a thick, bound document. It had an FBI seal on the cover. "Here are the transcripts from Danny's first session. The best parts are highlighted. He's just getting warmed up."

Sean read, tracing lines with his index finger. He read a highlighted line, grunted, then turned violently to another page.

Tommy smiled and let him go from page to page. With every turned page, he could see Sean's face getting redder. The document was authentic enough.

"Bloody hell!" Sean screamed. "Bloody hell!"

"He's getting real close to dangerous territory. Seems like he's going in chronological order. He should be to your staged auto accident by the end of the week."

Sean stood and tossed the report against the wall, pages went flying around the room.

"Sean, sit down. Sit down now," Tommy was calm yet stern. Sean sat back down and put his head down into his hands, muttering.

Tommy continued, "As you could imagine your brothers were not happy."

"What'd they say?"

"They asked me if I had any way to handle the situation," he added.

"What'd you tell them?" Sean moved to the edge of his seat.

"I told them I had a plan that would work, but it would cost them."

"What'd they say to that?"

"They told me to do it," Tommy said with a smile.

This seemed to relieve Sean. He eased back in his chair. "What's the plan?"

Tommy paused. "Well, Sean, that's why you're here. To listen to the plan and help me get it done."

"Tommy, I'll do anything you say. Just point in the direction."

"That's the spirit, Sean. But I need you in top form."

"Done. Anything you say. I'm yours."

Perfect. Tommy smiled as he sipped his beer. Sold.

chapter 5

"Do you really have to go?" Alex said genuinely into her new man's eyes.

"Yes, I do. My country needs me," Mitch said mock-patriotically.

The two broke into a slight, comfortable laugh.

"Seriously, Alex. The big guy needs me on this one. The Chinese are going to be tough to crack. And if they don't, Phil intends to hammer them. And..."

Alex reached across the seat and put her index finger over his lips to quiet him. "If I wanted a briefing, Mitch, I would have asked for one. Anyway, don't waste all that on a simple girl like me."

Mitch smiled. If there was one word that described Alexandra, simple was not it. Bright, funny, drop-dead-runway-model gorgeous. Those words better described her. She was the most exquisite woman Mitch had ever met. And that list included the First Lady.

And Mitch was no slouch himself, or so he was told. Just under six-foot with a round, soft face and features, Mitch looked much younger than his thirty years. He passed as "cute" rather than "handsome." But his Capitol Hill job had some power attached to it and that worked well for him. It was working with Alex.

Mitch glanced down at his watch. "I really have to go."

"Well then let me give you something to look forward to." Alex effortlessly undid the middle two buttons of her denim shirt with her left hand as she leaned over to kiss him from the driver's seat. When she pulled back Mitch had full view of her breasts and he couldn't help but stare. He looked back up into her golden eyes, her long, full hair just touched her shoulders. She leaned back over and they kissed like parked high schoolers. The chaos of the Dulles International departure lane swirled around them and not one person gave them a look.

Alex pulled away and did one button on her shirt. Mitch was still distracted as she started the car.

"Hey, hold on, this trip isn't that important," Mitch joked.

She turned and smiled. "There will be plenty of that for you when you get back. What day do you get back again?"

"Well, we'll be back in the country Wednesday."

"Can I pick you up?" she said in a breathy whisper.

Mitch paused, "I'd like that, but we land in Philly. Phil wants to spend Thursday at his beach house in Jersey preparing his recommendation for the subcommittee. We'll be back to DC Friday."

"Ooh, the beach. That sounds like fun." She noticed a slight bulge in Mitch's pants and raised an eyebrow. "Maybe I'll stop down. Wouldn't that be fun?"

Mitch got lost for a moment in the thought of Alex naked on the beach. "I don't know if Mrs. Stephenson would approve."

"I don't blame her. Your boss is a hunk."

"Take it easy young lady," Mitch said, wagging his index finger at her.

"Sorry, you know I only have eyes for you."

Mitch considered that for a moment. He heard the words and saw it in her eyes, yet, somehow, didn't believe it.

"Okay. Now I really have to go."

Looking down at his pants Alex joked, "Are you sure you want to go out like that?"

"That is what they invented briefcases for."

She smiled as he opened the door and left. She eased out into traffic. *A few more days*, she thought.

United States Senator Phillip Stephenson sat calmly, legs crossed, on one of the leather sofas in the airport's Captain's Club Lounge. His eyes were fixed on the big screen TV in front of him.

He had seen the tape at least fifty times since it had aired on *Dateline* almost a week before. The footage was brutal. He watched one more time as Chinese soldiers rounded up a small group of peasants that had been having a secret Catholic mass. The soldiers lined them up in an open field and opened fire. That tape was the reason he was on his way to Beijing.

Mitch plopped down on the leather sofa next to his boss. Both men were dressed comfortably for the eighteen-or-so-hour flight. Mitch was in jeans and a Harvard Law sweatshirt that he had earned. Stephenson was in tan khakis and a blue, button down oxford with the "President's Cup" crest on the breast pocket.

Stephenson's eyes were fixed on the horror in front of him.

"The tape again, huh?" Mitch asked.

"It gets worse every time I watch it. They will not get away with this," the senator replied.

"Calls at the office are 10-to-1 that we should do something," Mitch recited.

"Well, if those commie bastards don't commit to some human rights reform, they will find it very hard to export to this country."

"Commie. Now there is a word you don't hear much anymore. When did you get into politics, Phil? Right after the 'The Big One?'" Mitch joked.

"I may be old, but I can still kick your ass, my young friend."

"Speaking of kicking ass, how did golf go with the President?"

"You mean when he wasn't cheating? Pretty good. He 'guaranteed' me that he wouldn't even mention MFN and China in the same sentence until we got back. He owes me that." He paused, then added, "Anyway, I would have broke 80 if my knee hadn't acted up."

"That's what you get for playing football at a state school," Mitch quipped at the former Penn State star.

Stephenson took his eyes off the TV and looked over at Mitch. "Did I mention I could kick your ass?"

"You and what Red Army?"

"Keep it up, and I'll make you stay home."

Mitch gave a shocked look. "Gee, Dad, you promised that I could see real live commies. You promised."

Stephenson laughed and shook his head like a parent does when their toddler does something embarrassing but hysterical.

Mitch opened his briefcase and handed a newspaper over to the senator. "From yesterday. Check page 9."

Stephenson took the paper, a *Philadelphia Inquirer*, his hometown news. "Anything good?" he said as he thumbed his way to the page.

"Actually a bit from your past."

"Super." Recently Pennsylvania's favorite son, the two-time Democratic senator from the Keystone State, had come under some fire in the press regarding his position on the closing of the Willow Grove Naval Air Base in suburban Philadelphia. The downsizing of the military continued and the prevailing feeling was that Stephenson had not fought hard enough to keep the base open.

Stephenson found the page and took out his reading glasses. As he approached fifty, the only thing starting to fade was his vision. His eyes gravitated to a picture of him, ten years earlier as a Philadelphia district attorney. Across from his picture was a similar sized photo of Danny Sullivan, the man whom he prosecuted and convicted years before for killing an off-duty police officer. Underneath the pictures was a graphic timeline that noted the events in each man's life since the trial.

Stephenson's timeline was one to be proud of. A year after convicting Sullivan in a widely publicized trial, he was elected district attorney of Philadelphia. With two successful years as DA and a famous trial on his résumé, Stephenson took a chance and ran for the vacated US Senate seat. He won easily.

His first term was filled with tough decisions, and he often voted his conscience rather than the party line. But he was consistent in his approach, and he was rewarded with a second term, of which he was in his third year.

But the biggest note on his timeline was the negotiated release of a Chinese dissident who was facing death for his participation in Tiananmen Square. That dissident, now an American citizen, became an outspoken human rights activist and made it a habit of sneaking back into China to document human rights abuses. His latest video had kept a nation's attention for five solid days.

"I really cannot believe this footage," Mitch said as the video was played once again.

"Brutal," Stephenson said, shaking his head.

"You know, I didn't figure the average guy would get too worked up about this. A little outrage, then forget it. I don't get that feeling with this, though. I mean I was in college during Tiananmen and thought it sucked, but I wasn't going to any anti-Chinese rallies or anything like that. I was more worried about scoring with the ladies."

"You still are," the senator quipped, crediting himself with a zinger at Mitch's expense. Then Stephenson turned to Mitch and got serious. "You know what it is, Mitch?"

"No." He honestly didn't.

"People are fed up. They see everything that is happening in the world as it happens real-time, on CNN or MSNBC and it makes them sick. I'll tell you what, our constituents are fed up with the world we are giving them. They are fed up with ballplayers doing drugs or worse, with overcrowded schools, with kids killing kids. And with do- nothing politicians who lie to them and make a mockery of representative government," the senator said emphatically.

Mitch continued looking at the senator, even as the man turned away and faced the TV. He looked tired and his words showed it.

"So, Phil, what do we do today to change the world?"

Stephenson leaned forward and rubbed his eyes under his glasses with his thumb and index finger. "Let's at least try to do the right thing. That's a start."

chapter 6

Seven-thirty came incredibly early for Keith. His alarm clock sent a jolt through his body, and he opened his eyes wide. His friend Ed's favorite joke played in his head: Q: What's the best thing for a hangover? A: Drinking a lot the night before.

Keith could feel the dryness left over from the few beers he had had before going to bed. With nothing pressing on his schedule he was tempted to stay in bed like all the other yuppies that were recovering from an extended happy hour.

But he was trying hard not to be one of them.

He got out of bed and was in and out of the shower in less then ten minutes. He felt like a real, live human being again. He dressed and went to the window that overlooked Washington Street. The sun was up, and it was a clear morning. The street was empty, except for an unshaven young man with matted hair dressed in a wrinkled suit walking south and sipping coffee from a styrofoam cup. It looked like he was just getting in. Someone had once called that lonely walk home from the night before as "the walk of shame." Keith smiled at the thought.

He thought of Dave's e-mail from the night before and said to himself, "A week from now I will be at the beach. Nice."

Keith moved away from the window and sat down at his desk to plan his day. The thought of being at the beach was a distracting one. He loved the South Jersey Shore and was finally getting to spend a summer there after the ill-advised summer in the Hamptons with Shannon. They hadn't made it to the fourth of July. He thought of that whole Hamptons scene, of Shannon in a bikini, of Shannon with another man. Move on.

Keith reached over to his bookcase and pulled out a hardback book on how to get published. While the prospect of actually selling his concept of his "conversations" seemed like a long shot, it was time to try. Time to try something. He had a plan, a set number of conversations, a set mix; some funny, some controversial, some heart wrenching. Like the time he heard a couple decide to end their marriage in the course of a forty-five-minute bus trip. Or the time he had listened as two welfare mothers compared and contrasted the visitors' accommodations of the various prisons their husbands had been in. He had some good ones, but needed more.

And there was no time like the present.

He opened the desk drawer and pulled out the tape recorder, his constant companion. He stuffed it in his backpack along with some extra cassettes and batteries. He went into the kitchen and got two warm cans of iced tea and tossed them in the bag.

On his way out, he grabbed the publishing book and then locked the door behind him. He hadn't left anything unlocked since his Saab disappeared.

"I just cannot believe I did that," the blonde whispered.

"Come on, don't beat yourself up. It was a one-time thing. It happens," the red head said.

"Yeah, but it's not supposed to happen to me."

Keith was on the PATH train once again. This time he was two seats away from what looked like a pair of classic "Walk of Shamers." They were on their way back to the city, and, from their outfits, they'd get off in the Village.

The couple and Keith were the only three in the car and Keith pretended to sleep as they spoke softly. His backpack, faded jeans, and sweatshirt gave him the look of a college student. The two passengers occasionally looked over to see if he could hear them. He could.

After a short silence filled with the clack and wince of metal on metal, the red-haired girl turned to the blonde. "Look, she doesn't have to know. No one has to know. I'm sure not going to say anything."

"But she will know. She'll figure it out one way or another. She's smart like that." The blonde was upset.

"You're giving her too much credit. She won't be able to tell. Trust me," the red haired girl consoled.

"Trust you? Look where that got me."

"Don't blame me. You thought he was cute."

The two sat silent. Keith kept his eyes closed and fidgeted a little to make it look good.

"Maybe you're right. Maybe she won't know," the blonde reasoned.

The train pulled into the Christopher Street station. The girls got up and headed for the door. Keith opened his eyes to get a good look at them. The blonde was tall and wispy-model thin, dressed in hip hugger, retro jeans and a denim jacket. The red head had spiked hair, black lipstick and a long, leather trench coat. She was guilty of a variety of fashion "don'ts."

Keith closed his eyes again as the doors opened and closed and the train headed towards 9th Avenue.

Not bad for the first half-hour. Maybe he'd get enough for a book yet.

The PATH train rolled into Hoboken station at exactly 2:50 P.M. with Keith on it. He had planned to be back by three to catch the Flyers/Rangers playoff game at Stinky's Bar. Actually, that was only half of it. He was also meeting a high school friend of his sister's, Cindy Ciarrocco. Cindy had had a crush on Keith growing up, but their four-year age difference kept them both at arms length. But now with him twenty-eight and her four years younger, and with them both living in Hoboken, away from friends and family, it seemed like something could happen. And it probably would have already had Keith any confidence with women.

Keith was up the stairs of the station and onto Washington Street quickly. The promising morning had not turned into a promising day of eavesdropping on mass transportation. People were riding the trains and buses, it was just that no one had anything interesting to say.

It was on days like this that he felt what he was doing was sleazy. It was on days like this that he felt like giving up.

The clear morning had stayed a clear day, and it was definitely shorts and tee shirt weather. The streets were crowded again and the bars had their sidewalk gates and tables set up, adding to the congestion.

Keith got to Stinky's, a corner bar no more than twenty-four steps from his apartment, right at 3:00 P.M.

The bar was long and narrow with ceilings that were close to twenty feet high. Long necked fans dropped down and circulated the smoky air over the dark wood bar on the right and the series of tables on the left. Sun pounded through the windows on the Sixth Street side, giving it a much different look in the afternoon than it had at night. The bar itself ran three quarters of the length of the room and it was crowded. A 35" screen TV sat high up on a shelf on the back wall.

Most everyone was turned toward the set as Keith entered through the propped open door. There was a fair mix of girls and guys at the bar and at tables. Almost half had Rangers jerseys or hats on. A hostile crowd for any Flyers fan.

About halfway down the bar was a lone Flyers jersey. It was Cindy. She was talking to the bartender and Keith got an unobstructed view of her great profile. She had her long, black hair in a ponytail that cut down the middle of her back and the two 8's of her old Lindros jersey. She wore some makeup, but not too much; it only accented the features that were just fine as is. Her slim, athletic legs seemed to grow out of her khaki shorts. The big jersey hid a fit and toned body.

The patrons were focused on the TV and the room was oddly quiet for a bar. Keith cupped his hands and yelled: "Let's Go Fly-ers," followed by the rhythmic clapping that was a staple at Philadelphia's First Union Center.

He got everyone's attention, including Cindy's.

She smiled and waved him down. She then turned and gestured to a group of guys who were dressed in Rangers gear from head to toe.

"Hey killer, what's shaking?" he said as he leaned over and kissed her cheek.

"These guys have to go, Keith. They have been taunting me for an hour." She turned to the Ranger fans again. "So I told them that when my boyfriend got here he was going to kick their ass," she said with a wicked smile.

"Okay. Speaking of Derek, where is the boy wonder?"

"We got into another fight last night. He's such an asshole. Every bartender in Manhattan is an actor or has a screenplay, and he thinks he's something special," she lamented.

Keith listened and held comment. In Keith's view, Cindy's boyfriend Derek was an asshole and treated her poorly. But Cindy didn't need to hear that, Keith thought.

Keith noticed that her big brown eyes were starting to well up, so he changed the subject. "So how bad are we going to beat the Rangers today?"

Cindy's face brightened. "We're going to beat them like a bunch of limping baby seals."

"Now that's more like it." Keith waved the bartender over. "Hey, Mike, can I get two light beers?"

The beers arrived and he stood next to her as she sat on the stool. He was close to her. Why couldn't he make a move?

"So, do you still need a ride to the beach?" she asked.

"Yes, Ma'am. You are my ticket to the shore."

"Would you mind driving part of the way?"

"Not at all. Anything you want me to do." Keith meant it.

The puck dropped and everyone's attention went to the screen. Everyone's but Keith's. His eyes were still on the girl.

chapter 7

The President of the United States had lied. That in and of itself was not troubling to the senator. Except the President had lied to him. On the second day of the three-day China trip, the President made an impassioned plea to the Senate not to tie China's human rights record to US trade policy. The statement took away any leverage Stephenson had with the Chinese.

But the fight had just begun.

"So what's the count?" the senator asked as he put the plastic airline cup to his lips.

"Well, if we assume Crandall, Waterford, and Jackson vote with us, it would put it at 52-48. But there are at least four more votes that could go against us," Mitch replied.

Stephenson and Mitch had spent the better part of their long, marathon flight back to the states drafting legislation that would, in effect, remove the Most Favored Nation trading status from China. That legislation, if passed into law, would increase the price of almost everything imported into the states from China. It was not the first time they had worked on this bill and it was well known in political circles that if anyone were to champion this cause, it would be Stephenson. And now it was time.

Stephenson leaned over to Mitch, "Don't worry. I have some favors to pull. We'll get the votes," the senator assured.

"What about the dreaded Presidential veto?"

Stephenson smiled, "With all the Chinese fund-raising crap that has gone on, it would look like he was in bed with them. It would look bad, and I would be more than willing to point out the relationship." Stephenson sipped his water again. "Not to mention, it would make *him* look bad. And all that guy cares about is looking good. No, if it passes, it won't get vetoed."

"Not to mention he lied to you," Mitch added.

"Not to mention."

Mitch leaned back in the leather, first class seat, slipped off his horned rim glasses and rubbed his eyes. Had it only been three days? Maybe four with the flight, who could count? The days had been long and the food bad and their hosts even worse.

"Mitch, in as a few words as possible, how would you sum up the attitude of the Chinese officials?" Stephenson said, playing a sound bite game he often did with Mitch when they had some down time.

"How about 'Don't go away mad, just go away?'"

"Not bad. Mine was only two words," the senator noted.

"What are they?"

"Take a guess."

And that did sum up the trip and the resistance the Chinese officials showed. Stephenson would bring up the massacre, they would counter with Rodney King or a Kent State or the Diallo case. One brought up, through his interpreter, the fact that the senator himself had sent a man to death row. In short, they didn't see themselves as bad world citizens, just a country trying to clean up the subversive elements on their way to a democratic/socialistic hybrid society. In their view, they were no worse than the United States.

The stewardess stood in front of the two silent men. "Can I get you anything?"

Stephenson looked at Mitch and realized that he had been pushing them both hard. With another six hours to go on the hellish flight, it was time to kick back and relax.

"Yes, please. I'll have a scotch on the rocks," the senator answered first.

Mitch popped up from his slouched position. The senator was letting his hair down. About time, he thought. "I'll have three light beers."

The senator rubbed his eyes and laughed inwardly.

The drinks came quickly and Mitch had to rearrange his tray to make room for his new friends.

"Here's to the Chinese government," the senator raised his glass, "may they choke on their own arrogance."

"And may the rest of the world forget how to apply the Heimlich," Mitch added.

The two men bumped cups and then sat quietly. As the 747's engines hummed along, each man was confident that they were doing all they could do to straighten out a problem nation.

Stephenson reclined his seat. The scotch went down nicely. "So, Mitch, tell me about your new girlfriend."

"Oh, well, she's too good to be true, Phil. Beautiful and smart and, to top it all off, she really likes me. We get along great. I don't understand what she sees in me, but I'm going with it." He smiled a schoolboy smile.

The senator smiled. "What does she do again?"

"She's a flight attendant for Intrastate. That's why I only see her sporadically. She's actually based in Newark and does the Newark to D.C. flight most of the time. I can't wait to see her again."

"I'll have to meet her sometime." The senator meant it.

"Well she did joke about showing up at your beach house. I told her she would have to clear it with the boss," Mitch said.

"Oh, the missus. That would be a tough sell."

The senator's wife and two sons were in Denver visiting relatives. The beach house would be empty and he and Mitch could put the finishing touches on the speech and make some calls, pull some favors.

Mitch went on, "Yeah. Anyway, you'd really like her. She has an energy about her. It's hard to describe."

Stephenson considered that. He would have to meet her, sooner than later. Young aides were politically vulnerable animals, and he felt like a protective parent when it came to Mitch. He would have her checked out, just in case. It wouldn't be the first time.

Things that were too good to be true usually were just that.

chapter 8

Officer Watkins would not describe his assignment as hazardous duty. In the six times he had been assigned to the senator's beach house he had chased a total of three people off the beach: one couple who did not seem to have a hotel room and a guy who wanted to give an anal salute to, as he put it, "that ass kissing, phony baloney, politician." Neither qualified as real trouble.

Watkins walked methodically around the perimeter of the Stephenson house, or the "compound" as Avalon locals called it. The beachfront house was three stories of classic Victorian architecture nestled behind a line of trees that separated the road from the beach in the small coastal town of Avalon, New Jersey. Even in the moonless night it was impressive.

Watkins walked the north side of the house that faced Sea Isle and Atlantic City farther north, then to the front, and then he looped back south to the beach. His steps matched the rhythmic crashing of the waves. The air had a chill to it, and there was a thin mist. It was a cool May night. One more day until the population of the town went from about 2,000 to 30,000 with the influx of weekend warriors. Then the fun started.

Watkins' partner, John Smith, was inside the house "supervising house telecommunications." In short, he was watching the replay of the Phillies/Astros game. Watkins didn't mind the outside duty, he was thirty-five years Smith's junior and Smitty was retiring at the end of the summer.

As he got to the edge of the dunes, he looked back at the massive structure and wished it was his own. All the indoor lights were out except in the kitchen. The outside floodlights were muted by the mist and the house looked like it could be floating above the ground.

The senator was asleep in the second floor master bedroom which had a deck just outside its sliding glass doors. The senator's aide was on the third floor in a guestroom. 1:30 A.M. and all was quiet.

Watkins turned his attention back to the ocean and watched as the whitecaps formed a few yards out and then crashed to the shore. The dark sky and the dark sea came together on the horizon and made a large black curtain. Only the relentless whitecaps registered against it.

He had just started to walk back to the house when he heard a voice, or maybe voices, in the distance. He waited and the voices got increasingly stronger until three figures appeared out of the black night.

A man flanked by two women strode carelessly close to the shoreline some thirty yards from Watkins' position near the dunes. Their gait indicated that they might be intoxicated. Their voices cut through the sound of the crashing waves, but he couldn't make out what they were saying.

The three did not see the officer through the mist and probably would not have cared if they did. The women were concentrating on the man, taking turns kissing him.

"This ought to be good," Watkins said to himself. He stood observing, hands on his hips, ready to pull his flashlight.

The trio played in the surf, splashing each other. After a minute or so of that, the man, with a woman on each arm, moved toward dry land.

"Foreplay is over." Watkins felt like a color commentator at a porn flick. He would let it go a little further and then clear them off the beach.

As they moved closer and settled, he could make the figures out better. The man was average height and was wearing plaid shorts and a navy sweatshirt and had on a baseball cap. His hair looked to be dark, or red. He couldn't gauge the man's age, but he didn't spend much time looking at him. The woman closest to him was a tall blonde in a tight fitting, floral print sundress. Even from that distance she looked fantastic. The other woman was shorter and had dark, short hair. She was in shorts and an oversized sweatshirt and was very plain. She was dressed very much like the man.

"Husband and wife pick up a free spirit?" Watkins continued his commentary. The three never looked his way.

As the trio stood, the women continued to take turns kissing the man, and then each other. Then the brunette dropped to her knees in front of the man and started to work on his shorts. The blonde had a lip lock on the man and rubbed his chest.

While the brunette struggled with the shorts the man took to rubbing the blonde's breasts and whispering in her ear.

"The quarterback calls the play." Watkins could feel his mouth going dry. He thought to go get Smith, but the action might kill the old guy. Watkins looked down the beach in both directions like a kid trying not to get caught looking at his dad's girlie magazines. There was not a house light on for blocks.

The man moved to the ground and laid on his back with his feet facing toward the ocean. The brunette continued her struggle with the shorts and the blonde had pulled up the man's sweatshirt and was kissing his chest, working her way down. The two women seemed to be going for the same point.

Watkins squirmed as his pants' front got a little tight. He'd let it go for only a few more minutes.

The blonde stopped kissing the man and got on all fours, straddling the man's torso. She lurched up and straightened her back. She then slipped the straps of her dress down showing her bare breasts. She smiled.

The brunette was not out of view, but Watkins could only imagine what she was doing.

The blonde ran her hands over her own breasts and then slid forward on the man until she straddled his face, the dress completely covering the man's head.

"This is too much," Watkins said to himself as he reached for the flashlight. Half of him wanted to arrest them, the other half wanted to videotape it for the guys at the station.

The blonde woman began to bob up and down, continuing to rub her own breasts. She cocked her head back, closed her eyes, and moaned.

Watkins took a few steps toward the group with the intention of breaking it up. Pretty embarrassing stuff. As he got closer to them, the blonde suddenly arched up, opened her eyes and looked right at him.

"Oh boy," he whispered to himself.

Her look was not of surprise but of complete and utter bliss. Then the unthinkable; she motioned Watkins over.

He was, what seemed like, the longest seventy-five feet in the world away from her. She continued to motion him over.

Just ten feet away and the blonde spoke first. Her voice fit her figure. "Would you like to join us, officer?"

"I'm sorry, ma'am, I am going to have to ask you to leave the beach," he said half-heartedly.

She looked disappointed. "Too bad."

The blonde threw herself forward on to the sand in front of Watkins, off of the man.

The startled officer looked down first at her and then to the couple. Instead of seeing another act of oral sex, Watkins stared into the mouth of a loaded gun.

The brunette popped to one knee and squeezed the trigger, letting a round loose, headed for the officer's forehead. She squeezed again toward his chest. Both shots were deadly accurate.

Watkins dropped down. He was dead before he hit the ground.

The blonde looked up from her prone position and saw the dead officer and smiled. She rolled to her back and held out her hand. "Tommy dear, can you give me a hand up?"

Tommy got up and brushed the sand from his body. He pulled the woman up and they embraced. He helped her pull her dress back up. Then they kissed.

The brunette, though short and small, was strong and had managed to drag the body a third of the way back to the house. Tommy looked down the beach in both directions: nothing. He had checked houses earlier in the day and there was not an occupied house for three blocks. In close to twelve hours the town would be overrun with people. This was the last day that could have pulled this off. Tommy knew that timing was everything.

Tommy caught up with the brunette and grabbed an arm of the dead officer. They were over the remaining distance to the house quickly. The blonde cupped her hands under the sand where the blood had settled into a brown, clumpy mud. She scooped it up and walked it to the water. She repeated the action three times, determined to get most of it. The tide would come in and do the rest. On the way back to the house she kicked at the bloody trail.

The three met on the back porch of the house in silence. They had done their part, a little late, but in the framework of the plan.

Tommy took off his sweatshirt and gave it to the blonde who put it on. Tommy then reached into his pockets and pulled out black gloves. The brunette did the same and handed a pair to the blonde. They all put them on.

Tommy went to the body and looked for a pulse. There was none, as expected. The police officer was quite dead. He then undid the clasp of the officer's holster and slipped out his service revolver. He wedged it in his back waistband.

The three heard a car pull into the driveway and they froze. Tommy looked down at his watch. Right on time.

Officer John Smith was upset. Not only were his beloved Phillies down two to the Astros, but some college kid just pulled his pizza delivery van into the senator's driveway. Another summer just around the corner.

Smith met the delivery boy at the door, sure to not have the bell rung.

The young man was smiling and holding a pizza box. "Hi. I have a pepperoni for 5223 Dune Drive."

"You have the wrong house, son. This is 5423," Smith said.

"Huh. So this isn't yours?" the pizza boy said, looking at the box like it had given him bad directions.

"No, son, it's not," Smith assured.

He turned to leave, then turned back. "Oh, then this must be yours." In one swift motion he dropped the pizza box that had been covering his gun. He pumped three quick, silencer muffled shots into the man's chest. His body crumpled to the driveway.

The Phils would come back that night. Officer Smith would not.

With a duffel bag on his shoulder, Sean got out of the van through the side door and he helped James, the pizza boy, move the body to the side of the house.

Sean and James entered the house cautiously and quietly. James shut the door quietly. The only other noise was the voice of the Phils' announcer on the television set. They moved through the huge family room, through the dining area and into the kitchen.

Sean unlocked the back door and let Tommy and the others in. They silently met in the kitchen and Tommy used hand signals to move everyone into position. They all knew what their responsibilities were. They had gone over the layout a hundred times.

Sean placed his bag on the table gently and unzipped the main compartment. He handed out ski masks to all but the blonde. He handed Tommy a pistol. Then out came the handcuffs, the duct tape, and a black fabric case that housed several syringes.

The blonde went up the stairs first and headed for the third floor guestroom. The stairs were solid and did not creak. Tommy and Sean made mental notes. Once she was out of sight, the three men made their way up to the second floor master bedroom. The brunette watched the front door. The officers were to go off duty at eight in the morning and were only to check in if there was a problem. It was 1:45 A.M.

Mitch could not believe his eyes. Either he had a weird case of jet lag or Alexandra was sitting on the edge of his bed.

Mitch propped himself up and started to speak. "How did..." Alex put her index finger over his lips.

"I told you I might surprise you," she whispered.

Mitch started to speak but she hushed him again. She pulled the sheet and bedspread back and Mitch was naked underneath. Alex rubbed his thighs and then kissed them, moving her mouth between his legs. She took him in her mouth and Mitch let out a muffled groan. This had to be a dream.

He climaxed quickly and rolled onto his stomach. Alex began to massage his buttocks and moved her hands up his back. She climbed on top of him, straddling him and massaging him the whole time, working his tense shoulders. Mitch let her know his approval with every groan.

She kept the massage going with one hand and with the other she pulled a small dagger from a holster strapped to her thigh.

She leaned over and whispered in his ear, "Good night, Mitch." She went back upright and stopped the massage. Then with both hands she drove the knife through his top vertebrae and into his brain. It was a textbook kill. Mitch Slade died without even a whimper.

The three men entered the huge master bedroom quietly and quickly saw that the senator was not in his bed. It had been slept in, the sheets were in disarray. Tommy put his right hand up and motioned for the other two to stay still. Had the senator heard something? Possible, but not probable. The bedroom window faced the ocean and Tommy had not seen a light go on while they were outside.

Tommy shifted his feet across the deep pile carpet. The room was a large square, it must have been 30 x 30. Tommy remembered the floor plan; a bathroom was tucked in the far corner of the room. He passed by a large closet door and then a chest-high dresser. Ten feet from where the bathroom should be he still couldn't see the door. It was recessed behind a vanity built into the wall.

Then he heard the flush.

Tommy moved quickly and silently in front of the vanity. He heard the door creak open and the senator shuffled past him in the dark. Tommy moved behind the senator slowly. Then Stephenson paused and looked over in the direction of James and Sean. Before he could react, Tommy chop kicked the back of the senator's knee and it buckled, sending him awkwardly to the floor.

Stephenson groaned as he went down. Tommy went down to the floor to pin the senator with a knee to the back, but Stephenson rolled and clipped Tommy's bad leg. Tommy went down.

Stephenson rolled again, this time up on to his hands and knees, and as he tried to stand, a foot came out of nowhere and clocked him in the side of the head. The impact sent him into a wall with a thud.

"Don't kill him, Sean!" Tommy said with force through his clenched teeth.

Sean went to the senator. The kick had knocked him out. Sean felt for a pulse and found one. "He's fine. He'll just have a little headache."

Sean and James rolled the senator onto his stomach as Tommy struggled to stand. James cuffed Stephenson's hands behind his back and shackled the ankles as well. Sean pulled out his case, opened it and took out a syringe. "This will keep him out for a good twelve hours." He jabbed the senator in the ass with the needle.

Tommy was standing, testing the bad leg. James rolled the senator over and taped his mouth, just in case.

"How's the knee?" James asked.

"It'll be fine." Tommy grimaced.

Sean ignored them and worked on the senator.

All five intruders met back down in the kitchen. James and Sean had negotiated the senator's limp body carefully down the flight of stairs. Alex and the brunette had been waiting.

"How did it go?" Tommy asked Alex.

"As planned," she said with no emotion.

"No distractions or complications?" he added.

"None."

Tommy didn't want to think what Alex might have done to get the young man off guard. He had a good idea, but blocked the thought from his mind.

Tommy reached into the black duffel bag and pulled out a cassette tape. His gloved hand left it on the kitchen table. Then he said, "Okay. The three of you get him in the van. Sean, come out back with me. We've got one loose end to tie up."

The four followed the instructions.

Tommy and Sean stood over the body of officer Watkins on the back patio. The whole affair had taken less than twenty minutes.

"So, what's up?" Sean said looking out at the beach. He turned back to Tommy and froze. Tommy was holding a gun and it was pointed right at Sean.

"See, Sean, this isn't about Danny Sullivan. Not about the IRA. Nothing like that," Tommy stated matter of factly.

"What? What are you talking about?" Sean couldn't decide if he should rush him or wait him out.

"The kidnapping is real. Just not for the reasons you think. We have to sell it as an IRA job, a revenge sort of thing," Tommy said, waving the gun casually.

"I don't follow." Sean knew his gun was back in the duffel bag. He didn't have any defense.

"You will. See, the best way for us to make this look like the IRA was involved would be to leave indisputable proof they were here."

"What, like an IRA membership card?" Sean tried to break the tension. It didn't work.

"No, no. Good idea. No, what I had in mind was more definitive. Like you."

"Well, I'm not going to sit around here and wait to get caught," Sean said angrily.

"I didn't figure as much." Tommy lowered the officer's revolver and let a single shot loose into Sean's leg. Sean fell back on top of Watkins' body.

"That was for twenty-five years ago. You weren't supposed to shatter my leg, you asshole!"

"Is that what this is about? Come on, Tommy, that was a lifetime ago. I was just following orders. You had it coming. Let it end here," Sean pleaded through the pain.

"Like I said Sean, we have to complete the illusion."

"Don't do this, man. Don't do it!"

Tommy hadn't expected Sean to cower and grovel. *No matter*, he thought.

"Goodbye, Sean."

"You asshole! I hope you burn in ..." But the shots from the gun cut Sean off. For good.

His body lay limp and Tommy checked Sean's pulse. He was dead, lying right next to the slain officer. Tommy then leaned over and placed the revolver in Watkins' hand. He put the barrel into the sand at the edge of the patio, cradled his hand over Watkins' and pulled the trigger, firing a shot into the sand.

He knew that the body positions and bloodstains and the sequence of the shootings would drive FBI forensics nuts. But they would somehow conclude that Watkins had killed one of the assailants before losing his own life. Watkins would be remembered as a hero, not a voyeur.

The illusion was complete.

chapter 9

The white van rolled along Dune Drive at the posted twenty-five mile an hour speed limit with James at the wheel. There was no reason to hurry. The streetlights lit up the empty road, and the mist created a surreal setting. Even with the engine noise and the chatter of their police scanner, the four in the van could hear the faint crashing of the waves.

The van traveled the twenty or so blocks from the senator's house to 30th Street. They made a left at the blinking traffic light, went a block and crossed over Ocean Drive to the access road that would lead them inland.

The senator was making no noise. He had been placed in a large wooden crate marked "MACHINE PARTS" and loaded into the back of the van.

Alex and Tommy sat in the back seats and the brunette was James' co-pilot. They traveled in silence, each weighing the consequences of killing two police officers, not to mention kidnapping a United States Senator. They had done things like this before, but this was different.

Tommy had told the group that Sean would not be making the return trip, and not one of them batted an eye. It was Tommy's show.

The van eased along the desolate access road, marsh on either side, for about three miles until they got to the junction of Route 9. James turned right, and they headed north. Most of this part of New Jersey was forest with roads cut into it. There were a few businesses and houses along the route, but there were more trees.

Six miles later they passed the Sea Isle City turn-off, a driving range, and a bank. They made a left on Woodbine Road and went another three miles and then pulled over on the shoulder. James checked all his mirrors carefully to make sure that there was no traffic. He then turned the van onto a hidden dirt road. The road was the entryway to the closed Woodbine landfill.

The van jostled and creaked along the overgrown road about four hundred yards into the woods. The old landfill had been closed for over ten years and the road was a mess.

The van headlights shown on a clearing. In the middle of the clearing was a yellow rental truck. James flicked the lights three times, and the truck flicked three times back. It was safe to proceed.

The four got out of the van quickly, and a man emerged from the rental truck. He met Tommy half way and the two shook hands.

"Jacob, is everything ready?" Tommy asked.

Jacob stood a full head taller than Tommy, well over six feet. His thick and muscular frame, coupled with his dark Israeli complexion and perpetual five o'clock shadow, gave him a very intimidating look. "We are right on schedule. No one saw me come in. The holes are dug and the truck is full." The truck was full of yard sale furniture, part of another illusion.

"Great. Help James with the box," Tommy instructed.

James and Jacob opened the back doors of the van and carried the senator slowly over to the truck. James struggled with the weight of the box as he was much shorter and weaker than Jacob. Even in the cool night air, James had broken out into a full-out sweat.

As the men moved the box, Tommy and the women stripped down to their underwear. Tommy pulled a bag out of the van, unzipped it, and handed both the women new clothes. He couldn't help but stare at Alexandra as she covered her magnificent body with bulky clothes. Soon, he'd stare at her body all day long on a beach somewhere far away.

After they finished dressing, they put their old clothes, gloves, guns, and knife into the large duffel. James returned, out of breath, and stripped as well.

Alex went to a toolbox in the van, grabbed a screwdriver and began to detach the New Jersey license plates from the van. The brunette followed behind her and attached the New York plates. While this went on, Tommy hoisted the bag over his shoulder, and James picked up the shovels. They met Jacob near the truck and headed out into the old landfill.

The thought of burying any evidence from the crime at a landfill seemed almost too cute to Tommy. But this landfill was the perfect place to make the transfer and to get rid of the evidence. Even if the authorities knew to look there, they would dig up their fair share of baby diapers and refrigerators before they hit pay dirt. Metal detectors would be useless. Unless someone knew the exact burial spot, the bag would never be found.

Ten minutes after pulling into the fill they were ready to pull out.

They all met at the van. "Ready?" Tommy asked. They all nodded. "Let's go."

James and the brunette went to the driver and passenger seats of the van, respectively. Jacob went to the truck. In between the vehicles, Tommy and Alex stood face to face.

"Make sure Jacob drives the speed limit, okay?"

"We'll be fine, Tommy. It's less than a week. I'll meet you back here then. There is no way I am going to miss this payday," Alex said with a smile.

Tommy grinned. When it all came down to it, money was the bottom line. He liked that in her.

"You just take care of getting the money," Alex said pushing her finger into his chest playfully. She knew that part wouldn't be a problem. This time next week, they'd be retired.

Alex kissed him on the cheek and went off to the truck. Tommy went to the van. The truck went first down the dirt road, followed by the van. When they all got to the end, Tommy got out and went to the road to check for traffic. There was none, and he waved the truck through. The van followed. He locked the gate that sealed off the fill from illegal dumpers.

Tommy got in, and the van headed back down Woodbine Road, going the same direction as the truck. But the two vehicles had very different destinations.

chapter 10

Donna Van Ness was seriously wondering what the hell she was doing in that one-horse town. The thought played on her mind for a few seconds before the camera's red light gave her the cue.

"Today, look for early cloud cover to give way to afternoon sunshine with highs in the mid-sixties. Your Memorial Day weekend looks to be in great shape." The screen flashed an overused "5 Day Weather Forecast" graphic. Her voice continued. "Saturday and Sunday will be mostly sunny with highs in the low to mid-seventies at the beach; inland may hit eighty. For Monday, look for a few more clouds with a chance of late afternoon showers. Water temp today is 62 degrees, look for it to stay there all weekend. Now back to the...." Blah, blah, blah.

"And, you're clear," the cameraman said as the red light went off.

Donna's thoughts went back to: "Where was I? Oh yeah, one-horse town."

Donna was the pleasant voice and face of TV 39, the Jersey shore's NBC affiliate. The station was located along the access road to Avalon, in the marshlands of the small town of Swainton. Donna did the local weather when the national morning show cut to the local stations. She was also co-anchor of the local twelve o'clock news and did some reporting. It was not exactly what Donna saw as her life's work.

She walked off the set, past the technicians, and went to what passed for a dressing room. She sat in her worn chair and looked into the mirror: "And the big story today at the shore: a plumber from Absecon catches a really big fish. This is some huge fish, Bob. Must be twice as big as the huge freakin' fish that redneck caught last year." She smiled wryly and shook her head. "Or even better. The big story today: a homeless man from Atlantic City wins a million dollars at the Trop. Says he'll move into a larger cardboard box."

She sighed and slumped in her chair. This was the punishment she got for sleeping with her boss and then breaking the relationship off at the station in Chicago. Banished to a nowhere town with nothing news. She wished for something, anything, that could get her out of this town. If she could only get the chance.

Donna had about twenty minutes before the next weather update (as if it would change) and almost six hours before the noon telecast. She slid open the desk/make-up table drawer and stared inside. The choice of the day was news magazine or nails. She grabbed the nail file and polish and started work on her nails. She really should have a person who did that for her, she thought. But that was a city and lover ago.

Her nails occupied her thoughts, taking the place of her frustration. The station was small and the staff was few in number. The station manager, an overmatched company man named Jim, was more concerned with running a stable, little affiliate than with taking chances. Donna had come to him with several ideas for stories in Atlantic City: hookers, gamblers, developers. But Jim would not go for the hooker exposé type pieces. And that pissed her off.

One day the story would come, and she'd get out of there.

After the nails and right before the second to last update leading up to nine o'clock, Donna got a call on the "tip line" that she had made Jim set up.

"This is Donna. Talk to me," she said into the receiver.

"Oh, hi Miss Van Ness. I'm one of your biggest fans."

"Why thank you. Did you have a tip to call in?"

"Oh, right, right, I did. Sorry, I'm a little nervous," the man admitted.

"Just take your time." Her tone showed patience and compassion, while her body language showed the opposite.

"Well, I run from 68th Street to the inlet and back every morning on the beach."

"That's quite a run," she replied.

"Oh, yes it is. About six and a half miles. Anyway, this morning I was on my way, but I got stopped and was asked to turn back," he said in almost a hushed.

"Stopped? Who stopped you?" She could not tell if the man was fifty or fifteen.

"Well, it wasn't the Avalon police. They looked like FBI guys."

"Why do you say that?"

"Well, there were about fifteen of them in suits and sunglasses combing the beach. A few had metal detectors."

"Where was this? Did they say why you had to get off the beach?" she said rapidly.

"At the 53rd Street beach. They didn't say why. When I went out to Dune Drive to finish the run, that's when I saw all the police cars," the man explained, trying to keep pace with Donna.

"Police cars? Where?"

"On 53rd, in front of Senator Stephenson's house," he stammered.

"Police cars in front of the senator's house?" she continued.

The man took a deep breath. "Yes, ma'am. That's what I saw."

"How many cars?" Donna scribbled furiously on a legal pad.

"Well, there were all kinds. I'd say about a dozen."

"Were there any local police present?"

"Some cars and some guys. They didn't seem too happy," he editorialized.

Donna's mind raced. She had to move and move quickly. "Is there anything else you can tell me, mister..."

"Oh, my name is Mark Josephs. And no, that's about it," he said, thankful that was all there was to tell.

"Well, I would like to thank you very much, Mr. Josephs."

"Well, you're welcome. I hope everything is okay with the senator."

"I'm sure it is. Thanks again and goodbye."

She waved Jim over, and he took his time getting to her. "Whatcha got?" he said, envisioning another really big fish story.

"There's a ton of police activity in front of Senator Stephenson's house. A jogger called and said he was asked to leave the beach when he got within a few blocks of the compound. Says he saw the FBI," Donna said in one long breath.

"Sounds like a crackpot to me. Wasn't the senator in China a few days ago?" Jim challenged.

"Yes he was, but they have these amazing machines now called airplanes that travel long distances..." The prima donna had come up for more air.

Jim cut her off. "Okay, I get the point. What do you want to do?"

"Give me the camera and Scooter and let me check it out. It's just three miles away!" She was losing patience, and it came across loud and clear.

"Who'll do the weather at ten of?" Jim whined.

"Who cares!" She caught herself and started over. "Look, if it's nothing, we'll be back in ten minutes. If it turns out to be something, we'll break the story to the world."

Jim scratched his bald spot. "Okay, go ahead."

Donna went for the cameraman and they were out the door, into the news van, and on the way into Avalon.

When they got two blocks from the senator's house, they saw the scene that the jogger had described. There were no less than eight marked cars and several unmarked cars that formed a blockade on Dune Drive.

Donna spotted an Avalon officer she knew that was diverting traffic down 49th Street. She got out of the van and went toward him.

"Drew. Hey, Drew," she yelled as she approached.

"Just great," Officer Drew Coleman said to himself as he waved another car down the detour street.

"Drew, what the hell is going on here?"

"I can't comment, okay?" There was a strain on his face that Donna picked up.

"Is it the senator's house? Did something happen to him? Is he dead? Even better, caught with a dead hooker?"

He glared at her and felt the twinge to go for his firearm. "Look, there is some serious shit going down and I am not going to discuss it with you. Move on, or I'll arrest you."

"Is he hurt? Heart attack? Stroke? Heart attack with a hooker?" she said, wide-eyed.

"Donna, I am warning you!"

"Look. I have to file a story any way you look at it. I can either get the truth, or I'll have to speculate. Your choice."

Officer Coleman took a breath. "The chief will have a comment in the next hour."

She shook her head. "Too long. Every news van in the area will be here by then. I need something, Drew, anything."

The polished New York anchor was calm and composed, but he knew this could be big news. The time at the right hand corner of the screen read 8:31 A.M.

"Now, some breaking news from our affiliate in Atlantic City. Donna, this is Preston Shaeffer in New York. What can you tell us about the situation down there?"

The screen went split, New York on one half and Donna Van Ness in front of the police car blockade in Avalon on the other.

"Preston, I am standing about two blocks away from the summer home of Pennsylvania Senator Phillip Stephenson. As you can see, there is heavy police activity. Details are sketchy right now, but we have learned..."

A star was born

Tommy had nearly missed it. The long night with no sleep had caught up with him despite all the coffee. Pillows propped him up on his Manhattan hotel bed as he held the remote control. He had stayed too long on CNN and almost missed the story on NBC.

He watched and listened. The reporter didn't have much, but she had enough to speculate that something had happened to the senator and that it could be related to the pending execution of former IRA soldier Danny Sullivan. Perfect. Now everyone watching just got the idea that the two were related.

And then when the FBI identified Sean's body even they would have to focus their investigation on the IRA.

Now he could get some sleep.

chapter 11

They had made great time, even driving at the speed limit. The van cruised through New Jersey, across the Walt Whitman Bridge through Philadelphia, up to the PA Turnpike's Northeast Extension and onto Interstate 80. The plan had been simple. Once they heard anything about Stephenson on the radio, they were to pull over and find the nearest of the ten safe houses they had rented along the route. If stopped, they were to pose as a young doctor and his wife who were driving from Delaware, where the truck had been rented, to Youngstown, Ohio. They had valid driver's licenses and other documents to support their alter egos.

They would move into the new dwelling and keep the senator drugged and quiet and out of sight. Tommy had explored all possible escape routes and liked stashing the senator in his home state the best. Plus, with the high rental turnover with all the colleges in central Pennsylvania, no one asked questions when you paid six months up front in cash.

When the news came across the airwaves that something was going on in Avalon, they made the decision to get off the interstate and head for Safe House Number 6 in Lock Haven, PA.

But the decision may have come too late.

The police cruiser appeared out of nowhere in Jacob's rearview mirror, trailing a cloud of dust and red blinking lights. "Shit," Jacob uttered, checking his speed. He was right around sixty-five, what he thought was the posted speed limit.

"What?" Alex said and she leaned for a peek in his rearview mirror.

"What do we do?"

"Were you going the limit?" she said calmly.

"Yes. I mean, I think."

"Pull over."

"But..."

"Pull over."

The truck rumbled to the shoulder, kicking up dust and stone. Jacob began to sweat slightly. He was a sniper by trade, a skill that Tommy had needed when he recruited him out of the Israeli Army years ago. But Jacob had proven to be cool under pressure. He needed that coolness now.

Officer Pryce approached the truck on the driver's side. It was almost too easy. There were a few places on Route 80 where the speed limit went from sixty-five back down to fifty-five. This stretch of road just happened to have one of those speed limit anomalies. The guy driving the truck was clocked at sixty-seven. Not his day.

Jacob had the window rolled down and was waiting for the officer. "Good morning, officer."

"License, registration, and insurance, please," the officer said as only a state trooper could.

"They're all in the glove box, hon," Alex said calmly. "I'll get them." The officer watched her move for more than one reason.

"It's a rental," Jacob added, as if people rented trucks with an option to buy.

Alex handed the documents to Jacob who gave them to the trooper.

"I'll be right back." Pryce took the documents and went back to his car. Surely the news of the kidnapping and shootings had reached law enforcement by now.

"This can't be good. Why did he stop us?" Jacob said, showing a slight crack.

"Relax. If it gets ugly, it gets ugly."

Jacob turned as Alex produced a pistol from the small cooler at her feet. He turned back quickly.

After a long five minutes Officer Pryce was back at the driver side window. "Did you realize you were doing sixty-seven in a fifty-five mile an hour zone?"

Alex and Jacob looked at Pryce, and then back at each other.

"Really, officer? I thought this road was sixty-five?" Jacob said apologetically.

"In most places it is. Here it wasn't. Where are you headed?"

Alex, the strong wife, answered: "We're moving out to Youngstown from Wilmington. My husband just got his residency at Youngstown General. And I teach first grade."

"I see," he paused, "You two haven't been drinking, have you?"

"No, officer," they said in unison.

"Can you open the cooler please, ma'am?"

Jacob swallowed. He had a vision of trooper brains all over him. Alex pulled the cooler up and held it toward the two men. She slid the lid back. Nothing but diet soda. "We've been drinking caffeine like crazy this morning."

"What's in the back?" the officer continued.

"Mostly junk. We call it furniture. Plus a bunch of boxes. Want to take a look?" Alex responded calmly.

Jacob's heartrate went off the charts.

"No, ma'am, that's not why I'm asking. Most people who rent these kinds of trucks aren't used to the size and contents do tend to shift. And if you're going over the speed limit, you may have a tough time controlling the vehicle. Especially on this road."

"We hadn't thought of that. Thanks for the advice," she responded.

"We'll be very careful," Jacob added, his deep voice an octave higher.

Pryce ripped a ticket from his pad. "I knocked the ticket down to a busted tail light. Just pay it in time and you won't have points on your license or an insurance hike."

"Thanks," Jacob said as he took the ticket.

"And watch your speed the rest of the way."

"Yes, officer, we will. And thank you very much," Alex added as she leaned over to get closer to the window. Her loose fitting polo shirt opened up as she leaned over, giving Pryce a clean shot of her breasts.

Pryce smiled. "Have a nice day." He then turned and left. The blue and white pulled away and went a hundred yards to a turnaround then headed back east.

Jacob slumped in his chair. Alex pulled the gun out from between her legs and put it to his head.

"Now, honey," she started sarcastically, "we have two and a half miles to go. Please don't screw it up."

Ten minutes later the truck backed into the driveway of 23 Sunder Road, otherwise known as Safe House Number 6. There were ten such houses stretched from Vineland, New Jersey through DuBois, Pennsylvania. Each house had been rented by Jacob, who had posed as a graduate student the week before. Each house was "out of the way" and was prepaid for the first six months in cash. Move-in day was negotiated for the Friday before Memorial Day.

This house was located right off Route 220 in rural Pennsylvania. It was more than 400 yards from the next closest house, but a short drive to Lock Haven University.

Alex got out of the truck, unlocked the front door, and opened the garage door. Jacob backed the truck up as far as he could, right up against the house. No one could see what they were unloading.

"Get him, then the bed," Alex said, in command. "I'll pull the shades."

Jacob got the dolly down first and then worked the large box out of its resting place between a bookcase and a loveseat. Jacob was a big man, close to 6'4" and very strong. With some difficulty he got the crate onto the dolly, pulled back on it, and began to wheel it into the house. The load was uneven, and he struggled with it.

Alex checked to make sure the electric was on and it was. There would be no phone line, though it had been debated during the planning process. The phone companies asked too many questions. They would rely on the television for news regarding the kidnapping. The proliferation of all-news cable channels provided as good an early warning system as any. And if information was critical, it would be leaked to the press.

Jacob had convinced eight of the ten landlords to keep the cable on in their names. He'd pay the bill up front, explaining he wanted to save the cost of setup. Safe House 6 was cable ready.

Jacob wheeled the box through the kitchen and into the living room. Alex pointed to a back bedroom of the three-bedroom ranch, and Jacob dropped the crate off there and went back for the bed.

Alex had gotten a 13" TV from the truck and hooked it up to the cable box. She clicked through the channels and settled on one. There it was, Senator Stephenson's house, the house where they had been only seven hours before. The house where Mitch had died.

She listened intently for five minutes while Jacob got the bed set up. The FBI had not released many details yet. The news anchor and the on-scene reporter bantered back and forth about what they knew and speculated about what they did not. They mentioned Danny Sullivan and the IRA no less than six times in two minutes.

"The bed's together," Jacob interrupted.

They went to the back bedroom. Jacob worked on the crate with a crowbar and opened it quickly. And there he was, the senator from Pennsylvania, sleeping like a drug-induced baby. The two lifted him out of the crate and laid him on the bed on his side. The cuffs and tape were still in place. Alex uncuffed him and then recuffed his legs and hands to the four bedposts of the wooden frame.

"He's good another five hours or so. Why don't you get some sleep. I'll keep an eye on the news," Alex said looking at her watch.

Jacob nodded and headed for one of the other bedrooms to sleep on the floor. He wondered briefly if Alex would kill him in his sleep for the speeding screw up. She had killed for less.

Alex got the keys and went out to the truck. She carefully backed it into the garage. There was just enough clearance.

Outside the house a black SUV crawled slowly down Sunder Road with Jimmy Braxton behind the wheel. He slowed to notice that someone had moved into the Jenkins house. He had also noticed the beautiful creature that was moving in. The house had been empty for about three months, and now it looked like a college girl or girls were moving in. That was too good to be true.

"I'll have to welcome them to the neighborhood, Jimmy Braxton style," he said to himself. He checked himself out in the rearview mirror and pulled away.

chapter 12

Her fifteen minutes had come and the clock was ticking. The tip from the jogger had landed her instant stardom. Donna would be forever known as the face of the Stephenson incident. And the beauty of it all was that a full hour after the story had broke she was still the only reporter on the scene. The affiliates in Philadelphia had recalled traffic helicopters to shuttle reporters to the scene, but the closest they could land was Ocean City, a full twenty minutes away. Like a plane crash in the middle of a cornfield, this was not an easy place to get to.

Donna fixed her hair in the news van's mirror. She looked a little tired. She had been up since three in the morning, but the excitement of the breaking story was enough to carry her. She was just waiting for her next chance to address the nation.

She looked over at the house as she sipped her coffee and wondered what was going on in there.

Special Agent Thomas T. Jackson of the FBI stood in the kitchen of the Stephenson beach house and wondered just what had happened and how it had happened.

He had a small army of agents combing the beach for evidence outside while the forensics team worked their magic inside. He also sent a few newer agents out to knock on doors, to see if anyone saw anything.

Agents moved cautiously and silently in the house, a trademark of a well run, no bullshit Jackson operation. Some were taking pictures, others dusting for prints. Windbreakers identified who was who. Jackson could hear the faint footsteps on the next floor. Man, was this some house.

Jackson sipped on his styrofoam cup. A voice came from behind him. "You know, Tom, this happens twenty-four hours later and we have a hundred witnesses." It was his old partner and long-time friend, Special Agent Michael Thompson.

Thompson was tall with curly, dirty blonde hair. He was the same height as Jackson. The two had come into the bureau together over twenty years before and had become instant friends. They were called the "twins," which was ironic because Jackson was an African-American and Thompson was pale white.

"You're right about that. This town is dead. No pun," Jackson replied.

"None taken. This place is real clean, Tom. Whoever did this knew what they were doing."

Before he could comment, his cell phone rang and he picked it out of his coat pocket. "Jackson." He paused to listen. "That's very interesting, sir. Yes, that is interesting." Pause. "Yes, sir, no screw-ups on this one." Longer pause. "Yes, sir, every square inch of this town will be looked at." He rolled his eyes slightly as the assistant director went on and on. "Yes, sir, everyone will be watching this one. I understand. Bye."

"Was that our dear friend? How is he doing?" Thompson chided.

"Not well."

The two men moved to the kitchen table, away from any other ears. They both stared down at the cassette player that held the only information they had to go on.

Jackson spoke, "The assistant director is getting more pressure than it sounds like he can handle. The President called him, personally, at home."

"Ouch."

"Yeah. And he is trying to inflict his pain on me." Jackson took a deep breath and put both hands to his eyes to help him concentrate. "Mike, what happened here? How do you see it?"

Thompson thought for a second. "Well, looks like there are at least two, probably four. My guess is the cops were probably killed by two separate groups of intruders. A set on the beach, a set at the front door."

"Okay. Let's take the back," Jackson directed.

"My guess is that Watkins sees or catches someone trying to enter the house. He's young, so he fires a round, maybe misses, fires another, gets the dead guy in the leg, then finishes him. Then the second guy gets him."

"They don't exchange fire?" Jackson asked.

"Not likely. Judging by the wounds, the kid was killed instantly."

Jackson nodded. Thompson had always been great to bounce ideas off of, and Jackson had asked for him specifically. "So he doesn't see the second guy?"

"My guess not. Pitch black night. Probably didn't see him until it was too late."

Jackson paused, then: "What about out front?"

"Okay. The officer in the front, the old guy, saw the killer, he was shot in the chest. Either he didn't hear what had happened out back, or he went first. Someone gets him to the front door and lights out."

"And the senator and the aide, Slade I think, they don't hear a thing?"

"They came off an eighteen-hour flight from China, plus the ocean sounds must have drowned out any noise. Killers could have used silencers. We'll know from the slugs," Thompson explained.

"True. But Watkins didn't have a silencer," Jackson pointed out.

Thompson paused and thought. "Okay, maybe the front goes down first, the bad guys are up the stairs and into the rooms before the shots are fired."

"Maybe, but then there would need to be at least three in the front. Stephenson put up a fight. I am sure there were at least two bad guys in his room."

Thompson thought that through, too. "You know, it sounds corny, but maybe the gunshots sounded like thunder. Just a thought."

"Maybe. So how did they escape? Sea, land, or air?"

Thompson pulled out his note pad. "Roland has the time of death between 1:00 and 3:00 A.M. You know Roland. He can't commit until he cuts them open. That would give them five to seven hours before the shift change. They had to plan on that."

"We're checking the small airfields in the area. My guess is they didn't fly out of here," Jackson added.

"Probably right. It would be one thing to kill him and then fly, but they have a big man to carry around. And I hope they didn't fly because they could be very far away by now," Thompson said.

"Think they landed a boat on the beach?" Jackson queried.

"Possible. But it would have to have come from somewhere, and we are checking marinas."

"If you could figure on a six-hour head start, wouldn't you just drive out of here calmly and disappear?"

"Seems logical," Thompson said as he shrugged.

Jackson changed the subject. "But here is the million dollar question. Did the IRA really do this?"

"Sure looks like it. Someone is looking to get Danny Sullivan out before he fries, for whatever reason. Maybe they thought Sullivan would name names to save his ass. Then there's the tape. Irish accent. Anyway, who else has motive?" Thompson added.

"Name them. Stephenson is a politician after all, which means he pisses off half the population with anything he does. And he has made some enemies overseas."

That comment seemed to bother Thompson, and he folded his arms. "So, you don't think it's the IRA?"

"I just think it's a little too clean," Jackson said.

"Okay. Let's play devil's advocate. Sullivan aside, the tape has an Irish accent."

"Could have been imitated," Jackson countered.

"So we're looking for Rich Little?" Thompson joked, but was serious.

Jackson smiled. Maybe Thompson was right, he thought.

One of the agents who was working in the house, Kittridge, came over to the two men and cleared his throat.

"Yes?" Jackson asked.

"Sir, we just got a positive ID on the dead bad guy."

"Who was he?" Thompson jumped in.

"You won't believe this. Turns out that it's Sean Flaherty," the agent said, reading from his notepad.

"Irish. Why does that name sound familiar?" Thompson asked.

"Irish all right, as in Irish Republican Army. Sean Flaherty was an IRA bomb maker that was supposed to have died in a car accident about six years ago," Kittridge answered.

"I'll be damned," Jackson muttered.

"Found the prints on Interpol. His death had been confirmed by an IRA mole," Kittridge added.

"Who better to bring in for this job than someone who was already dead?" Thompson said as Kittridge folded his notepad and went off.

"Looks like you're right, Mike."

"Wasn't hard to be right on this one," Thompson admitted.

"Let's get the press together, and let's make a statement. Let's tell them that the senator has been kidnapped, and let's let them know about the tape."

"Shouldn't be hard. There's only that one reporter, a woman. No one else has been able to get on the island. We've blocked it off," Thompson said with a smile.

"Nothing like securing a crime scene. You know what, Mike, bring her in here and let's talk to her. Maybe we can use her." Jackson smiled back.

A half hour later, televisions across America were tuned to another appearance by Donna Van Ness. "NBC News has confirmed that United States Senator Phillip J. Stephenson was abducted early this morning from his summer home here in Avalon, New Jersey in a raid that took the lives of his aide, Mitch Slade, and two Avalon police officers. We have also confirmed that the kidnappers have left a list of demands. Or should I say 'demand.' Although they did not identify themselves, they have demanded the release of convicted death row inmate and Irish national Danny 'Mad Dog' Sullivan whose execution is days away. Sullivan, who has ties to the Irish Republican Army, was convicted by then Philadelphia Assistant DA Stephenson in one of the most celebrated trials in Philadelphia history.

"The demands give no specific timetable but do stress that the health and welfare of the senator is directly related to the health and welfare of Danny Sullivan.

"This is Donna Van Ness, NBC News, reporting from Avalon, New Jersey."

chapter 13

Traffic on Fridays in northern New Jersey was always a mess, a bigger mess on summer Fridays, and a disaster on the Friday before Memorial Day. To make matters worse for Keith, his beach house was at the other end of the state. He and Cindy would have to drive through all of the New York traffic only to be greeted with the Philly traffic after Long Beach Island. The trip on a good day was two and a half hours; they were looking at four hours or more as they left at three in the afternoon.

"Can you believe it? Can you believe what happened to the senator? I used to see him on the beach jogging all the time last year," Cindy asked Keith as he opened the passenger side door.

Keith threw his backpack in the back seat and slid into the passenger seat of Cindy's standard issue pharmaceutical sales rep car. He looked her straight in the eye, "No. I can honestly say I cannot believe it."

"It's too weird. Way too weird. It's like nothing is sacred anymore."

"Nothing is," Keith emphasized.

The four door sedan pulled out from in front of the yogurt shop. The car moved slowly down Washington Street, having to stop every block for the never-ending series of traffic lights.

"Sorry I was late," Cindy said as they stopped again.

"No problem. You're my ride. I leave when you leave," he said.

"Well, it is a problem, and I am sorry. That asshole Derek showed up at my apartment just as I am about to leave. Ahhhhhh!" She let loose.

Keith let her vent. He was becoming more and more convinced that he didn't need to say anything bad about Derek; the boy did well enough on his own.

"Then he wastes two hours of my time, our time, trying to convince me to take him back. What an asshole!"

Keith said nothing.

Cindy looked over at him. "You alive?"

"Yes, but I think you know what I think of Derek, so no use stating the obvious," he said.

"You're right. I'm sorry. He just pisses me off so much. I just had to vent."

"No problem," Keith replied. Cindy lost none of her beauty when she got angry, he thought.

"So, were you able to find out the deal about getting onto the island?"

"I called the borough today and sat on hold for forty-five minutes. Had nothing better to do at work with the relocation so close," Keith explained.

"What did they say?"

He paused, "Well, they said we could get on. They also said they had no idea how long it would take."

"Great," she said, dropping her forehead to the steering wheel.

"And the beaches from 29th to 70th may be closed tomorrow because of the investigation," he added.

"Even better. I may have to come to your beach." Cindy's house was located on 42nd Street and Keith was on the bay off of 21st Street.

"That's not it though. Apparently the spring storms did a number on the beaches from 10th through 14th."

"How bad?" She didn't want to know.

"Well, there is no beach there. All gone."

"You're full of useful facts, aren't ya?"

Keith went on, "Here's a couple more. They started to dredge the inlet and hope to have the beaches rebuilt in the next three weeks."

"That doesn't help me this weekend," Cindy replied.

"Maybe it'll rain," he said with a smile.

Cindy looked over at Keith, "You're going to be walking if you keep this up. Why don't you turn on the radio before you get in any more trouble." She gave him a smile that could make a happily married man leave his wife.

Mr. Jones glanced at his watch then continued to review the press release. It was 4:15 P.M. and they would make the announcement at 4:45 P.M., after the market closed. That would give the analysts a long weekend to review the move. He found the after-hours press release a good way to keep National Merchandising's stock price stable. Many times moves were misinterpreted and sent stock prices all over the board. Jones wanted stability through this transition.

The timing, however, hurt his employees. They would be called into meetings around the country and be given the news. They would have a long weekend to consider their futures.

Jones sat back in his leather chair and put the paper down on his desk. On the wall facing him was a large bookcase that had two 32" televisions built in. The one to the right was off; that was used for closed circuit telecasts only, typically with overseas import offices. The TV to the left was tuned to CNN's extensive coverage of the Stephenson kidnapping.

Jones had paid careful attention all day. Most of the broadcast was rehash or blabber from a so-called expert in the field. He hit the mute button and the set came alive with sound. He listened for a few minutes, then, satisfied nothing had changed, he muted the sound.

He went back to the piece of paper. Everyone had plans for the weekend, but none bigger than his.

He pressed a speed dial button on his phone. "Hicks, it's me. The release looks fine. Let's go with it."

A light came on his phone and he punched the button. "Yes?"

"Mr. Jones, Mr. Tarman is ready when you are to go over the employee evaluations."

"Tell him I'll be right in," he answered back.

"And we'll be right back with more on the Stephenson kidnapping." The screen faded from the anchorman to a graphic overlay with the words: "A NATION HELD HOSTAGE: THE STEPHENSON KIDNAPPING".

Tommy got off the edge of his bed and headed for the bathroom of his hotel room. He turned the shower knobs until the water was just right, then went to the sink. He stripped, then leaned on the marble sink and stared into the mirror. He studied the lines of his face for a few seconds. Some of the scars and nicks were new, he thought.

A long day, he thought. Tommy had been to visit the graves of two old friends, two friends that were dead because of him. He stared in the mirror, and it began to fog around the edges. The two names played over and over in his head: Antonio and Kevin. He could see their faces, one a good looking Italian kid, the other a large, mentally challenged kid from the neighborhood.

Antonio had been killed while on a hit. Tommy had taken the contract, and he and Antonio both knew the risks. But they hadn't expected that one of them would get killed, and Tommy blamed himself. There had been a lack of information.

Kevin was different. A 6'5" man child, Kevin was mentally handicapped. Tommy had used him as muscle, just for show, when he went out to collect debts. He never made Kevin do anything, he just had him stand behind him as he talked over payment plans. And it worked well for both, as Tommy was able to keep Kevin clean and away from the other Westies who would have had Kevin do worse.

But in the height of the FBI's investigation into the Westies, Kevin was brought in for questioning. They bombarded him with questions and accusations for over ten hours. Confused and unable to comprehend the situation, Kevin attacked the agents, breaking one's collarbone and another's leg. Two more agents could not subdue him, and in the struggle, Kevin was shot in the stomach. He died on the operating table and on Tommy's conscience.

Tommy looked back at the mirror, and it had fogged over completely.

Three blocks away, Mr. Jones walked into the company's executive conference room and found Tarman standing at the end of a large oblong table. The table, which sat twenty comfortably, had countless stacks of employee files arranged in neat piles.

"Sorry we have to start this now, Rick," Jones said knowing that the sentiment carried no meaning.

"Not a problem," he replied as he adjusted his round framed glasses.

Jones sat in his customary seat in the middle of the right-hand side of the table, and Tarman sat across from him.

"This may take some time, but we have to get moving," Jones reminded.

And they did have to get moving. The 4:45 P.M. announcement would effectively merge fourteen buying and support divisions of National Merchandising into one central buying office in New York. The consolidation was the largest of its kind in retail and would take almost a full year to complete. While competitors struggled with how to manage their expense structures, Jones just took a large bite out of his.

National's move would give them great economies of scale—fourteen buying offices for the price of one. Also, he would get the best personnel from fourteen buying divisions to be his "super merchants." The other thirteen people not picked would be looking for work.

That is what they were there to do, make the decisions. When it was all over, he would have a hungry, motivated buying and support staff that would cost him about eight percent of what he had been paying to get the same results. It was a bold move. But not his boldest.

The sun was still hanging in there over the bay just outside Ocean City, but at a little after 7:00 it was on its way down. Keith and Cindy had been on the Garden State Parkway for about four hours, and they were still a good twelve miles from their objective, Avalon. They had listened to both the traffic reports and the kidnapping updates all the way down the tree-lined parkway. The news about traffic was not so good. But they didn't need a radio station to tell them that, they had been inching along for about twenty minutes and had gone about three miles. Traffic was not better on any of the local roads. There were no shortcuts.

The radio said that the FBI was monitoring traffic coming in and stopping traffic leaving the island. This was contributing to the delays. Plus, the FBI had closed off one of the two roads that ran the length of the island, making it hard to get on from the lone access road.

Keith had been driving since the Cheesequake rest stop up north, part of the deal. He didn't mind, the windows were down, there was a great breeze, and he could smell the ocean. Plus, he had great company.

"I figure once we do get there, I'll jump out on Ocean Drive and walk," Keith said, breaking the silence.

"Why?" Cindy said, looking like she was being punished.

"Well if the traffic is as bad on the island as it is here, I would hate for you to take me in one direction and have to fight traffic all the way back," he reasoned out loud.

"Oh. Okay. Are you sure?"

"Sure. I need to stretch my legs a little after this," he added.

Two hours and twelve miles later, Cindy switched seats with Keith. She kissed him on the cheek goodbye and said she'd "definitely" catch up with him over the weekend.

Keith started walking slowly north along Ocean Drive as the red car pulled away. The sky was dark, but car and house lights lit his way. He took a deep breath of sea air and felt at home.

He made it to 21st Street and crossed the bridge back to the bay. Two blocks later he was standing in front of the rental house.

The house was huge and pink with South Beach Miami teal accents. Even the second floor wraparound deck had the color scheme. This house would not be hard to find in a drunken stupor.

His sneakers crunched the white pebble front yard as he made his way to the front door. The door was unlocked, and he went in. His first thought was, "This is big." He moved left into the living area that looked in on the kitchen. Various duffel bags lay on the floor and on the sofas. He dropped his and went into the kitchen. He looked out the back window to the bay and saw their slip and the boat they had rented for the summer. This was going to be great.

There was a note scribbled on a paper plate and taped to the refrigerator. "To whom it may concern. We're getting faced over at the Princeton."

Keith smiled and made his way back out of the house. He would have plenty of time to check the rest of the layout. The Princeton Bar and Grill was only a few blocks away, and he needed a beer.

chapter 14

The senator spoke into the microphone slowly and deliberately. He had trouble with some words. The drugs had put him in an eighteen-hour haze, so they had been forced to do a number of takes.

"One more time," Jacob insisted through his ski mask as he reset the tape.

Stephenson's feet were shackled to the thick wood bedposts, and his hands were cuffed behind him, allowing him to sit up. He was a mess; matted hair, pale and shaking. He had some trouble keeping his balance, like a newborn getting used to the mechanics of sitting up straight, and fell over twice during filming. His captors were not amused.

After six tries, he was awake, able to both balance himself and speak fluently.

"This is United States Senator Phillip Stephenson. I will be brief. The people who have kidnapped me are very intent on having their demands met." He had no idea what they were, but he assumed cash. "They tell me if those demands are not met that I will be killed a week from today, Saturday, June 3rd. There will be no negotiations. Please wait for further instructions." Jacob shut the camera off and left the room.

"Very good, senator," Alex said like a first grade teacher giving encouragement. "I am sure you are normally a very persuasive speaker."

The senator glared at the woman behind the mask. He thought of screaming for help, but didn't know if that would accomplish anything. And despite being an athletic man, there was no way in his current state that he could overpower either of them.

"So, what are your demands? I mean, it's only fair to tell me, right? I may be able to help you get what you want," the senator asked.

"It's sad. Even in your darkest moment you still act like a politician," Alex said as she sat next to him on the edge of the bed.

"Well, if you must know."

"I must," he insisted.

"We are ransoming your life for the release of one of your favorite people, Danny Sullivan," she said.

"All this trouble to get that animal out of jail?"

"Oh, you were no trouble at all. Mitch and those police officers, now they were trouble. Emphasis on 'were.'"

"They're dead?" he said in disbelief.

"As doorknobs." She paused, "Are you hungry? We don't want you to die on us just yet."

Stephenson was speechless. Mitch dead? The woman was callous, he thought.

"Not hungry then? Oh well, you let us know."

Jacob came back into the room after packing the videotape for pickup. He pulled a gun out of his waistband, walked calmly over to the senator and pressed the gun's barrel against the cuffed man's right temple.

Alex leaned over and whispered, "This won't hurt a bit."

The prisoner froze in panic. He closed his eyes and started to mumble a Hail Mary. He thought maybe he should not have cooperated with the videotaping, maybe he should have stayed a district attorney. He thought of his wife and kids.

Then click. Not the click of the gun's trigger, but the click of handcuffs being unlocked behind him. Alex took his right hand, the one with the cuff still attached, and hooked it to the bedpost. The senator was too frightened to move. The gun was still at his head as Alex cuffed the left hand to the other post.

Jacob left and came back in with the syringe case. He opened it, drew a needle full of a clear liquid, walked over and stuck the senator on his shoulder. There was no struggle.

Alex stood over him like an angel, an angel of death, the senator thought.

She leaned across him to the opposite ear, her breasts pressing against him and whispered, "This shouldn't take long. Sweet dreams."

The senator felt tingling in his extremities and was getting lightheaded. He started to get delirious and angry. He was going to take his chance.

Jimmy Braxton had downed about six beers at happy hour with some buddies, but the women weren't biting; so he grabbed a twelve pack and decided to pay his new neighbor a visit.

The black SUV pulled up across the road from the house. He grabbed the twelve pack and uncoiled his long, lean frame in stages out of the truck. He strode confidently across the dark dirt road. It would have been rude of him not to welcome a beautiful new neighbor. This approach had actually worked a couple of times before for him. Jimmy's limited intellect didn't go as far as to think that maybe the girl in the truck was married or otherwise attached. When he saw a pretty girl he thought "single."

He went to knock on the front door, but heard screams from within the house. Sounded like a man calling for help. He put the beer down and went around back for a look.

There it was again, he thought. It sounded like a muffled scream. All the windows he passed had the shades pulled down. It was coming from the back of the house.

He got to the room where light hit the pulled shade and figured that was where the ruckus was. He could hear movement, strained movement. He stood in front of the window as he pondered his next move. Maybe there was some kind of sex game going on? Maybe it was like a two on one? He hoped. His twisted thoughts went down strange roads.

The senator had fought his best as the two successfully gagged him. Jacob held his shoulders down while Alex stuffed a sock in his mouth and taped over it. The senator struggled, even as a fading mute. The drugs had won over him.

Jacob and Alex both stood up at the same time and their feet got tangled. Jacob fell toward the window and grabbed for the sill to support him, but got the shade instead. He ripped the shade out of its brackets as he fell to the floor.

"Oh, shit," Jimmy said as the shade came down and he got a view of the room. Hot babe in a ski mask. Tied up guy on the bed that looked like the kidnapped senator guy.

Jacob got to his feet and came face to face with the peeping Tom. Everybody froze for a second, then Jimmy took off. Jacob turned and went for the kitchen door.

Jimmy had slipped and fell but was back on his feet and was back in gear. He could see his truck from the side of the house. It was so close.

Jacob exploded through the kitchen door on the side of the house like he was shot from a cannon, clipping Jimmy in the side and taking him down hard, shoulder to ribs.

Jacob rolled off Jimmy as he struggled to gain his breath back. Jimmy got to one knee as Jacob got to both feet. Jacob went to kick the prone man in the ribs, but Jimmy lurched up and grabbed the foot and pulled Jacob to the ground. Jimmy Braxton had been in his fair share of fights.

"Come on, bitch," he said taunting Jacob as they both got to their feet.

Jacob, clearly the bigger of the two men, rushed Jimmy again and tackled him as he tried to move away. That worked momentarily, but Jimmy was back up on his feet quickly and drove his boot into the bridge of Jacob's nose.

"Take that, bitch!"

Jimmy stood over the man as he took his mask off, using it to help stop the blood volcano that was his nose. Jacob tried to get to his feet, and Jimmy went to level another kick to the head, but his legs wouldn't move. He felt his back, and blood, a lot of it, stained his hand. He felt faint and turned to see the babe in the ski mask aiming to finish him off. He closed his eyes and felt a ripping pain in his chest and then nothing.

"Get up and get him in the house," Alex ordered Jacob as she moved closer to the boy to make sure he was dead. She stood over him, gun with silencer attachment in hand, and felt nothing either way. She reached down and searched his pockets for truck keys and fished them out.

Jacob was finally on his feet, his face a crimson festival, and grabbed the boy's feet and dragged him to the kitchen door. Jimmy's head bounced hard off the two cement steps as he was taken into the house.

Alex got to the black truck, started it, and pulled it into the driveway. She got out, opened the garage door and pulled it in.

It took them a little over a half hour to repack the van, senator and all. They knew the possibility of movement existed, but didn't expect it this quick.

"Do you think anyone knows he came here?" Jacob said with a nasal twang. His nose was a mess.

"Maybe some buddies, who knows. We just need to be out of here," she said, hiding her anger.

"The explosive device and accelerator are in place. The timer is set for an hour," he said back.

"Well then, let's get out of here."

The truck pulled out of the garage without lights on. Jacob jumped out and closed the garage door behind them. They got onto Sunder Road, turned the lights on, and headed back for Interstate 80.

An hour later a small explosive device went off in the house and started a fire. The accelerator took over from there and in seconds the house and Jimmy Braxton went up in flames.

chapter 15

The beach Keith was standing on didn't exist a week ago. He stared into the large, three-foot diameter, rust colored metal pipe as is it spewed sea water, sand, as well as mollusk and crustacean parts on the beach.

Seagulls, the pigeons of the beach, hovered by the mouth of the great pipe hoping to pick off a piece of crab or other sea life. This was dredging, this was man's way of fighting beach erosion.

The sun was bright, and the cool northern breeze from the ocean reminded the beachgoers that it was not quite summer yet in New Jersey. Keith stood, arms crossed, barefoot in the sand, watching the onslaught. The noise from the rush of water, combined with the screech of the seagulls, made it hard to even think. His hangover was slowly going away, another night of partying, and the relentless rush of water seemed to take the edge off.

The pipe reminded him of one of those 1970's environmental commercials that showed waste being dumped from sewage pipes into the ocean. He was waiting for the Native American, tear running down his cheek, to pop out from behind the dunes.

Seven days ago a dredge boat from the Carolinas parked itself in Townsend's Inlet, the waterway that separated Avalon from its neighbor to the north, Sea Isle City. The large vessel's job was to replenish the sand that had been eroded by storms from the northern tip of the island. Avalon was missing six blocks of beach.

Crews ran metal pipes from the boat 400 yards along the sea floor on to the inlet beach and then another couple of hundred yards along the dune line to the spot where they wanted to build a beach.

The hydraulic dredger then began to dig up the sea floor. The centrifugal pump forced all the sand, along with anything else, through the pipes and onto the waiting beach-to-be. The process had been going night and day since set up. The flow only stopped for crews to move the pipes further down the coast.

After a few more minutes of mind-numbing pipe watching, Keith started his walk back to home base. Three blocks away, his group of seven or so friends were hard to miss; all members of the party were in different states of lounge in their beach chairs while a PSU flag waved above them in the wind.

The 21st Street beach was more crowded than usual, the overflow from the closed, and not yet built, beaches. His group consisted of Steve and Dave and their girlfriends, Jill and Andrea. They were all in their chairs. Steve's rugby buddies, Ronny and Howard, were off playing beach boche ball. Steph and Amy were laid out on beach towels watching for men. Ed and Karen would be down soon, it was only noon. They all nursed hangovers of varying degrees.

"What's it look like down there?" Steve asked over his *Philadelphia Inquirer*.

"Pretty cool, you should take a look," Keith said noticing that his pale friend was picking up some red.

"Maybe later. You know, they gave a stay of execution to that asshole Sullivan," he said from behind the paper.

Dave put his football magazine down, "Makes sense."

"They should fry the bastard anyway. You can't back down like that," Steve pointed out.

"Maybe. Maybe they want to show a sign of good faith?" Dave countered.

"Well, the chances of Stephenson coming back alive are slim and none. Don't get me wrong; I like him. The only Democrat I ever voted for."

Keith angled toward the two. "I don't see what they would do with Sullivan anyway. I mean, how do they expect to get him out of the country?" Keith interjected.

"They probably want him dead as bad as anybody. He's a potential leak. He needs to be plugged," Steve replied.

"Seems desperate," Dave added.

"Desperation is relative," Steve answered, then went on to sports section and gave his critique of the Phils' pitching staff.

Keith closed his eyes and took a deep breath. He missed being with his friends. Though he lived only ninety miles away, it was hard to see them with everyone's ever-complicated lives. This summer would allow him to catch up and forget about Shannon. He closed his eyes and leaned back.

"Hey, stranger," the voice came from right in front of him no more than five minutes into his nap.

Keith opened his eyes to a vision. Steve put his paper down, Dave put his magazine down, and even Ronny and Howard took a break from their game. Cindy could do that to men.

"Hey, what's going on, Cin?" Keith said.

"Not much. How are you guys making out?"

The guys were in a trance. Cindy's body had a black Brazilian cut bikini clinging to it. Her hair was pulled back in a pony tail, her long legs were tan already, her eyes hid behind reflective lens sunglasses; she could have passed for a pro volleyball player/model.

"We're doing okay. Don't know if you remember Dave and Steve from high school." Cindy turned and pulled her glasses down. The boys waved, trying to look cool and then went back to their reading material. The other girls tried not to pay attention.

"Oh, yeah. Didn't you three used to get into trouble all the time?" she said with a smile.

"Something like that," Keith answered for them.

Cindy looked the group over. "Where's the tall guy with blonde hair?"

"You mean Eddie?" Keith answered.

"Yeah, he was always funny."

"He'll be down soon," Keith said.

The two looked at each other as everyone else tried to look away.

Cindy smiled, then said, "Anyway, we're having a 'Free the Senator' party tonight. You guys interested?"

"I think we could be persuaded. We could stop by after the Windrift. What time?" Keith saked.

"Nine, ten, whatever," Cindy said running fingers through her hair. "Hey, your sister is down at our house."

"Really? She couldn't come by to say hi?"

"Nope. I wanted you all to myself," she said, raising an eyebrow.

"Hey, guys, up for a party at Cindy's after the Windrift?" Keith asked the group. Heads nodded.

"We're in," Keith spoke for the group.

"Great. I'll see you then. Or maybe I'll see you at the Drift just to make sure you show up."

"Either way. Sounds good to me," Keith said as coolly as he could.

Cindy stood up, leaned over and kissed Keith on the cheek. "Bye."

As she walked away she was getting more attention than the plane flying over head trailing a "1/2 PRICE DRINKS AT THE SPRINGFIELD" banner.

At 3:30 P.M. the boys were ready to get off the beach and get started on their next hangover. Dave, Steve, and Keith carried their beach chairs with them as they hit 21st Street and started the walk home.

The brunette had showed up at Tommy's hotel room with the videotape and the VCRs just after four o'clock Saturday afternoon. And then she was gone.

Each safe house had a drop point nearby where the tape was to be left. The brunette had to retrace the escape route and check each of them. She finally struck gold at the point near Safe House Five. Tommy didn't care to know where she had picked up the tape.

Tommy had slept little in the past thirty-six hours. Not all his thoughts were on the mission. He missed Alex and worried about her. She was smart and self-reliant, but also antsy. He worried about her getting bored and speeding up the timetable or deviating from the plan. She would have to be patient, and that was hard for her.

Tommy put leather gloves on and began to set up the VCRs. He used gold cables to connect them together so he could do tape-to-tape recording. A stack of three blank tapes sat on his bed. Once he was set up, he played the original tape using an earpiece to listen to the audio.

Perfect, he thought as he watched it again.

He pulled the first blank down and slid it into the other VCR. Alex and Jacob had done a fine job.

At 6:00 P.M. the line at the Windrift, the quintessential beach bar located on the border of Avalon and Stone Harbor, was not as bad as it would be an hour later. It would get bad, snaking for a full block, but Keith and his friends got in before the rush.

They had staked out a nice spot in the corner of the "beach" part of the bar. The Drift, as it was affectionately called, was part inside bar, part outside bar, part restaurant, part hotel. The outside portion of the bar was right up on the dunes. The ocean could be heard there and the breeze off the sea was something unto itself. A band played inside that no one could hear.

The beach area was fenced off and was about thirty feet deep and more than sixty feet long. The Windrift had long been an older hang out, but over the years all ages came "drifting".

Ed and Dave came back with a round of light beers and Keith grabbed one to help lighten their load. The girls were talking to each other about this and that and occasionally they would comment on an outfit or a man. The guys stood to the side of them. Steve, Ronny, and Howard played liar's poker with dollar bills and Dave and Ed joined after unloading their beers.

Keith's skin was a little burnt, a healthy, red glow that he could feel, but it wasn't painful. He saw a lot of that in the faces in the crowd. The beach floor was getting packed. People wove their way through little clusters of friends, trying to get somewhere else or just looking. There was an undercurrent of excitement associated with the first happy hour of the summer and Keith could feel it.

He leaned up against the wood fence and the edge of the dunes and thought of Cindy and that bikini and thought it was time he made some kind of move. She was flirting with him, wasn't she? That's what the guys said. Shannon had to be banished forever, erased from the hard drive. But close to a year later, it was still hard to forget.

Steph came over and leaned next to him. "I'm going for shots, wanna come?"

Keith considered that for a moment. He looked across the crowd and saw her, saw Cindy. As she got closer, weaving through the crowd, a guy was trailing her, holding her hand. It couldn't be, but it was. Derek. Before she could make eye contact, he turned to Steph, "Shots? What a good idea."

There was more than one way to erase one's hard drive.

chapter 16

"Get up lazy ass," Steve said poking Keith in the ribs with a cold bottle of water. Steve was sweating as he was just back from a morning run.

Keith opened and closed his eyes several times, trying to focus on his friend's face. "Go away."

"Come on, boy, the day is getting old. Ed is already up," Steve said a little too loud.

"What time is it?" Keith's throat was dry and swollen.

"Hell, it's already nine," Steve replied.

"Bullshit. Ed wouldn't be up at nine." Keith rolled over. He had flashes of getting in as the sun was coming up. There were the shots, then a trip to Wildwood, then an all-night bar, Moore's, then hitchhiking back. Ouch.

"Come on, get your butt out of bed. We're having breakfast—bacon, egg, and cheese sandwiches with mimosa chasers."

Keith pulled the seashell patterned bedspread over his head in a weak effort to drown Steve's voice. "Go away."

Steve laughed and put the water down on the nightstand next to the bed. He was about to razz him one more time but decided against it and left the room.

Keith tried desperately to figure out the sequence of events. The Windrift and Cindy and shots. He didn't make it to Cindy's party, he was pretty sure about that. It was a blur. It would come back to him.

He fished around on the nightstand for the bottled water and got a hand on it. It was cold and liquid and, at that moment, beautiful. He struggled to sit up in the twin bed and finally did. He looked around, trying to get his bearings. He had woken up in the "orange" room, a ten by ten room with bright orange, mosaic, floor to ceiling wall paper. It was the room reserved for the last person to go to bed or the drunkest. Keith assumed he was both. The color hurt his eyes. It was so bright, even with the shades drawn. Alone in the orange room dressed in his stale and smelly clothes with nothing but his thoughts. This was rock bottom.

"Okay," me muttered, "what did I do?" He checked to make sure he had his underwear on and then for tattoos. Okay on both accounts. He shuddered that hangover shiver. He could feel the alcohol pulsing through his body.

His mind jumped. What was Cindy's deal anyway? Comes on to him like that and then shows up with her sometime boyfriend at a place she knew he was going to be? Who needs that?

He opened the bottle and drank the water slowly, the liquid hurt against his throat. It was too early to do this. He lay back down and rolled over.

The "pop" of the champagne bottle and the chatter woke him. It sounded too close to be coming from downstairs. He opened his eyes to see a little party going on in his room, all around him. Steph was sitting on the edge of his bed, pouring carefully, mixing champagne and orange juice into cheap plastic champagne glasses. Steve and Dave were leaning against a dresser. Howard sat on the floor reading the paper and Ed, all 6'6" of him, was stretched out on the other twin bed. He was fast asleep.

"It is alive," Dave announced as Keith sat up. A small cheer went out.

"What time is it?" Keith moaned.

"A little past noon," Steph said pouring another glass. "You have the record for latest sleep so far."

"And you deserve it," Steve added. "What were you thinking last night?"

"Not much, obviously." Keith felt better, relatively speaking. "Why aren't you at the beach?"

"Take a look," Dave said, opening the shade. The sky was a cool gray and the rain was steady. Weatherman was wrong again.

"And when it rains at the beach, what do we do?" Howard chimed in.

"Drink!!!" All said in unison.

"And since you couldn't make it downstairs, we figured we'd bring it to you."

"Great," Keith said as Steph handed him a glass. He took a sip and shuddered. It was going to be a long day.

"So, how does it feel to be off death row?" Youngman asked through the plexiglass. He never thought those words would come from his mouth. He was not sure how he felt about it.

Danny sat on the other side, playing with a cigarette, paying little attention. He then looked at his lawyer and smiled, "Great."

"Now, you know this might not play out for you. I just want to reiterate that. It's just a stay."

"You're a ray of sunshine, aren't ya? The first bit of good news I get, and you shit all over it. Lawyers. You're a killjoy, that's what you are."

Youngman took a deep breath. Why did he even try? He should have given this client up years ago and let some crusading, anti-death penalty, ACLU do-gooder deal with Danny. But this case gnawed at him; it was a loss, and he wanted to see it through.

"I just didn't want you to get any false hope," Youngman cautioned.

Danny rose in his chair and got up against the divider. "Let me tell you something. I'll take false hope over no hope at all. Don't underestimate the power of positive thinking."

Point taken, the lawyer acknowledged. Youngman could not imagine the mental anguish of death row, the day after day grind of living knowing that you were alive just to die, that your demise was a "to do" on someone's day planner. The mind game that someone actually controlled the amount of time you had left to breathe.

"Lousy weekend, huh?" Danny said back in his chair.

"Not lousy, just unexpected." Danny was right, though; it had been lousy.

Saturday had been "FBI Day" on death row as agents questioned Danny on and off for twelve hours. They wanted information on the kidnapping; surely Danny had to know something. They cajoled and threatened, but Danny didn't have any answers for them. Youngman believed he knew nothing about it. And they were coming back today. But what leverage did they have? What could they possibly threaten a man on death row with? A really bad death?

Youngman knew today would be deal day. Information for getting off death row. Life with no parole vs. certain death.

"The FBI is here again today for questioning," Youngman stated simply.

Danny smiled. "I hope it's the two boys from yesterday. I liked them. It would be like a family reunion, wouldn't it?"

Youngman leaned forward. "Danny, I think they are going to offer you a deal. Tell them about the kidnapping, and they'll help you."

"Problem is, I don't know anything."

"Sure?" Youngman pressed.

"Listen, I may not know it all, but I am smart enough to know what I don't know. Follow?" Danny said like a bad guy in a thirties prison movie.

"Yeah, Danny, I follow."

Tommy had a busy Sunday planned for himself, á day of running errands in the big city. He had watched the copies of the tape and was satisfied with the quality. He had purchased each of the three blank tapes at separate stores in three different cities over the last few months. Each tape was a different brand, different duration, different quality. The FBI would try to track down each tape, but he paid cash, wore disguises, went to stores without video surveillance. Anyway, they would be too late.

"Keith, the phone's for you. It's your sister," someone yelled from the other room.

Keith had made it out of bed and was showered and all cleaned up. "Be right there."

He found a phone in one of the bedrooms and picked it up. "Hey what's up?"

"We have a slight problem." His sister was no-nonsense even before she went to law school.

"We do?" he said unaware.

"Yes we do. Cindy just got paged by her landlord. Her apartment was broken into last night."

"That sucks," he said sarcastically.

"That's right, it sucks. Anyway, she's a mess, freaking out, you name it. Not to mention she overdid it last night and has been puking all morning. She's got to get home, but I don't think she should drive."

"And?" Keith decided to make this difficult.

"And you're her guy."

"What about Derek, why can't he drive her home?"

"Derek is back out of the picture. Cindy found him in the outside shower with some teeny-bopper. She booted him and then inhaled a tray of shots," his sister said.

Keith sighed. He felt bad for her regarding the apartment, not Derek. He would also hate to cut the weekend short. But it was raining, and he was done drinking. And, after all, Cindy was his ride and his friend. "All right, how do you want to work this?"

"Don't worry about that, we'll get her over there."

Ten thousand miles away in Hong Kong, the divisional footwear manager, Charlotte Tsang, pointed to a 2-inch, black, plain pump. The image appeared real time in Jones' New York office on one of his televisions. Charlotte was National's representative in Hong Kong and handled all the relationships with Chinese manufacturing. National did close to four billion dollars at cost on direct imports from China and Hong Kong alone.

Jones sat at his desk and watched the TV intently. To his right was a round disk the size of a personal pizza that allowed him to talk to Hong Kong with a press of a button. This was teleconferencing.

Charlotte continued her presentation, showing some riding boot samples. All of the product she was showing had been produced in Taiwan only a few years before, but now all of the factory owners opened in China and took advantage of the cheap labor force.

She was finished with her presentation and stood facing the camera, waiting for questions. And they would come. They always did.

"Charlotte, let's go back to the plain pump. What was the first cost?" Jones' voice rang in the studio.

The camera moved off of her and swish-panned to the pump. "$9.34 first cost," she answered nervously.

"So we can land it at about $13.20, put it out at $40.00 and run it at $29.99. That would be a 56% margin at the low. We are definitely not getting that domestically."

The camera moved back to Charlotte's demure but nervous face. She did not see the man asking the questions. She only heard his voice. It was unnerving for her.

"That's a great job, Charlotte. Great job. I can see that being big, like 200,000 units big." He paused as the woman practically ran off screen. "Now, if everyone could leave the studio, I'd like to talk to Henry for a few minutes."

Henry Simpson hooked himself up as the technicians cleared the studio. "We have about three minutes of satellite time left, Chuck. What's on your mind?" Henry was American, the name a dead giveaway. He had known Jones for close to thirty years and had come out of semi-retirement to run the Hong Kong office after Hong Kong was given back to the Chinese.

"Is everything all right over there, Henry?"

"Well, they're a little bit nervous with the threat of sanctions. I mean it never does happen, but it still makes us all nervous. That news magazine piece did not help. Papers here say that MFN could be revoked. But they always say that every time the vote comes up. Anyway, if MFN is revoked, most people in this office figure that's it for them. And sanctions could be worse," Simpson said.

"Well, Henry, if either happens, we will all have to worry about our jobs. Imports are about 25% of our business as you well know. Chinese imports are almost 90% of that," Jones pointed out.

"I know, I know." Simpson switched gears, "Any news on Stephenson? We just got the kidnapping news this morning."

"Well, any grandstanding he had planned is now on hold. Word is he didn't get what he wanted from the Chinese and he was going to make them feel some pain. I honestly don't think he has enough votes."

"I hate to say it, but we'd be better off if they never found the guy. Not a nice way to think," Simpson added, almost—but not quite—ashamed of himself.

"Henry, business is not always politically correct all the time." Jones paused then added, "Tell your people not to worry, I have a pretty good feeling about this one."

The ride back to Hoboken could have been worse. Well, not really, Keith thought. The rain pounded the earth as hard as Keith's head pounded from the night before. Between the two, it was impossible to do over forty-five miles per hour. Not to mention everyone on the road seemed to be panic stricken from the deluge, like an army of driving school dropouts. Par for the course.

Cindy was feeling no better. She had said nothing and just stared out the window at the rainy coast. Her landlord was unable to tell what was missing because he had no idea what she started with. To make matters worse, like most other young apartment dwellers, she had no renter's insurance. Her expression said that she was expecting the worst. She was a contradiction: beautiful girl, beautiful face, totally distraught.

Keith had a soft rock radio station on to help take the edge off but that backfired when a song came on that brought Cindy to tears. They drove the rest of the way in silence, just the pounding of the rain.

Once in Hoboken, Keith parked the car in front of Cindy's Bloomfield Street apartment. The streets were desolate as the town cleared out on holiday weekends. Cindy took a deep breath as if to summon her courage, then put her head in her hands and began to sob.

Keith leaned over and put his arm around her and in his best big brother tone said, "I know this isn't easy, but let's go up there and face this together. It sucks, but you still have your health, your family, and a great set of legs." The last part was not so much big brother.

She looked up and laughed. Keith wiped the tears from her cheek. Then a perfect moment to kiss her, and Keith leaned away and opened his car door.

The door to Cindy's apartment had been forced open and with no one home on her floor, there was no one to hear it.

Cindy's building did have a coded entry pad, but there were ways around that. People would buzz anyone in.

Cindy walked into the apartment slowly, scanning from one end to the other. Keith followed, and having been there before, noticed several things missing right off the bat. But Cindy remained composed, maybe his speech had helped.

She moved through the small kitchen quickly but long enough to check the fridge. She then went to the lone bedroom. Keith stayed in the living area. It was not exactly a separate room because the kitchen/living room was open and formed one room.

A few minutes later Cindy came out from the bedroom. She went to the refrigerator, got two diet sodas, came into the living room and plopped down on the couch. She handed Keith a soda as she joined him. The sofa was across from a decent sized entertainment center that was missing a VCR, TV, and stereo.

"I'm not calling the police," she said calmly.

"Are you sure?" Keith asked.

"Yeah. It would do no good. Everything missing is electronic; assholes even took my alarm clock. Anything with a plug. No way to trace it."

Keith had expected her to be a little more emotional, hysterical even. Instead, she was angry.

"No, I'm not going to call the police. I am, however, going to hunt down the assholes that did this and stick their little pricks into electrical sockets."

Keith smiled nervously, not knowing if she was joking or having a breakdown. "Are you okay?"

"Yeah. This is the first time something like this has happened to me. Never been mugged or had my car broken into, nothing. This is lousy. I now know how you felt when your car was stolen."

"Not a good feeling," he reiterated.

"I don't know what I would have done without you, Keith. You're the only man I seem to be able to depend on. Thank you very much." She leaned over and hugged him. He hugged back. It felt great.

"Anytime," he said as they separated. "Why don't we see if we can get someone to fix that door for you?"

"Okay." She paused and stayed on the sofa as Keith got up. "Even if I can get the door fixed, would you mind if I stayed at your place tonight? I just don't want to be here, alone."

Keith stared at her beautiful, slender face. How could he say no?

Tommy had dropped off his first package of the day and returned to his hotel. It was a one-page note to his current client with instructions for their next meeting. It was not really necessary for them to meet. Payment would be handled through wire transfers, but he wanted to see the man.

chapter 17

"What? Could you repeat that?" Graham Roswell said into the phone. The line went dead. He slowly put the phone down, his mind trying to reconstruct the quick sentence. "Holy shit."

Roswell, a twenty-year-old research intern for the morning news at NBC, ran to Jonas Ranford's office with what he thought was an unbelievable lead.

"What is it, Graham?" Ranford said without looking up from his newspaper. It was 6:00 A.M. on a holiday Monday and he was not altogether pleased that he was working. The hazards of being a news director.

"I just took a call, it was a guy. He was talking very fast, words were almost incomprehensible."

Ranford looked up at him. "Calm down, boy. Take a deep breath and start from the beginning."

Graham took a full breath. "I just took this call. It was a man, a man with an Irish accent."

"Irish or Scottish?" Ranford questioned.

"Irish, I guess. Anyway, he told me that there was a videotape of Senator Stephenson reading demands...."

"Where?" Ranford was now interested.

"He said it was taped to the inside of an out-of-order urinal in the lobby of the Dorset Hotel."

"Did he say anything else?" Ranford said.

"No. He hung up right after that." Roswell was nervous.

"Did he sound legitimate?" Ranford pressed.

"Well, yeah, I guess so. I mean he didn't sound like a kid trying to order a hundred pizzas or something. He was direct and brief. He didn't stay on the line to try to convince me he was for real."

"And he had an Irish accent?" Ranford asked again.

"Sounded Irish," Roswell said with some conviction.

Ranford ran through the possibilities mentally. It was probably a hoax, but what if it wasn't? When in doubt, send an intern.

"Okay Graham, take a cab uptown to the Dorset. Buy a pair of latex gloves, come to think of it. I don't want your prints on the tape if it is for real. If the thing is there, call me from the lobby. Actually call me either way. I'll get things moving here just in case."

"Shouldn't we call the FBI or something?"

"Screw them. Let them get their own leads. Now get your ass in gear."

Tommy had placed one call to each of the big three networks directing each one to a different scenic location in the Big Apple. The tape at the Dorset was his favorite; it was a block from National Merchandising's offices.

The second video was taped under a pay phone down by the World Trade Center. The third was put in the drop off box at a video store on the Upper East Side. He was careful to make sure no stray camera, at an ATM booth or from a nearby office lobby, recorded his leaving the tapes. As if it would matter; after all, he was just a ghost.

He really enjoyed running the media all over town like a pack of news hungry Pavlovian dogs. But they were only one piece of the game. The next object, the next game, was to make the FBI look incompetent, especially the man who had killed his friend.

"Hello?" Keith mumbled into the receiver of his phone. The clock on the wall read 6:25 A.M. This better not be a wacky morning show playing a joke.

"Uh, yeah, is, um, Cindy there?" a male voice asked.

Had to be Derek. Pretty good, Keith thought, six words and almost a sentence.

"Yeah. Hold on," Keith replied.

Keith got up off the sofa, which he had failed to pull out the night before, and went toward his bedroom. He and Cindy had spent a nice evening together after the locks and door were fixed. They saw a movie, had a nice dinner, it was almost like a date. But there was no close, no final move by Keith to show he was attracted, interested, whatever. They fell asleep watching the local news. All the footwork, no knockout punch.

Keith went into his bedroom where he had carried Cindy at some point. He shook her gently. "Cin, phone is for you. Might be Derek."

She looked at Keith not sure where she was, and then it clicked. She took the cordless phone from him. "I left your number on my voice mail. Hope you don't mind."

"No problem." *I like being a doormat*, his inner voice commented.

Keith left the room and shut the door behind him and went for the shower. The water felt good, and it drowned out the sound of any conversation Cindy was having with the boy wonder.

Memorial Day and he had no hangover. He knew there would be guys and girls at the beach house that could not claim the same. Two more miracles and he could be canonized, he thought.

He wrapped himself in a towel and opened the door. His bedroom door was still shut so he went into the kitchen to get something to eat. A nice bowl of cereal seemed as good as anything.

A few minutes later, Cindy came out of the bedroom. She sat next to him at the small kitchen table.

"Sorry about that. He was the last person I expected to call," she said sheepishly.

Keith nodded and kept munching on his toasted cinnamon cereal. They were friends and nothing more. He kept reinforcing that with his behavior.

"Anyway, now that I'm up, I really have to get going and get used to being in that apartment," she continued.

Keith finished chewing. "Okay." It suddenly occurred to him that Derek sounded like he was on a cell phone. Maybe he was right outside. Keith didn't feel like a doormat, more like wall-to-wall carpet.

"So, thanks again. I don't know what I would have done without you," Cindy offered.

"Hey, no problem. What are friends for, right?"

She shook her head affirmatively, leaned over, kissed him on the cheek and then left without another word.

So there he was at 6:45 in the morning, wide awake and nothing to do. He had two choices: go back to bed or go work out. He decided to work out and get some of the lingering poisons out of his body. Then maybe he could spend the rest of the day writing.

Graham found the videotape right where the caller said it would be. He called Ranford with the good news, and he was then urged to get his ass in gear.

"Pure gold, kid!" Ranford shouted as he watched the video on the TV in his office. "Let's get a copy made. The feds will be here the second the thing airs, and they'll want the original. If we hurry, we can lead off the seven o'clock hour with this."

Roswell sat, mouth gaping, sweaty, as his boss rewound the tape. He was sure the FBI would want to talk to him. They might ask him questions for hours, but there wasn't much to tell. It all made him very nervous.

"Snap out of it, boy. Take this to production, they'll know what to do. We can make 7:00 A.M."

Graham nodded, got up, and, with gloves still on, he took the tape and left the office.

The screen first showed footage from the Stephenson compound, police lights and all. Old footage. The voice over: "Good morning. A major development in the Stephenson kidnapping case. Reporters here were contacted early this morning and given the location of a tape that has imprisoned Senator Phillip Stephenson pleading for his life."

The tape played. The Senator looked out of sorts. He had only four days to live.

chapter 18

It was not a time to take chances, so he wore a disguise. A bushy mustache and a matching black wig erased the gray hair. He accessorized the wig with a Yankees baseball cap, something he never wore in real life, and a matching nylon warm up jacket. Jeans and a black duffel bag completed his look. No one would recognize him.

He had followed the instructions to the letter, though he wasn't much for taking orders. He boarded the 11:15 P.M. New York bound New Jersey Transit bus at the Hackensack Terminal and sat in the back right as instructed.

The note was insistent that he come and not one of his lackeys. This would be as safe a place to meet as any, the note had explained. There was only one other passenger on the bus, an elderly black man that sat in the first seat.

He sat impatiently, constantly checking his watch. He should have sent Tarman, but crossing his partner would be an unnecessary risk. He was naïve, he admitted to himself, to have ever believed that this would be a normal business transaction. Though his contractor was all business, he was not a businessman.

At exactly 11:15 P.M. the bus pulled out of the station.

The bar was smoky and dark and although the private party was far from over, it was for Keith. He had gotten the invitation on his e-mail from John Timmons, a guy in MIS at his firm, about the bachelor party for Henry Figueroa, another guy in MIS. And while Manhattan was more than a decent place to have a bachelor party, Timmons explained Figueroa wanted to keep it local.

The party had actually turned out to be a lot more mellow than Keith had anticipated. There were no girls, no shenanigans. There was, however, a lot of card playing, drinking games and flat out drinking. And Keith had gotten his ass kicked in every game he attempted.

"John, John, I gotta go. Can't be late for the second to last day of work," Keith slurred as he leaned on his buddy.

"Dude, are you gonna make it? You're faced," Timmons said between puffs of his cigar.

"Under control, my man. I just have to get out of here before I do some real damage."

"How you getting home?"

Keith reached in the front pocket of his backpack and pulled out a bus schedule. "I can catch the 11:21 P.M. right out here on the corner. How about that? I take it to the port authority and then get on the Red Apple home. Piece of cake."

Timmons was distracted by some raised voices at the poker table and then turned back to Keith. "Dude, you can stay at my place if you want. Screw work. We're done Wednesday."

"Thanks, but I got it all figured out." Keith's eyes were a bit glassy and his movements a little off.

"Whatever you think is best, my friend. I will see you tomorrow. Thanks for coming out."

Keith smiled and they shook hands. He made his way out of the bar and right onto Main Street in Bogota, New Jersey.

He stood on the corner and peered down Main Street in the direction the bus would come. He saw several headlights but they blurred into a kaleidoscope of white light.

He leaned up against a lamppost and it reminded him of Shannon. When he got really drunk, most things reminded him of Shannon. His thoughts were not of anger but of reconciliation, forgiveness—all things he would not consider sober.

The slight, early summer breeze reminded him of playing stickball when he was a kid late at night under the streetlights in Philadelphia. Now he was a slightly older kid trying to find his way. And that made him think of Shannon.

He fished in his backpack for his tape recorder and finally pulled it out. He pressed the 'record' button with the intention of stringing together the most stirring sequence of words ever known to man. An Ode to Shannon. He felt the words bubbling up inside, ready to form beautiful thoughts.

He took one last deep breath and bent over and threw up on the curb and his shoes. His stomach emptied in a dozen or so muscle contracting convulsions. He wiped his mouth on the sleeve of his jacket and slipped the recorder in his pocket.

He instantly broke into sweats and struggled to take his denim jacket off. Once off he put it in his left hand and looked to flag a bus down with his right. A minute or so later a bus did pull over. He got on and flashed his pass and went to the back to sit.

Keith finally plopped in to the second to last row of seats and slumped. He noticed a man in the seat behind him, but he was a featureless blur.

A voice came from behind him. "Hey, pal, can you move. You smell like puke."

Keith was, if anything, a well-mannered sloppy drunk. He stood without saying a word, got into the aisle, negotiated his way to a middle seat and fell into it. Time for a nap.

The 168 Local was nothing like the 168 Express that commuters took into the city during morning rush hour. The local snaked its way through Bergen and Hudson County towns like Ridgefield Park and Fort Lee, stopping at lights, doing no more than twenty-five miles per hour. It was a scenic ride, but it took forever.

Tommy Fortune stood at the corner of Broad and Grand Street in Fort Lee. He was dressed in black jeans and a black denim shirt. His hair was slicked back, giving it the illusion that it was not so red. He had a black duffel bag in one hand and a $1.75 in the other. He'd get on for under two bucks and get off with a couple hundred thousand.

As he waited for the bus, he went over the timetable again in his head. The bus was about three minutes behind schedule, but he knew those schedules were loosely based on reality.

The bus arrived, the door opened, he paid his fare and went to the back where he sat in the middle of the back bench of seats. He looked forward and noticed two other passengers. Perfect. The bus engines whined as they made their way up a hill.

"Once again, I am impressed with your work," Jones said under his mustache. "But this a little too cloak and dagger, isn't it?"

"Glad you like the way things are going. As far as this, we needed to meet one last time. This is too delicate," Tommy said as he looked ahead and not at Jones.

"Fine. You know your plan is working well, but wouldn't just killing him have been easier?" Jones asked.

"That would not have suited your purposes."

"True. It would have solved the problem, but there would have been too many questions. This was the way to go. You created a real Potemkin Village. Good thing that Sullivan is so closely tied to Stephenson."

"Stephenson will be dead soon enough," Tommy assured.

"How are you going to accomplish that?"

"Trade secret. Don't worry, he will be done by the end of the week in spectacular fashion," Tommy added.

"Good. No loose ends. Killing him is the only way to insure he doesn't cause any trouble, ever. The man just does not get it," Jones said with contempt.

Tommy did not like Jones for many reasons and was tired of talking with him. They sat in silence as the bus rolled along West New York, giving the passengers a fantastic view of the Manhattan skyline. The Empire State Building had its yellow lights on.

"This is my stop. The bag has the money you asked for. The remainder will be wired when I hear of our man's untimely demise at the hands of his kidnappers." Jones stood and pulled the signal cord and the bus stopped at the next corner. "I hope it tides you over." Jones walked down the aisle whistling 'Tie a Yellow Ribbon'.

Keith had a knack for waking up right before his stop came and once again he was right on the nose. The 168 pulled into the port authority drop off zone at 12:10.

Keith arched his back and winced. Though he was still drunk, he could feel the hangover begin. His head was a jack hammer festival, his mouth a cotton parade.

The bus swung into its bay as Keith stood with his backpack. He took one step forward and realized he was missing his jacket. He turned and walked backward as the doors opened. His balance was a little better.

He saw a black blur in the back seat. He mouthed "excuse me" as he leaned over the seat in front of the man and grabbed his jacket. The blur smiled, he thought.

Tommy had seen enough drunks in his life to know that this young man was toasted. The kid must have put his jacket down and then moved his seat. As the drunk made his way to the front of the bus, Tommy stood and reached for the heavier of the two duffel bags. He rubbed his lower leg to make sure the gun was still in place.

What was that? he thought, reacting to the drunk kid. Something dropped out of his jacket. It hit the floor with a metallic thud. The kid picked it up and looked at it. It was a tape recorder. The kid clicked it off, then went down the bus steps.

Tommy could not believe his eyes. He watched as the young man made his way down the platform stairs.

chapter 19

Tommy knew a few things. One, the kid had not listened to the tape. Two, he would have to get to him before he did. If that meant killing him, so be it.

Keith carefully went down the stairs leading from the platform to the second floor concourse that was bustling with activity despite the late hour. The two block long buildings of the port authority were in the middle of the city that didn't sleep and looked it.

The fluorescent lighting created the illusion of daytime, but the closed shops that encircled the second floor concourse told a different story. Only the newsstands and the bar stayed open this late.

Keith got on the down escalator that passed by the open-air security center. He watched the men sit at large control boards and glance up at video cameras that gave them views from all points of the large buildings. The men looked bored.

At the bottom of the escalator he turned right toward the newsstand and the Ninth Avenue exit.

Tommy followed Keith at a discreet distance. He surveyed the entire lower level from the escalator and saw no police. There were cameras inside, but outside he could take some chances on the street.

Keith stopped abruptly and turned. He shuffled back to the newsstand. The newsstand was more of a convenience store, a huge square in the middle of the concourse where middle eastern men and women stood behind counters and took money. Keith grabbed a bottle of water and a bottle of aspirin and went to pay for it.

Tommy stopped casually behind a paperback bookrack and kept a close eye on the drunk. He knelt down and expertly switched the gun from its holster to the duffel bag.

Keith paid for his hangover relief, opened the water and took a sip. He started to walk.

Tommy watched as Keith began his way toward the street exit. Tommy followed and caught up with him, getting about five feet behind him. He could smell the booze on him. He looked ahead through the glass doors and saw no police, only a few people waiting for a cab. Tommy put his hand into the duffel bag like he was looking for something. He undid the safety and put his finger on the trigger. He kept his head down.

Twenty feet from the door, without warning, Keith made a sharp left down an escalator that seemed to pop out of the middle of the floor. Tommy almost missed it.

"Where is this guy going?" Tommy said under his breath.

Keith went down yet another escalator to the basement of the port authority where the Red Apple buses departed. He went to platform 213 and boarded a Red Apple bus with exclusive service to Hoboken.

Tommy stopped in front of the bus and weighed his options. He had no choice, he would have to follow. There was a risk being recognized, but there was more risk in walking on the bus and blowing his brains out. Tommy got on the bus, paid the fare and went to the back where he could see everything.

At 12:30 A.M. the bus pulled away from its platform and then abruptly stopped to let a young girl on. She looked upset. She sat right next to Tommy's problem.

The bus whined and groaned out of the building and toward the Lincoln Tunnel, then under the Hudson River. The tunnel was a surreal series of tile and off yellow lights.

Minutes later the bus passed through Weehawken and into Hoboken, making a left on 14th Street and then a right on Washington, headed downtown. Cars were double-parked all along the route and it made the journey a slow one. The bus was crowded compared to the 168, and at every street someone rung the bell and got off. Tommy looked outwardly cool, but his mind was racing.

Keith woke to find Cindy sitting next to him on the bus. She looked upset and a little tipsy.

"Hey killer," he said thick tongued.

"Hey yourself," she said quietly.

"Where'd you come from?" Keith had to remember where he was.

"A party in the city."

"Are you okay?"

"Let's just say it's Derek related." Cindy dropped her head.

"Oh."

"I'd rather not talk about it."

"Same here."

There they were. Both under the influence, both vulnerable, both having had a bad run with the opposite sex. Any thoughts of friendship Keith had about Cindy were going out the window as she leaned close to him looking more like a runway model than his little sister's friend.

"Here's your stop," she said as a small line of people formed at the door waiting for it to open.

"Hey, how about getting a drink?" Did he say that?

Cindy looked at him. She knew what he meant. "How about we sit at the bar and talk."

Keith nodded his head. The less he opened his mouth the better. They got off the bus and went right into the bar at the corner.

Tommy exited through the bus' side door and watched in disbelief as the drunk and the beautiful girl went into the bar. "This kid has got to be Irish."

Tommy looked around for a perch. Going into the bar would be too risky and he highly doubted that the kid had even thought about the tape recorder. There had to be a clean way to just get it from him.

Tommy spotted a pizza parlor across the street with a large front window from where he could keep an eye on his new friend. He made his way across Washington, went in, ordered a slice and sat at a window table with a full view of the bar.

He thought about his next move, thought about what the tape would have on it. No names, but it did have information that would lead anyone to come to the conclusion that the kidnapping had nothing to do with Danny Sullivan or the IRA. He needed the tape and didn't necessarily want to hurt the kid or the girl.

Ten minutes later the couple came out of the bar. Tommy made up his mind to mug them. He would wait until they got off the main street and he would hold them at gun point and rob them, tape recorder and all. He'd only hurt them if need be.

He quickly exited the pizza joint and went across the street to catch up with them. But it didn't matter. The couple stopped a few doors down from the bar and the drunk kid pulled out his keys and opened the door by the yogurt shop. They disappeared behind the door.

Tommy stood on the street and shook his head. He watched the light on the third floor go on and then off less than a minute later. He went over to the door and jostled the handle. It was a thick metal door and was locked. He checked the names on the mailbox. Third floor: Keith Garrity. Now the drunk had a name.

Tommy walked a little further down the street to a pay phone and made a call. "It's me. There's a problem. I'm in Hoboken. Yes, that Hoboken. I need you to sit on someone."

chapter 20

The sex had been great. Great? she thought. Maybe not great, but definitely different. Not what she had expected. Great might do. Donna racked her brain for the right word, then lost interest.

She sat on her deck that faced toward ocean. She didn't have the unobstructed view of the beach that she hoped one day to have, the house being three blocks from the ocean, but she could hear the waves hit the beach. She sipped her coffee, naked underneath her thick terry robe. She watched as the sun began to rise.

It was just supposed to be what she called "courtesy sex." Someone had provided her with some great inside information and she wanted to show her gratitude. She also wanted the source to have a reason to keep feeding her great information.

But she had been pleasantly surprised and the agent had spent the night. He was indeed a "special agent." She put her coffee down on a deck table and closed her eyes. She took a deep breath that almost pushed her large breasts out of the robe altogether.

"Good morning," a voice came from behind her.

Donna leaned to see Agent Thompson standing at the screen door that led to the deck. He was showered, standing there in his dark suit and sunglasses, though they were not yet necessary.

"Good morning yourself," Donna replied.

Thompson moved to the railing, "Nice view."

"Not bad for a Sea Isle rental," she admitted.

"Not bad at all."

"So, what's on the Stephenson agenda today." She couldn't wait to get back to business. Thompson smiled.

"I'm on my way to New York to meet Jackson. He spent the day tracking down videotapes yesterday."

"You and he seem to get along real well. Have you worked together before?" She undid the belt on her robe.

"Always another question with you, huh?" He paused, "I've known Tom for over twenty years, but..." He stopped.

"But what?"

"Listen, I was best man at this guy's wedding, we've been friends a long time. But...I don't know."

"Don't know what?" Donna could not let things go.

"Just between you and me?" Thompson said, unsure.

"Sure, reporter hat off."

"Tom has some weird ideas on this case. Says he doesn't like how it all fits. Says it's too clean. Says he doesn't like what forensics came back with."

"Really? So, he doesn't think this is an IRA kidnapping?" Donna showed some surprise.

"I don't know. I don't know what he thinks. We're all going in one direction, but I think he may be off in another," he said, staring off.

"If it wasn't the IRA then who?"

"Good question. We have a dead IRA soldier and a demand to release another. Seems clear to me."

"Have you talked to anyone about him?"

"That's not how it works. This is Tom's case. He has us moving in the right direction. It's just I don't know if he is the best guy for this," Thompson said, looking back at her.

"Why do you say that?" Donna was thinking on the record.

"Well, his wife passed away last year and I think he never recovered. He's not the same guy. It may be affecting his judgement."

Donna nodded, implying both sympathy for Jackson and understanding for Thompson's position.

"Listen," he looked at his watch, "I have to get going."

"So soon?" Donna opened her robe and laid back, running her hands over her breasts.

Thompson walked over to her and kissed her stomach. "I really have to go."

"How can you leave me like this?" Donna said, a little hurt.

"Years of practice."

He left the deck and she heard the front door below close and a car start. She covered herself up. For the first time she had wondered who had used who.

Keith woke up on the floor both hung over and alone. Nothing new. The sun came through his window and he checked his clock. 6:30 A.M.

Keith rolled onto his back. The floor was not carpeted and while hardwood floors were a great feature of Hoboken architecture, they were not a good sleeping surface. He rolled his head left and noticed that Cindy was not on the sofa where he was pretty sure he had left her the night before. He thought to get up and check the bedroom for her, but when he rolled his head the other way he saw a note taped to his computer screen.

"Keith, thanks for letting me crash. You're the best. Call me. Luv, Cindy." She dotted the 'I' in her name with a smiley face.

Keith closed his eyes and began to grade his hangover. On a scale of one of ten it was a nine with a bullet. It was as bad as the Wildwood hangover from the weekend.

He rolled onto his back. "This has got to stop."

Jacob had set his watch alarm for seven o'clock, the end of Alex's shift. They had taken turns watching the drugged senator and the television, each spending six hours alone to sleep and the other twelve together.

His watch beeped and his eyes opened instinctively. As his eyes adjusted to the dark, he saw a figure approach him. It was Alex and she was completely naked. She moved slowly and gracefully, her body was toned, accented with dancer's legs and cheerleader's curves.

"Time to get up," she said as she knelt next to Jacob who was laying on his back on the floor.

She went for the zipper of his pants, but he put his hand there to stop her. "Don't do this, Alex."

"Why not? I'm bored and horny."

"Because Tommy will kill me. That's why."

"Well, if you don't give me what I want I'll tell him it happened anyway. Better yet, I'll tell him you raped me. How about that?"

Jacob moved his hand away and said nothing more.

The deal was simple. While the firm packed up for the relocation to Dallas, any non-relocating employee was required to come to work until May 31st to collect their severance checks. Even though their client files had long been moved south, along with most of their office equipment, they were still required to show or lose the easy money.

"Showing up" meant different things to different people. The secretarial pool checked in at nine and by eleven were out to a Broadway matinee, returning at four with a full review. Timmons and Figueroa were running a huge video golf tournament down in MIS. Others brought in books or televisions or both. The whole thing had a "last day of school" feel to it.

Keith had done some reading and then some writing in the last three weeks, the duration of his lame duck employment. The company had been helpful in placing non-relocating employees and provided résumé writing courses for those not moving. The week before, Keith went to that class to kill a couple of hours. Today, though, he would nurse his hangover.

Keith got in at nine and went right to the men's room and splashed water on his face. He then took his bagel and orange juice to what was left of his cubicle. As soon as he sat, his phone rang.

"This is Keith."

"Dude, you made it. Figs owes me a five spot. I said you would." It was Timmons checking in.

"Glad I could be of assistance," Keith replied.

"Man, you sound like shit." Keith heard someone shout 'it's in the hole' in the background.

"Feel like it, too," he confirmed.

"Well, I know it's early, but I wanted to know if you wanted to join us for a night on the town after the company party?"

"Go away, John," Keith said quickly.

"Now that is not the right attitude. I'll tell you what. I'll call back later when you feel better. My shot's up. Gotta go." Timmons hung up.

Keith put his head down on the desk and left his phone off the hook. He looked up and realized that food was not a good idea at this point. He got out of his chair to take a walk.

The floor Keith's cubicle was on looked like the other two the company occupied in the mid town office building; they looked like one of those model cities where they simulate a nuclear bomb explosion. Everything seemed to be in pieces, shadows of their former selves.

Moving men in jumpsuits were taking things apart and putting them on dollies and taking them away. Keith wanted to hop on one and get out of there, anywhere. After a complete circuit around the floor, he went back to his desk and started to eat his breakfast, very slowly.

James had tried to get into the kid's apartment but some lady had her dog out on the deck next door and it barked anytime James touched the fire escape ladder. So, James had spent the night drinking coffee and waiting for Garrity to make a move.

And when he did, James tracked the Garrity person into the city and trailed him to his office. He had not seen the tape recorder in question, but surmised that the kid was not acting like someone who had stumbled onto evidence in a major kidnapping. The kid stumbled along in a haze. Either way, he would have to report status back to Tommy. And Tommy hated loose ends.

At five, with his head flat on his desk, Keith heard a loud cheer. The signal that the New York office was officially closed for business. And though many of the remaining employees in the building had not yet secured jobs, they had made it through to the end of the severance rainbow. All that was left was to pick up the checks in the morning.

Keith lifted his head off the desk and suddenly felt human again. At that instant Timmons appeared with a six pack. Keith gave him an incredulous look.

"What? What are they going to do? Fire me?" Timmons popped a beer and handed Keith one. "This is just the beginning."

Keith opened it and took a sip. "Not bad."

"Thatta boy. So, you going to the party?" Timmons said.

"Sure. Why not. Where is it again?"

"Downtown in the Puck Building. They spared no expense for the 'See-you-later-you-poor-unemployed-bastard' send off." Timmons' first beer was done and he opened another.

"So, what's after that?" Keith asked.

"Glad you asked, my resilient friend. I see us at that party for about an hour, hour and a half tops. Then we head down to Moran's. The weather should be perfect. From there we head to Scores for the Mets/Dodgers game." Man's best friend, a strip club sports bar.

"That may be a little too aggressive for me. I will probably bail at Moran's. It's a nice little ferry ride home," Keith responded.

"Whatever. Me and Figs figure we stay out all night and show up for the checks in the same clothes."

"Like I said, I'll bail at Moran's."

"Sure," Timmons said sarcastically.

"Have you cleaned your desk out yet?" Keith said changing the subject.

"Not completely. I'll get the rest of the crap tomorrow."

"Yeah, I mean I have my bag and a box of crap."

"Leave it. You don't want to carry that all night. Your file cabinet still lock?"

"Yeah." Keith's head was starting to clear.

"Then leave it. I was talking to some of the moving guys and they said they're waiting for the place to clear out tomorrow before they get the rest of the furniture and stuff out."

"Cool."

Keith killed his beer and the two headed out.

Timmy MacKenzie had just pulled up and his brother-in-law James jumped into the white van.

"Where have you been?" James said with urgency.

"Traffic man, chill," Timmy responded calmly.

James could smell the beer on Timmy's breath and was not surprised. Timmy had a variety of addictions, and on top of that he was lazy. But James needed some help and Timmy owed him money.

James had waited in the lobby and when he spotted Garrity getting off the elevator, he quickly went outside.

"See those two, getting into the cab?" James said.

"Yeah, yeah. The two guys in suits?" Timmy pointed.

"Yeah. Right there. Follow them."

Timmy pulled the van out and followed the cab

The room the company had rented at the Puck building was architecturally impressive. It was huge, measuring in yards, not feet, and was almost as big as a football field. The light bleached hardwood floor was only outdone by evenly spaced, majestic, white floor-to-ceiling pillars the circumference of California redwoods. Windows ran from waist high to close to the top of the thirty-foot ceiling.

Keith and Timmons entered and went right for the drink table, while a middle of the road wedding band played. About fifty of the hundred or so non-relocating employees were there already. Buffet lines were forming.

The band sounded pretty good, but Keith was convinced that the room's acoustics could land a busted muffler a record deal. After getting their drinks, Timmons went over and talked to the band about playing something a little more progressive. Keith wandered over to one of the spectacular windows. The sun's glare was muted by large, gossamer drapes that ran to the floor. He stared out the window and wondered if once again he would bump into Cindy. And what if he did? What would he do? She was beautiful and confused. A slave to Derek, like he himself was a slave to Shannon. Not to mention, he thought, she also dotted the I's in her name with a smiley face. Could he love someone like that?

Keith turned and joined the party and for the next hour he and Timmons and Figueroa ate and drank one more time on the company, determined to get their money's worth.

The party ended for them when the band broke into the "Electric Slide." The sight of their drunk former co-workers group dancing was too much to take. So, they headed outside, flagged a cab and were back on their way. The white van followed.

"Told you. The weather is perfect for this," Timmons said as the three of them stood in the crowded outside plaza known as Moran's.

"You were right. I do like it down here. This bar reminds me of a bar at the beach," Keith said as Timmons and Figueroa scanned the crowd.

"So, you're a shore boy? Where?" Timmons said.

"Avalon. In New Jersey."

"No shit? That's the town in the news with the kidnapping, right? Man, that is a haul."

It seemed that everyone had now heard of his little shore town. "Yeah, exit 13," Keith said.

"Ouch. I'm in Spring Lake. Me, Figs, his fiancée and three other couples." Timmons gulped and finished yet another beer. "Need one?"

"Sure."

"Let's go Figs. I see shots in our future."

They left Keith standing there, next to a green wire table overrun with half filled plastic cups. Time had gone quickly at Moran's and the large Maxwell House clock across the Hudson River said it was 9:20 P.M. There was still a pretty good crowd on hand as he heard more than one Wall Streeter complain that the market had a tough day.

Keith turned around to get a different perspective and then he saw her—Shannon. There she was, standing and talking to three guys with slicked back hair. They were hanging on her every word. Her blouse was unbuttoned one button too many (typical) and each of the friends took turns ogling her ample cleavage.

Keith instinctively spun the other way, his heart falling to his feet, his face getting flushed, his ears burned. He slowly turned back toward her group. He felt sick. Why was she here? Why now? He watched the men watch her, laughing way too hard at the things she said, captivated by the way she pulled her fingers through her short black hair.

Part of him wanted to get a running start and jump into the Hudson. Part of him wanted to go up to her and say 'hi' and calmly walk away. He did neither and just stood and watched through the crowd. He knew that she would never see him, she was blind as a bat and was not wearing her glasses. To her, he would look like a navy blur. To her, that is what he must have been.

Timmons and Figueroa returned with a tray of alcohol. There were fours beers and about a half dozen shot glasses filled with ugly, brown liquid.

"What are you looking at?" Timmons asked as he put the tray down.

"See that girl over there, short black hair, with the three Gordon Gecko look-a-likes?" Keith nodded in her direction.

"Yeah, the one with the great body?" Timmons saw her and Figs shook his head affirmatively.

"That's my old girlfriend."

"Dude, nice work," Timmons waited for a return on his high five. "Dude, don't leave me hanging."

"So, Keith, what happened? Why is she your old girlfriend?" Figs said, sipping his beer.

"One night I found her wrestling naked with another guy."

"That blows," Timmons said.

"It sure does," Keith responded in a whisper.

Timmons passed the shots out. "I have a toast to our boy Keith. To the man who dated a woman most of us only dream about." They tapped plastic shot glasses and down the hatch.

Figs passed out the second round. "A toast. I have never seen her wrestle, but I'd love to see her box." Down the hatch. The three shook off the impact of the shot and when they looked up, Shannon and the men were gone.

"Wow, maybe she was a mirage," Keith said, feeling the alcohol's effect, a quick head rush.

"Dude, you tell us." Timmons went for a beer.

Keith paused and considered that. Maybe she was now gone for good. "Boys, we're going out on the town; my treat. And we are going to get lucky."

The night was young.

The white van followed yellow cabs all over the city. First to the Red Lion in the Village, then to Dorian's up town and then to Scores around two.

James had watched his substance dependent brother-in-law drink a six pack in their travels. But Timmy seemed as sharp as he was going to get.

At 4:30, Figs had passed out in his red velvet chair. A mostly naked Brazilian girl danced at their table as Timmons made small talk and slipped her twenties. John Timmons was not human, Keith thought. Keith, on the other hand, was, and was fading quickly.

"Johnny, hey Johnny," Keith slurred.

"Yeah?" Timmons said half-paying attention.

"I gotta go. You guys'll be okay?" Keith said.

"Yeah, sure. Figs' cousin has a place around the corner and is gone on business. Right Figs?"

No answer.

"Anyway, why don't you crash with us?" Timmons showed no signs of slowing down.

"Nah. I gotta go. How long are you staying?"

"Until I can get one of these girls to come home with me." Timmons gave up another twenty.

"What about Figs?" Keith blurted.

"Good point. I'll have to get him one, too."

Keith smiled weakly and waved as he stood up. "Later." For someone nursing a bad hangover, this was not exactly a health night.

Keith got outside and the cool night air woke him up a bit, but there was no getting around it; he was knee walking drunk. There were no cabs in front of the club, so he made his way up to York to try his luck there.

Keith walked slowly, digging his hands into his pockets as the early morning air had a chill to it. He passed by a few limousines and other cars along the street. He would have to go about half a block before he'd see a cab. He passed by a white van and didn't give it a second look. He was focused on the intersection ahead and getting a ride.

He didn't notice the men getting out of the van. The two men walked quietly behind him. One man passed him along the right and then suddenly stopped. Keith felt his legs buckle and a sharp pain to head. Lights out. The two men carried Keith to the back of the van and loaded him in. They'd give him a ride.

chapter 21

Keith had always wondered how characters in thriller novels knew when someone was really trying to kill them. And then how would a person in real life determine that the fix was in, that their ticket was on its way to being punched? For Keith, finding himself bound and gagged and half-naked on the floor of an unrecognizable apartment qualified as something more than worrisome and just short of all out panic.

He had only been awake a minute or so, just long enough for him to get his bearings. He was careful not to make a sound. Had he been drugged or simply clubbed over the head? He couldn't tell, but whichever it was, the after effect made him wish for his worst hangover. What was this? What had he done? Keith suddenly thought of those stories he had heard about businessmen disappearing at night and waking up in Central Park missing a kidney.

He heard some noise as his head cleared but it seemed far away. From his prone position his eyes scanned the apartment and he could swear that if he didn't know better, he was in his grandmother's apartment. There were family pictures on the walls and in frames on every flat surface, crowded on tables, as if this person had eight hundred grandchildren and had pictures of them all. And the room had that musty, grandmom smell.

He could now focus better on the noise. It was coming from behind him and sounded like pots and pans banging. He stayed still, moving only his eyes, looking for an exit, but his vision was limited. He could see two windows in the wall behind a sofa, black curtains drawn. The only light came from a skylight directly above him. At least he knew it was daytime.

Then there were other sounds, they wafted through the window as the drapes flapped back and forth in the breeze, letting additional light in periodically. The sounds were cars and car horns and voices of kids playing.

His focus was jarred by the slam of a refrigerator door, then the beeps of someone setting a microwave oven timer, then the hum of the microwave itself. Then someone belched, loudly. So, he'd been kidnapped by a hungry, belching, bad guy? Why couldn't he have been taken by a sultry, blonde nymphomaniac? Another burp rang out.

Then he noticed a visitor at floor level. Approaching him was a gray, fur ball of a cat. It began to rub up against him, purring as it did. Shannon had a cat. Keith hated cats. This was his "Dante's Hell."

The microwave and kitchen sounds stopped and gave way to the creaks of the floor as the belchman headed toward him. Keith figured he would be better off if his captor still thought he was unconscious, so he closed his eyes and didn't move. He just listened.

The creaks moved past him. Another belch. A TV went on and then a pop of a can. Belchman turned up the volume.

Keith's mind raced, but he tried to keep his breathing steady and deep, giving no outward sign that he was awake. Then another creak toward him and he could feel someone getting close to him. It was all he could do to keep still, to not open his eyes or close them harder. Belchman got up close to his face and he could smell the alcohol on his breath. "Still out," the voice muttered and he creaked away.

Time moved slowly for Keith as belchman ate and drank and watched TV. His mind spun out of control and he had to stop himself from screaming. Nothing good could come out of this. Could it? Would this guy kill him? Or take an organ? Or keep him tied up forever? Was this some kind of white slavery deal? What? Why? What had he done?

The TV played on. Belchman listened to continuing coverage of the Stephenson kidnapping. Keith recognized the voices of the anchors and reporters and tried to visualize them and take his mind of his current predicament. He didn't move a muscle.

Then a phone rang. Belchman answered.

"Yeah. No, nothing's going on here. Yeah, sure, I can be there in twenty-five. Sounds too good to pass up. I'll be there."

Belchman hung up the phone and turned the TV off. He creaked back over to Keith. He first checked his work, the tape and rope that had his hostage immobilized. He leaned over to check Keith again, this time fumbling with his eyelid. A moment of terror as belchman opened Keith's eyelid. It was all Keith could do to give a blank look."Nothing," belchman said, satisfied that his hostage wasn't going anywhere. He got up, went to the door, opened it and was gone.

Keith let a huge sigh and opened his eyes only to find the gray fur ball inspecting him again. Great. He figured he had at least fifty minutes to find a way out as belchman said he needed twenty-five to get where he was going and then twenty-five back.

First, he tried to wriggle free of the rope, but quickly found that if belchman could do one thing right, it was tie a knot. He blinked his eyes hoping to wake up from his nightmare. Where was he?

He sighed again. He was lying flat on his stomach, stripped to his underwear, bound and gagged. His arms were tied behind him and the rough, flexible edge, probably from duct tape, scraped at his back when he moved his hands. His legs were bent at the knees and his ankles, tied together and taped over, elevated behind him. His ankles and wrists were tied together as well, and with a little effort he could touch his feet with his fingers. It was uncomfortable to say the least. And even if he could move or roll, his neck was tied off rather tightly to a very sturdy looking radiator. He was starting to get an odd respect for belchman.

"I am going to die," he mumbled through the gag. He tried to wriggle some more and got nowhere. Any calm he had left was moving toward hysteria as time ticked away. He arched and pulled and tried to roll and almost choked himself. He rocked and tried to bang his knees against the floor, but could not get any leverage. Was there someone downstairs? He banged his head against the floor. Please, someone be home.

But there was no answer, no bang back, no scream to "cut it out." Keith broke and began to sob. *Some hero*, he thought to himself, *very clever*.

Then some faint hope. He heard a police siren in the distance. And it got closer and closer.

Saved? But how? It made no sense. Somehow the police knew he was lying there on the floor roped like a calf? The siren grew louder and closer and drowned out the other street sounds that came from the window. The sirens now pierced his ear drum and he felt hope for the first time. Tick Tock.

Then the siren died. He could hear angry voices, some shouting, the sounds of a crowd forming, more voices, the constant murmur of the street. Then a second siren, not like the first, broke into the street symphony.

More noise. More shouting. Wild obscenities.

Time moved slowly as no police officer came crashing through the door to save his life, revolver blazing. In fact, it sounded like the ruckus was breaking up, like the cops had come to restore order to another incident and were doing so. All that commotion and not one outward sign that anyone, except the cat, knew he was there.

Minutes passed and his situation got no better. He had very bad dry mouth that was not helped by the gag. His stomach hurt and gurgled and if he had to throw up, well then… He didn't want to think about that. Belchman would be back soon. Maybe death wouldn't be that bad.

Keith lost focus and his thoughts drifted to the things he wished he had done in his life. Karaoke popped into his head. Asking Alice Renfro to the prom. Throwing a beer into Shannon's face at Moran's.

Shannon. Now it was coming back to him. He saw her at Moran's. Then he went out with Timmons and Figueroa to the Village and then Scores and then what? Nothing.

The events outside were coming to a close. He could hear car doors closing and he struggled to move. A siren started and then trailed off. The murmurs faded, the ruckus dissipated. He tried to scream but all he got was a muffled sound and a head rush.

Keith then began to move frantically, trying to work his hands free, but it was having no effect. As he wriggled he noticed that the gray fur ball was pawing at something on the wall. It stared and then pounced at the wall. What was there?

And then Keith saw it. The cat was chasing a spot of light and was hell bent on catching it. He quickly realized that the spot of light was a reflection off of the face of his watch and as he moved his hands, the spot moved and the cat moved with it.

Keith arched and lifted himself onto one shoulder, the rope on his neck becoming very tight. He moved his hands blindly against the shine from the skylight and the spot made its way across the room. The cat followed aggressively, jumping and pawing at the light.

Keith quickly moved the spot of light from the far wall to the middle of the sofa that was flush against the street side window. The cat vaulted onto the sofa like it was chasing the last cat treat on the face of the earth.

Keith craned his neck and positioned his hands and caught the light just right, creating a spot right in the middle of the drawn drape.

Officer Ward had been here before. The routine was the same. The old man would get drunk, very early in the morning, and would begin to threaten bodily harm to his wife of the last thousand years. His wife would get upset, call the police, the old man would calm down, no charges would be filed and everyone would go home. It was as regular as stopping for doughnuts and coffee.

But not today. The wife had had enough of the old man and stabbed him several times in the leg, leaving the carving blade in the leg on the last jab. It was a bloody mess, hysterical neighbors and all.

But, all was back to normal within forty minutes. The old man was taken to the hospital and would live. He wouldn't file charges. Thirty-Fifth Street could go back to its business.

As Ward and his young female partner, Jimenez, were getting into their car, they heard the shrill and screech. They looked up to see a cat plummeting toward the earth, wailing all the way.

The cat landed awkwardly onto some trash bags and scurried away. Jimenez looked at her partner and started to get out of the car. "Guess we're not getting out of here that easily," Ward commented.

Officer Ward was not sure what the law was regarding hurling cats out of windows, but he was sure there was something on the books. It didn't really matter, Jimenez was pissed and it looked like she was going to lead the way.

Jimenez judged the catapult point to be the apartment on the third floor, unit 3E. Mrs. MacKenzie was listed on the mailbox in the lobby and the two made their way up the stairs to the third floor. They got to the apartment, knocked on the door and announced themselves as the police.

Keith's head almost exploded with excitement and relief. Saved for real. The officers knocked again and Keith tried to respond, but couldn't make enough noise through the gag. Panicked that they would leave him there, he did the only thing that could make enough noise; he began to pound his head against the floor.

"You hear that?" Jimenez questioned.

"Yeah, sounds human," Ward confirmed.

"Want to break the door down?"

Ward smiled, remembering the famed 'breaking down the door' incident when he was a rookie years ago. He thought not. "I'll go find the super," the officer said.

About five minutes passed as Jimenez listened to the banging. Finally the super and Ward returned. The super, a thin, short man somewhere over sixty and under a hundred, fumbled with his key chain looking for the right key, apologizing the whole time in broken English. He found the key and opened the door. The officer's drew their weapons, entered cautiously and quickly found the source of the pounding. It was a half-naked man tied up on the floor.

Jimenez went to him and knelt down next to him. "Is there anyone else here?" The man shook his head no as Officer Ward moved efficiently through the kitchen, then the bathroom and then the sole bedroom. He returned a minute later and declared the apartment clear.

The super stood at the door, a little stunned at the sight of the man. Jimenez worked on untying him.

"Who lives here?" Ward asked the super.

"Mrs. MacKenzie, an old lady. She's been here thirty years," the super responded.

"Do you know where she is?" Ward continued.

"Yeah, she's in Florida, visiting family."

Ward took out a notepad. "Does anyone live with her?"

"No, but her grandson comes by to feed the cat. He stays here sometimes."

The whole exchange meant nothing to Keith as he waited to be untied and de-gagged. Jimenez finally got the gag off his mouth. "Thank you so much," Keith said, his words crackled against his dry throat and mouth. Jimenez smiled a flight attendant smile.

Ward started to write down some notes from the super as Keith was undone. Ward finally dismissed the man as the last of the rope was cut loose.

Keith tried to stand up. Wicked head rush. Both officers helped him steady himself and assisted him to a chair. Ward looked at him not knowing what to think. He had some ideas.

"Sir," Ward started, "did a friend leave you like this?"

Keith looked at him not realizing the implication.

"Excuse me? What do you mean?" he answered.

"Did, you know, things get a little out of hand and someone tie you up and forget to come back?"

"What are you talking about? I was kidnapped. I left a bar last night and was jumped and brought here." *Have another doughnut you asshole*, Keith thought.

"So, you were kidnapped?" Ward replied slowly, conveying cynicism. "Do you know why you were abducted or who the men were? It was men wasn't it?"

Keith paused. It didn't seem like New York's finest were taking him seriously. He didn't know what to say next.

Jimenez broke the silence, "Why'd you throw the cat out the window?"

"It jumped all by itself. Said something about the Mets' lousy start this season. There's a little Mets hat here somewhere." He paused, this time for effect, "I was tied up, remember?"

Jimenez glared back at him.

Ward stepped in, "Getting back to the tied up part. You don't know the guys who tied you up. You said you met them at a bar and maybe they asked you back here for a beer and things got a little out of hand..."

Keith closed his eyes and realized he had to get away from these two. One had him pinned as a boy toy and the other as a cat killer. He felt more comfortable tied up on the floor.

"Listen, I've been tied up for awhile. Do you mind if I get my clothes back on and use the bathroom?" Keith asked.

"No, go ahead," Ward said.

Keith got up and went toward the bathroom. On the way he spotted his clothes in a pile on the kitchen floor and grabbed them. He closed the bathroom door as the officers exchanged glances.

The bathroom was small, but had a window that led to a fire escape. He had a plan. Keith dressed quickly. Once done, he flushed the toilet and ran the water. He climbed onto the fire escape as the sound of the water through the old pipes covered the noise he made. Down the escape, he dropped into an alleyway and ran.

He kept a low profile as he made his way onto the street, careful not to bump into the belchman, who must have been overdue. His hair was matted and he looked like hell in his wrinkled suit.

He finally was able to flag a cab down and got in. He gave the cab the address of his office building. He did have to pick up his check from the firm and get his stuff from the office. He would have to figure out all the rest later.

chapter 22

James had slept only a few hours in the last two days and his hands were beginning to shake. He had trailed the kid since the Monday night Tommy had called and on Wednesday morning the whole thing seemed like one long day.

The white van pulled up in front of 618 Washington Street and parked. They had waited to go in until after the commuter rush out of the small town was over. Most cars would be off the street and most commuters would be well on their way. There was no rush now.

The van idled in the metered parking space in front of the yogurt shop as the brunette left through the sliding door. She carried a bucket and mop and was dressed in sweatpants and a sweatshirt. She looked the part of a cleaning lady. She dropped two quarters into the meter before heading for the door.

At the door, she pulled out a small set of keys and found the right one on the second try. She entered and closed the door. She made her way up the stairs.

Once she was in, James shut the van down, went to the back of the van and stretched out on the dirty, metal floor. It felt good to be horizontal. He looked at his hands and they shook out of control from all the caffeine and spotty sleep.

His surveillance had been thorough. In less then two days he knew more about the Garrity kid than he needed to. He also knew that Garrity had not acted like someone who had heard Tommy's conversation. Or if he did, he didn't take it seriously. No, this kid was in the middle of a week long party. Not to mention, James had slipped a listening device into his suit pocket while they were both on the bus the previous morning. No. They would get the tape and be done. It had to be in the apartment because it wasn't on the kid. No loose ends.

The brunette came back after thirty minutes and got into the driver's seat.

"Well?" James said, sitting up.

"It's not there, okay?" she replied angrily. She started the van and pulled it out from its spot.

"What?" James' face turned red.

"You heard me. It's not there!" the brunette yelled.

"Did you look everywhere?"

"What the hell do you think I have been doing? I certainly didn't clean the place! And that apartment is not that big. Trust me, I wanted it to be there as much as you did." She turned and focused on the road ahead.

They were silent as the van made a right down Sixth then another right onto Bloomfield. They were headed toward the Lincoln Tunnel.

chapter 23

There were lows and then there were lows. Showing up for the last day of work in wrinkled, day old clothes, with a hangover, having just been kidnapped and mistaken for a boy toy ranked right up there with finding Shannon in a naked half nelson with another man. He needed to get his life back into shape and soon.

The cab let him out at the side entrance of the building on 52nd Street. On the elevator ride up to the fifteenth floor, Keith was able to get his clothes in some semblance of order.

He got off the elevator and walked quickly, almost at a slow jog. On a normal day he would have passed dozens of people on the way to his cubicle. But all the employees that were left were on the sixteenth floor, in line waiting to collect their well-earned severance checks.

Keith made it to his cubicle, pulled file cabinet keys out of his desk drawer and opened up the cabinet. He pulled out his bag and "the shoe box".

The shoe box had been given to him by his mother on his first day in the real world of business. It originally contained all the things that she knew her son would forget to buy once he left home: band aids, a mini sewing kit, an extra toothbrush, nose hair clippers, etc. Over the years Keith had added other items like a hairbrush, an extra set of keys, a pocket size thesaurus, an extra stick of deodorant, aspirin. All would now come in handy.

He grabbed his bag and the box and went to the men's room. It took a little doing, but he made himself almost presentable in ten minutes, emphasis on almost. His eyes were in lousy shape. The large black circles helped to underscore their general puffy appearance. Plus, he had a little bit of rope burn on his neck.

He packed up his stuff and got on the elevator. It was 10:30 A.M.

"Hey Keith, nice look for you," Jack Johnson said as he got onto the elevator. The ultra-tight, three piece suited veteran of the firm was in white tennis shorts and a peach polo shirt. He waved as the doors closed on him.

The sixteenth floor was a floor of almost all conference rooms. There were two large ones separated by a moveable divider so it could be opened up into one large room for company meetings, or four smaller rooms. There were also two executive rooms that were very well appointed and only used by VP's and up. There was a line outside each of the four non-VP rooms.

Above each entrance was a sign with letters denoting what line you were to stand in: A through F, G-M, N-S, T-Z. In an amazing bit of luck there was only one person in the G-M line.

Keith got into line behind Moira Hanson. Moira was the main desk receptionist, who, as part of her job, could not stop talking. She was in her late fifties and had been with the company since she her late teens. Rumor had it that her severance package approached six digits. She and her husband were finally retiring and moving south to Clearwater. Keith was sure he was going to hear all about it. Maybe it would take his mind off of what had happened.

"Hi, Moira," Keith offered.

"Oh, hi Keith," she said as she turned, and then looked him over. "Now Keith, were you out with that John Timmons last night? He was drunk when he came in and was with a very young lady. He said she was a dancer. They were very loud."

"I'm afraid so, Moira. A lapse in judgement on my part." Keith took a breath. At least Timmons was no worse for wear.

"Well, I guess everyone deals with this kind of thing in their own way. You know, this is very sad, very sad. I've been coming in here for almost forty years."

"Six for me, though it doesn't compare."

She ignored him. "Yes, it is a sad state of affairs. Dallas, after all these wonderful years here. Who would have thought?"

Before Keith could answer, Moira put her hands to her face and turned her head, sobbing. A second later she was called into the room.

Leaving the room Moira went into was Melissa Gaffney, the attractive but married auditor that many men in the firm fantasized about. She stopped in front of Keith, and smiled. "Late night?" She leaned over to adjust the knot in his tie.

Keith was so distracted by the auburn hair and the way she smelled that he hesitated to answer. "Something like that."

She leaned back and brushed some dirt off his lapel, and her green eyes lit up. "You know, if I weren't married…"

"If you weren't married, you wouldn't waste your time on someone like me."

She laughed, leaned back in, and kissed him on the cheek. "Don't be so sure. I'll see you around."

"In my dreams," he said with a smile.

She laughed again as she walked away and disappeared onto the elevator.

Now he was fully distracted. Melissa could do that to a guy. His thoughts turned to what Moira had said, that it was a sad day. The only company he had worked for since college and now they were gone. All six years of his professional life reduced to some checks and a handshake. That was business.

The aspirin was beginning to take the edge off the head pounding, but he still felt like a walking, talking beer. He was sure he smelled like the floor of a frat house basement.

Ten minutes had passed when Moira came out of the room dabbing her eyes with a tissue, trying valiantly to hold back more tears. She shuffled past Keith and said nothing, too upset to talk.

Then Doug "Spanky" Spankowitz, the VP of Human Resources, came to the door and waved Keith in.

The conference room was bare, save for a banquet sized card table, two chairs and a series of accordion files on the other side of the table.

Doug shook Keith's hand and the two men sat on their respective sides of the table. Doug reached down into one of the accordion files and pulled out a manila folder with Keith's name on the tab. He let out a deep breath, as if to say 'here we go again.'

"Well, Keith, we have only a few things to go over and you'll be on you way, unless you want to bear your soul and tell me how much this organization has meant to you and how much you'll miss it?" There was an uncharacteristic edge to this normally stoic man's voice.

"I'll just take the money, if that's okay with you."

"Great." He pulled out the first envelope from the folder and handed it to Keith. "The first check is the severance we extended to all employees equal to 10 weeks of salary. Please open it and verify the amount then sign this." With that, Doug slid over a piece of paper with an 'X' marked and highlighted for Keith's signature.

Keith opened the envelope, checked the amount, nodded and signed the paper.

"The second check is a week's pay for each year of service. You have been with us six years, correct?" Doug droned.

"Yes." Keith took the check and opened it and it looked fine. He signed another sheet of paper.

"And the last check is for unused vacation time." And the process continued.

Keith, like all other employees, had known what the severance package was and he knew what the amounts would be. He knew he would walk out of the room with over ten thousand dollars net.

"Now. All your profit sharing is tied up in..."

Keith's mind jumped to the image of being bound and gagged less then an hour before. What was that? Were those guys going to be looking for him? Who were they? What did they want? What had he done?

Doug continued on. Keith was an accountant. He knew he had rolled his profit sharing money over into a qualified account.

"So, looks like we are all set. I just have a few forms for you to sign and we're all set," Doug said.

Keith signed the forms in a daze, totally distracted and almost jumped out of his seat when Doug got up to shake his hand.

"Are you okay?" Doug said.

Keith got right up and rubbed his hands over his face. "Yeah, sorry. Long night."

"Well, Keith, the firm thanks you for your service and wishes you luck in all future endeavors," Doug finished.

Keith shook Doug's hand, put his checks into his backpack, turned and left.

The cellular phone beeped and Tommy flipped it open. He listened, then stood.

"I don't understand what you are trying to tell me," Tommy said into the mouthpiece.

The nervous voice crackled on the other end. "Uh, um, he's gone. I don't know how. Some cops came to the apartment and let him go. That's what the super said," Timmy stammered.

Tommy's face grew red, almost the same brightness as his hair. "Why did you leave him alone? You were supposed to stay with him until I called, right?"

"Yeah, that was the deal. You're right, Mr. Fortune, that was the deal. But I had to run out, ya know?"

"No. No I don't know. You listen to me you stupid piece of shit, you better find him or just keep running. Because if you don't get our friend back to me in the next hour, there will be nothing left of you worth saving."

He flipped the phone closed violently, paused, then opened it back up. He dialed James but the call would not go through.

The white van was stuck in traffic a hundred feet under the Hudson River.

Keith sat in the back seat of the cab and fiddled with some of the things in his shoe box, trying to mentally piece together what had happened the night before. What did he really remember? What was he doing in that apartment? It all seemed surreal—belchman, the cops, the cat.

The cab emerged from the Lincoln Tunnel on the Jersey side and headed toward Hoboken. "Look at that traffic over there," the cabbie said, trying to get Keith to look. "All that traffic. Ya know, I have to sit in that on the way back." The cabbie continued to look into his rearview mirror at Keith.

"I said, look at all that traffic..."

"Look, you asshole, I see the traffic, okay?" Keith screamed into the rear view mirror. "If you have a problem, then let me out right here. Otherwise, shut up!"

The cabbie didn't say a word the rest of the way into Hoboken. The cab pulled up a block from Keith's apartment and Keith jumped out and took two hundred dollars from the ATM machine. He handed the cabbie a hundred dollars for a $35.00 fare.

Keith then went into the bank and deposited the three checks for just over ten thousand dollars. Since the checks were out of state, he would have to wait for them to clear. So, for reasons he was not sure of, he cash advanced two thousand dollars on his credit card.

He left the bank and headed up the block for his apartment not knowing if he would find the belchman there, or worse.

"Where have you been?" Tommy screamed into his phone.

"Stuck in traffic in the tunnel. What's the problem?" James answered back.

Tommy paused, "Do you have the tape?"

"No. It wasn't there. We'll have to ask the kid."

"Well, the kid got away from your dipshit brother-in-law," Tommy said with a calmed anger.

"Shit."

"Yeah, James, shit alright. I need you to go back to his apartment and wait for him. I don't care what it takes."

James dropped his head. "Tommy, come on. I haven't slept in two days."

"Then you'll have to go a few more hours, won't you," he said.

"Alright," James conceded.

"And James?"

"Yeah, Tommy?"

"Just kill him this time."

chapter 24

His building seemed to stare back at him as he stood in front of it. His heart was not only in his throat, it pounded in his feet and temples. What would he find?

He entered the building slowly, turning the key noiselessly and slipping into the foyer. The beat of his heart was the only thing he could hear. He started up the staircase and it creaked under his weight. He began to sweat. It beaded on his forehead. After each step he took he stopped and listened. Nothing. He finally realized that if someone was waiting for him they wouldn't be making a bunch of noise.

He moved a little quicker and made it to the second floor landing without having a heart attack. Half-way there. His hands were moist and his legs were wobbly. He took a deep breath.

"Mr. Garrity, we have a problem." The voice was cold and came from behind him.

Keith spun to it and came face to face with his second floor neighbor, Ms. Osbourne.

"Mr. Garrity, we have a problem," she repeated.

Keith composed himself. "A problem with what, Ms. Osbourne?"

Ms. Osbourne, by all accounts, was an original sixties burn-your-bra-leave-your-husband feminist. Now in her sixties herself, her new passion was policing noise and making the building as quiet as possible.

"Well," dramatic pause, "your cleaning lady made all kinds of noise this morning, a real ruckus. I honestly don't know how she got anything clean making all that noise. Woke me from a sound sleep." She punctuated the last words with a semi-shriek.

"But, Ms. Osbourne, I don't have..." Keith stopped himself. He was still sweating, still wobbling.

"Don't have what, Mr. Garrity?"

"I, um, I don't have an excuse for the noise she made. It's totally unacceptable. I will speak with her now. Is she still up there?" Keith looked up toward his door.

"No. She left in a big noisy hurry about an hour ago." Ms. Osbourne folded her arms.

"Well thank you, Ms. Osbourne. I'll call the cleaning service right now."

"You'd better. Seems to me that maybe you should do your own cleaning. Big shot like you must think that's women's work, huh, Mr. Garrity?"

"Like I said, Ms. Osbourne, I'll get it straightened out." Keith shot another glance up the staircase.

Before she had a chance for another scathing remark, Keith took two steps at a time and was up to his apartment door. He heard the door shut below. He stood and contemplated his next move. They were looking for something? He turned the lock to see what the cleaning lady had done. He opened his door and held his breath. No bad guys, only clutter.

Keith quickly surveyed the damage, stepping over piles of this and that, checking all three rooms of his less than spacious one bedroom apartment.

The mess was not what he expected, like in the movies where everything was pulled out of its home and thrown without regard. No, this was more of a controlled mess; everything had been gone through: kitchen drawers, bedroom closet, CD rack, the bathroom.

Whatever it was, it was not a robbery attempt like he had seen at Cindy's. Her apartment had things missing, like electronic equipment. Keith's apartment resembled a scavenger hunt gone bad. And that was it, Keith thought, they were looking for something specific. They must have had his keys, the keys he noticed were gone when he dressed in the belchman's lair.

What could he possibly have that someone would want badly enough to abduct him and then ransack his apartment? The answer was simple: Nothing.

The whole situation, the series of complicated events, was taxing a brain that was nowhere near working at full synapse-firing potential. He finally sat on his cluttered bed, not knowing what else to do.

"What the hell were they looking for?" he said out loud. In times of high stress he tended to think out loud, usually to the amusement of co-workers. "What were they after? What in God's name were they looking for?"

"Did they find it?" he continued as he got up from the bed and went into the hallway. He got to a point of the floor where he could see into all three rooms. There was no starting or stopping point to the mess.

He took off his shirt, went back into the bedroom and put on an oversized tee shirt he had gotten for participating in a walk-a-thon. "If they found what they were looking for, wouldn't they have stopped looking? Wouldn't the mess have stopped?" He was out of his pants and underwear and quickly slipped into a pair of shorts.

"It doesn't make sense." He took a second to collect himself and went to the kitchen for something to drink, something to help the dry mouth.

He left the kitchen and went back to his spot in the hallway, plastic bottle of red liquid in hand. "What could I have of any value? What could I have that was of value that wasn't on me and wasn't in this apartment? After all, they had me." He moved into the living area and stood. "If I had what they wanted, just mug me or kill me, right? No, they must have thought it was here. But it wasn't. What then?"

He scanned his memory and ticked one off after the other, "No car, no Swiss bank account, no safety deposit box." He stopped and looked down at his bag. It was the only thing he owned that was not with him and not in the apartment.

He went to it and dumped the contents on the floor. All the stuff from his shoe box hit the hardwood. Then some papers, his cell phone, then the thud of his tape recorder. The tape recorder? He picked it up and pressed the rewind button. Nothing. Batteries must be dead, he thought. He took the tape out. It was at the end. What was the last thing he recorded?

He put the recorder back in the bag with his cell phone and then went to his bedroom. He picked up jeans and a pair of boxers from off the floor, along with some socks and two shirts. He stuffed it all into the bag. He was moving, not knowing why. He took a PSU hat from his bedpost and slipped on socks and his basketball sneakers. He stood, went back into the living area and put his wallet in his back pocket. He went to the window and stared at the street. Keith watched as a van pulled up.

The white van stopped in front of the yogurt store and parked. James and the brunette rushed out of the van, slamming their doors as they did. They walked briskly toward the front door of the building. They used the keys once again to get in and went up the stairs quickly, but quietly. They were not quiet enough.

"Who are you?" a voice screeched behind them as they headed up the last flight of stairs.

James spun, surprised, and went for his gun. The old woman stood motionless, staring at the weapon. James did not hesitate. He squeezed the trigger and the woman went down.

Keith had got into the hallway just in time to see the couple, the small woman, the larger man, the gun, the "pithip" of the silenced shot, Ms. Osbourne going down, limp. He gasped. They turned, and saw him. He went back into his apartment, shut the door, and locked it.

Seconds later, Keith's front door practically exploded as James' foot broke through it. Slivers of wood joined the other sundry items on the floor. James looked right toward the window and then left into the apartment.

The brunette came from behind him and went into the apartment. She checked the bedroom, bathroom and kitchen while James guarded the door. She came back and shrugged. There was one door they hadn't opened, a utility closet door in the short hallway.

James nodded her over to the door and they both approached it, guns drawn. James turned the knob lightly and got the resistance of a locked door. The kid was inside, locked himself in like a little kid trying to hide. "Goodbye, Mr. Garrity."

James stood back and was able to steady his hand enough to pump a half dozen shots into the door. The metal and wood around the lock disintegrated and the door eased open in the hazy aftermath.

"Shit."

Keith had locked the door behind him alright, but that closet had a ladder that led to a hatch that led to the roof. He was through the hatch and on the roof just as the bullets came.

Keith scampered across the connected Hoboken rooftops like a street urchin in a Dicken's novel. The block was only twenty units long and he knew at some point soon he would run out of real estate.

Inside the apartment, James started to sweat as he ascended up the ladder and became lightheaded when he got to the top and squeezed his frame through the opening. He could see the object of his aggression no more then twenty yards away. "Got him," he said softly.

Keith turned and saw the man with the gun. He stopped and looked down on the edge of the roof. A way out. He got on his stomach, gripped the drain pipe and rolled off the edge of the roof.

"Hello ladies," Keith said as he hit the deck hard. The two girls in sunglasses and bikinis, laying on beach chairs, stereo on, sat up and screamed in unison.

"Listen!" Keith yelled back at them. "There is a guy on the roof with a big gun, coming this way. I am begging you to go in, lock the door and call the police."

One of the girls looked up and pointed to the figure on the roof while the other gave Keith a hard time. Then the second girl looked as the figure got closer and both retreated to their apartment.

Keith went to the far edge of the deck and climbed over. He stuck his feet in the spaces between the metal posts and held onto the railing. He faced back toward the roof. He had seen one innocent person get killed and didn't want to see anyone else hurt. If he could only stall for a little time while the girls called the cops.

James got to the drainpipe where Garrity had disappeared and looked down to see him standing there, almost daring him to shoot.

Keith got the first good look at one of his tormentors. He was not the belchman; he was younger, better dressed and groomed. About his own age, maybe older. Keith felt lucky, "Hey asshole! You are just not getting it done!"

James knelt down and aimed, wasting no time. Keith jumped off the deck landing hard on the top of a closed metal dumpster, two floors down. His knees buckled, he crumpled and rolled off the dumpster onto the cobblestone alley. He got to one knee and could not see the roof from his angle, which meant the man could not see him, could not shoot at him. He limped down the alley, hugging the wall.

James was pissed. The sweat got heavy on his brow and he was soaked through his shirt. "When I get my hands on him..." he muttered. He leaned over to inspect the drainpipe. If the kid could do it, so could he. He arched his back up and wiped the sweat from his face. He leaned back down for a better look and put pressure on a loose brick. It gave way, his hand slipped and James fell awkwardly, landing head first on the hard deck. Fade to black.

When the brunette heard the siren, she made tracks for the van. She pulled into traffic and made a right down Sixth Avenue. If she saw James, fine, but she was not going to jail because he overreacted and shot some old lady. Tommy still needed her, their work was not done.

Keith got out of the alley unscathed and out to the sidewalk on Sixth. He stepped into the street to cross and froze at the sight of the white van. From fifteen feet away he heard the engine gun and the tires squeal.

He went forward across the street and the van nipped his heels as he dove headfirst onto the hood of a parked compact car. He rolled off back into the street as the van's white reverse lights lit up.

He got to the sidewalk and ran up the slight incline toward Washington Street. Another car came down Sixth, a small one way street, and blared its horn at the van coming in the wrong direction.

Keith got to the corner as a Red Apple bus pulled up. He got on and took a seat where he could see the van. The bus eased into traffic and headed downtown.

It had become too real.

chapter 25

Special Agent Tom Jackson stared at the mounds of paper on his desk. Every one a lead, a tip, something that would lead him to the kidnappers. But it had been almost a week since the daring abduction and Jackson felt no closer to the perpetrators than he did the day he was assigned the case. To his dismay, none of the piles of paper had led to much of anything.

He leaned back in his chair and looked out the window at the buildings in his view. They were there, somewhere, somewhere in the big city. He could feel it.

Jackson stood and took his suit jacket off. The large man went to the window and kept looking as if the answer was there somewhere. So much bothered him about this case. The forensics for one. Watkins had powder marks on his right hand, though he was a left-handed shot. The dead terrorist was shot in the leg and the chest at close range. Watkins would have had to fire both shots, with the wrong hand, and would have had to have been right on top of the bad guy. Not likely.

Jackson rubbed his face with his large paws. It was too clean. No witnesses, nothing. It was like a case he had early in his career that had not been solved. A man with a good job, good upbringing, clubs his wife and twin sons to death one night with a baseball bat. Twenty-five years later and the guy is still out there. Could he be headed down that road again? Would the Senator ever see the light of day?

Another thing. Why did the kidnappers go strictly through the media with their demands? Like they wanted the exposure, the airtime. Sein Finn, the IRA's political wing, had steadfastly denied any involvement, but no one believed them after the breach of the cease-fire. Did the kidnappers really want Sullivan out? If they did, they were taking their time.

Jackson sat back at his desk. He knew the longer things went the less likely the Senator would return in one piece, if he was still alive. Not one person would consider any other perpetrator other than the IRA. Not one news story, not one newspaper article. No search for the truth. And no one in the bureau wanted to hear otherwise, either. The assistant director would listen to no other theory. Nothing that came from the CIA made sense either way. He had a strong sense that everyone wanted to cover their asses more than they wanted to find Stephenson. Even Thompson turned a deaf ear, would hear none of it. After Ruby Ridge and Waco, government agencies played it by the book. It still didn't feel right.

Jackson pulled his wallet out and slipped a business card out. Maybe someone with the right motivation would listen.

Donna was trying to decide whether to get a chicken cheese steak from Donnelly's or a plain old meat and cheese version. She stood at the counter as the clank of furious stainless steel spatulas chopped meat and onion against the grill's hot, metal surface. She had almost made up her mind when her cell phone rang.

"This is Donna."

"Donna, Agent Tom Jackson. Do you have a minute?"

Donna could hardly hear over the noise of the lunch crowd. "Hold on." She elbowed her way out of the deli and out onto Dune Drive. "Sorry, I can hear you better now."

"I had a spare moment and wanted to know if we could share some info, off the record of course."

"Of course," she said and she took a note pad out of her purse and cradled the phone awkwardly against her shoulder and chin.

"How are things in Avalon? Any late breaking news?"

Donna paused. There had been nothing for days. She had been reduced to local interest pieces, like interviewing the guy who did the Stephenson landscaping, the aerobics instructor who had Mrs. Stephenson in her class, etc. Everyone had a story. "We're moving along okay. Anything to report from your end?"

Jackson had her. "Well, I've been thinking that this might be too clean a job. The ends meet too exact."

"How do you mean?"

"Well, I have some conflicting information that may lead us down a road that does not involve the IRA."

"Really?" she said remembering Thompson's comments.

"Yeah. Seems like no news outlet would even consider another approach, another possibility."

"I see."

"Well, there are just some things that don't sit right with me. But there's just too much evidence pointing to the IRA, I mean Flaherty and Sullivan and all." Jackson couldn't tell if she was biting or not. If he could get her to broadcast a story, anything, that would suggest a different direction, then maybe the powers above him would try to cover all bases and let him move off the IRA.

"Seems overwhelming." Donna thought it sad that an agent had to call her to try to get a theory going. "But you may have something there. A smart reporter could take a different direction."

"Just a thought."

"Interesting." Donna yawned.

"Well, look, Donna, I have to go. It was nice talking to you. I'll be in touch."

"Same here, Agent Jackson." She killed the power on her phone and stood for a brief second. A beautiful day at the beach, she thought. Not a cloud in the sky.

"Was I getting a chicken cheese steak or a regular?" she said as she went back into the deli.

chapter 26

The dollar bill was rejected for the third time.

"You have got to be kidding me!" Keith yelled at the machine as his dollar bill spit out once again from the PATH's automated turnstile.

"Come on!" he yelled again. His hands were shaking as he heard the departure bell chime.

It suddenly seemed senseless to him that he pay the dollar when men were coming to kill him. Why not just jump the turnstile, he thought. But that was just the way he was. He didn't steal, didn't lie and he had never told a girl he loved her unless he meant it.

The temperamental machine finally ate his wrinkled dollar bill and he was through the turnstile. He sprinted across the empty landing and down the stairs to the platform. The doors for the 33rd Street train had just closed.

He looked desperately in both directions, first the right and then the left, trying to draw some compassion from the driver. Not in New Jersey. He dropped his head.

A second later the doors magically parted and he hopped in the car. Keith stood at the door as the train seemed to refuse to depart. He watched nervously for men with guns to come down the stairs and come for him. But they never came and the train finally jerked, then whined, then was on its way. He moved back from the doors and sat in a molded, plastic, yellow seat. He put his bag on his lap and slumped.

The other passengers paid him no attention as he tried to get a grip. Sweating and slightly shaking, his labored breathing expanded and contracted his chest, his mind raced. *Why didn't I go to the police*, he thought? Maybe it was the warm reception from the cops he had gotten in Manhattan or the old Philadelphia street instinct that told him to run from cops even if he hadn't done anything. Maybe both.

Somewhere under the river his breathing returned to normal and the sweating stopped. He noticed three other people on the train with him; a couple in black leather jackets and a young girl reading a book. He closed his eyes as the lights went out and then back on as they went toward Manhattan. He knew he couldn't stay underground forever and would have to come up with a plan.

The Hoboken police took the frantic call from the girls at 640 Washington Street and were on the scene within ten minutes.

Officer Bowden stood on the deck right next to the dead guy. He looked over the deck and thought how large it was. *Not bad*, he thought.

Semansky was in with the girls getting a statement when Oliver came back out.

"Ollie, whatcha got?"

"Our dead friend's name is James Madison."

"No way, the third president of the United States?" Bowden said between sips of coffee.

"No. Not that James Madison. Not to mention, Jefferson was the third president, you asshole."

"Whatever," Bowden said, taking no insult.

"Our James Madison has six priors, all for drugs in Bergen County," Oliver said, reading from a pad.

"So our boy has some yuppie on the hook for some cash and comes to collect and it gets ugly?" Bowden threw out.

"That, or he was thinking of running for president again and was trying to get this guy to vote for him."

Bowden didn't laugh. "The only way on to that roof is from an apartment on the block. Let's find our drugged up friend."

Oliver nodded.

"Thomas Jefferson, huh?" Bowden said.

"Yeah. Thomas Jefferson. Madison was the fourth president."

"Well, that was because he had all his money tied up in the Dolly Madison ice cream franchise. Like, when you are making that kind of dough, why go into public service."

Oliver looked at Bowden and simply walked away.

The PATH train slowed into its first stop at Christopher Street. The black leather couple got off as a couple of teenagers with short, weird, haircuts carrying roller blades got on.

He felt for his watch and realized it was gone. He had no clue what time it was and that bothered him.

The train stopped at 9th, 14th and 23rd Streets before it settled in at the end of the line, 33rd Street. Keith had been thinking the whole time the train made its way under the city. He had a plan.

He got out of his plastic chair, out of the car, and to the concourse. He made his way up the stairs to street level and emerged on 33rd and Sixth, a block from Herald Square, and quickly hailed a cab.

It may have been a mistake to come back to New York, but it was his best chance out.

Timmy MacKenzie, a.k.a the belchman, had had a rough morning. First the pot he bought was lousy stuff, then the guy that he was supposed to watch got away. Now he had this Tommy guy all over him. Not good.

Timmy figured that maybe if he tried to find the kid that the Tommy guy would appreciate the effort and not come after him. After all, what was the big deal about some bar hopping yuppie? And as Timmy figured it, the port authority building would be as good a place as any to look for him. If he didn't see him there, he'd call it a day.

The cab dropped Keith off at the south port authority building on 8th Avenue. Keith had been in this building almost every day over the past six years and he knew it well. He entered the side door on 40th Street and kept his head down.

In some of the great thrillers Keith had read, the hero had thrown the bad guys off his trail by booking plane tickets in his name to various cities all at the same time. The idea was that the bad guys would track the credit card purchases and get totally confused. Seemed like a good enough idea to him, but with a twist.

Keith first walked around the perimeter of the concourse looking for people who looked like they were looking for someone. After fifteen minutes, he felt comfortable that no one was watching the ticket counters.

Keith made his way past the newsstand complex and went to the first in a series of ticket counters. All bus tickets were purchased at this kiosk. One could get tickets to anywhere in the country from here. Keith looked up at the departure board as the ticket agent came over.

"Can I help you?" a tall, thin man with bad skin and a poor mustache asked.

"Yes, I would like to purchase some tickets," Keith replied.

"Where would you like to go today, sir?"

Keith looked over the destination board. "I would like one way tickets to Boston, Washington, D.C., and Buffalo."

The clerk gave him a puzzled look.

"Is there a problem?" Keith questioned.

"Well sir, the Boston and Buffalo buses leave within three minutes of each other," the clerk pointed out.

"Oh, that's fine."

The clerk typed in something on his keyboard. "Total comes to $124.50."

Keith handed him a credit card. He got the card back with a receipt and the three tickets.

"Thank you very much," Keith said.

He put the tickets in his bag and went to the next counter where a nice Asian woman waited on him. This was a national bus line and he figured he'd go to some exotic destinations like Vegas (he had never been there) and Key West. He paid with the credit card and took the tickets.

He repeated the process at the next two counters and bought all tickets with his credit card, except the ticket to State College, PA., which he paid for in cash.

Thoroughly satisfied that he would send his hunters in all directions, he went to kill some time. His bus left in an hour and he wanted a change in appearance.

He went up the escalator to the second floor, where most of the shops were. He went into an electronics store first and bought a cheap digital watch and some batteries for his tape recorder.

He then realized he had been too clever. If the men after him had tracked his card purchases, they could be on their way to him now. And he needed an hour.

Keith ducked into a bar and sat. He needed a beer but was not feeling quite right. The TV showed the local 12:00 P.M. news. He saw the words "breaking story" and "Hoboken" on the bottom of the screen. That couldn't be good for him.

Timmy sat at a table in the Silver Bullet Lounge on the first floor of the port authority building. It was the first place he saw to buy alcohol and he went to it. He was gnawing on a roast beef and cheese sandwich and washing it down with a beer. He watched as people entered the 8th Avenue entrance, hoping to see the kid that got away.

He finished his sandwich and then the beer and remembered that there was a bar on the second floor and headed there.

Keith was wondering why he went into the beauty salon. He was also wondering what the port authority was doing with a beauty salon. It did make some sense, he thought; there was a bar, a bowling alley, restaurants, why not a beauty salon?

The woman at the counter smiled. "Well sir, what can I do for you?"

"Uh, I'm not sure," Keith said, running his fingers through his hair.

"Well, my name is Mabel." The woman had a light Jamaican accent. She was eye to eye with Keith as she stood there smiling. Big featured and big boned, she was very pretty.

"I'm Keith and I was thinking of making a change today," he admitted.

"What kind of change did you have in mind, darlin'?"

Keith looked around at the photographs, impossibly beautiful women in hairstyles that could not be recreated. Then it hit him. "I have this urge to be a blonde."

"Don't we all, honey. Don't we all." Mabel laughed.

"I'm in kind of a rush. Can you do it in an hour?"

"Sure darlin', whatever you need." Mabel moved out from behind the counter and walked down the narrow, empty salon aisle that had bulbous hair drying contraptions on the right wall. She put her hand on a chair and motioned for Keith to come back.

"Here goes nothing," Keith said.

Timmy got a beer "to go" in a styrofoam cup at the bar on the second floor and sipped it as he canvassed the building. He was catching a great buzz.

After a fifteen-minute circuit around the concourse he went back to the bar for a refill. He stayed there for awhile as all the walking was taking its toll on his out of shape body. He sat on a stool and watched a Grand Prix from a country he had never heard of on an all sports channel. A few more beers and a shot of Jack and he was ready to get back to work.

"Ta da," Mabel said as she spun Keith's chair to have him face the wall mirror.

He sat there shocked. His hair was bleached California-surfer-dude blonde. He looked totally different with it. That is what he wanted.

He could feel Mabel becoming impatient in back of him, waiting for some feedback. She put her hands on her hips and cocked her head. "Well?" she said.

Keith ran his fingers through his hair and it felt strange, smoother. "I love it."

"Really? Don't be lying to me young man."

"No, I really love it." He looked at her reflection in the mirror then arched his neck around to look at her directly. "Really, it is exactly what I needed."

Satisfied that the boy was telling the truth, or at least lying hard enough, she came in back of him and put her hands in his hair, styling it, imagining what else she could do with it.

Keith looked down at his watch. He had fifteen minutes until the bus left.

"Darlin', if you have the time, I'd like to do one more thing," she said as she played with his hair.

"What?"

"Oh, just a little snip, some gel and a blow dry. Ten minutes tops," she promised.

He smiled at her in the mirror. "Sure."

Ten minutes later, he had short spiky blonde hair; a nice departure from his accountant hair.

With five minutes to get down two flights of stairs, Keith paid Mabel and gave her a fifty-dollar tip.

"Thank you, darlin'. I hope to see you again real soon."

He turned to her. "You didn't see me this time."

Keith exited the shop and was into the stream of people. Two flights of stairs and he would be away.

Then he saw the man from the apartment, belchman, coming out of the bar. It looked like him, Keith thought, but could it be? Then he let out a loud burp and Keith froze.

He was coming right for him, but the man hadn't recognized him. The belchman seemed to be looking around at nothing in particular.

Keith dropped to one knee and pretended to tie his shoe as the man stopped at the railing that overlooked the first floor. Keith watched him sip his cup and stare off. He checked his watch: two minutes.

Keith stood and casually made his way to the escalator. He moved two steps down and was able to hide behind a man in a business suit. Keith kept his eyes on him the whole time. The man seemed to be in a daze, like a guy who lost his wife at the mall.

The businessman moved two steps down and Keith was exposed again. He turned his face away and looked to the right. At the bottom of the escalator he looked back for him but he was gone. *Had he spotted him*, Keith thought?

He felt a wave of panic hit him. He strode more quickly for the next escalator that would take him downstairs. The red numbers on the port authority clock seemed to scream 12:59 P.M! He started a slow jog.

Keith had half a mind to bolt back onto the street, try to get lost and hold up in a hotel. But something carried him to the escalator, down to the ground floor and to his bus.

No one had grabbed him, jumped him or shot him. He got onto the bus just before it pulled out, gave the driver his ticket and went to the back. He slumped in his seat and leaned his head against the window as the bus moved through the dark garage.

He was safe for the time being. The problem was that he didn't know what he was trying to be safe from. And that bothered him.

chapter 27

The trip to State College, where he had graduated college, would take some six hours. Plenty of time to figure out what was going on.

After about an hour on the bus he decided to rewind the tape in his recorder and play the entire thing, not knowing what was on it, not sure if it had anything to do with his experiences of the previous twelve hours.

Two hours into the trip he thought he had his answer.

The tape started out with a few conversations that he remembered from the week before. Then there was some stuff from the bachelor party, then the puking episode that he vaguely remembered.

Then Keith heard himself getting on the bus. It was coming back to him. Then the voice of a man asking him to move his seat and then the sound of him moving. He had left the recorder on.

Then the conversation.

He could make out most of it, but there were some parts that the bus engines trampled over. He tried to remember the faces of the men in the back seat, but had no luck. It was a small consolation, but he now knew why the men were after him. He had recorded the Stephenson kidnappers.

Keith sat still in his seat, listening to the conversation over and over, trying to pick up all the words. He stared out the window as the bus moved along Interstate 80. In that part of Pennsylvania at that time of year, the highway was a paved corridor surrounded on both sides by trees and mountains. It was beautiful, Keith thought.

Another two hours passed and he had everything he could get off the tape. It was clear to him that someone had paid to have the senator kidnapped. But he had no idea who. If he hadn't been abducted and Ms. Osbourne hadn't been shot in front of him, he wouldn't think much of the tape. But those things had happened and it was real and those men wanted the tape and wanted him dead.

Keith put the recorder down and stared at the sign coming up on his right. They were coming up on Bloomsburg, where Ed had gone to school. A small town he had visited many times. The bus would stop there, one of the reasons the trip took so long; there were five stops made along the way. He would play it by ear.

Keith pulled his bag on his lap and did a quick inventory. He had clothes, money and his phone. Enough to get by on for the time being.

The bus pulled into the station in Bloomsburg and was back out and on Route 80 by 5:00. Next stop was Lewisburg.

Denise Carrington was growing weary of the juvenile delinquents she counseled as part of her graduate psychology course. It was bad enough that she had to drive the fifty miles from State College to Lewisburg by herself twice a week, but now the kids were getting violent.

Denise had just finished a counseling session with a thirteen-year-old professional car thief. He had been uncooperative, rude and abusive, calling her a "stupid college bitch." He ended the session by lunging over the table at her. She had defended herself well, breaking his nose and pinning him to the floor with a knee to his neck until one of the guards could relieve her. This was not on the agenda for his therapy, and she would probably have to explain herself to her professor.

Denise pulled her ten-year-old station wagon out of the correctional facility parking lot and noticed the yellow gas gauge light was on. She headed into town for some gas.

The Three Rivers bus sputtered into the tiny bus station located at the edge of Bucknell University's campus. The burning smell and smoke coming from the rear of the bus forced all the passengers off. Keith sat on the curb and watched as the bus driver assessed the damage. He came back to the passengers with, "It's busted."

The bus driver did have good news for them. There was another bus that had left New York at 6:00 A.M. and would be there at 11:00 A.M., a mere five hours away.

This was not good news. Keith thought that waiting around in one place could be hazardous to his health. He spotted a Gas 'n Go across the street. *When was the last time I ate*, he thought? He got up off the curb and went across the street.

Keith's eating habits had come a long way since his college days of chili-cheese dogs for breakfast, lunch and dinner. But, in times of great stress, he reverted back to old, bad habits.

Keith came to the register with two hot dogs, a soda and a package of butterscotch krimpets. He arranged his food on the counter for the cashier to ring up. The kid behind the counter didn't seem like the "Bucknell type". Medium height, he was a normal looking kid except for the three nose rings.

"Anything else?" The nose ringed cashier asked.

"No thanks. That's about it," Keith replied.

Keith paid the man and then tried to assemble his booty into a configuration he could carry. The bell on the door rang and opened and he jumped slightly. But it wasn't a bad guy. It was a very pretty girl, dirty blonde hair, thin but not model-thin. She got behind Keith as he struggled to move along.

"Dude, want a bag?" the cashier tried to help.

"Yeah, that would help." Keith turned back to the girl, "Sorry, I thought I could get it all. Just be a second." The girl had on a bulky PSU sweatshirt.

The nose ring boy got all the food into a bag and Keith was set. He turned back to the girl, "You go to Penn State?"

"Yes, I do," she answered politely.

"Cool. Me too." Keith turned and walked out of the store. He sat on the front curb of the store and unpacked his feast like a little kid who had just spent his whole allowance on candy. He chewed on the first hot dog as he watched the bus smoke.

He was halfway done with the second dog when the pretty girl came out of the store. She gave him a quick look and a half-smile and went to her car. Unexpectedly, she came back his way and stopped in front of him.

"Hi. How are you getting back to school?" she asked.

She had caught him in mid chew. He held up his index finger while he finished quickly, the international sign for "give me a second while I swallow this down."

"I'm taking the bus," he said pointing over to the bus station with its black smoke and stranded passengers. The driver stood near the back of the bus, arms folded, shaking his head.

"That doesn't look very promising," she said.

"Well, it is my lucky day. There'll be a bus by in about another five hours," he said.

The girl laughed nervously. "Well, I am going back to campus if you want to catch a ride." She regretted it almost as soon as she said it.

"You're not some kind of serial killer, are you?" Keith asked.

"No, not by the classic definition. How about you?"

"Not in the classic definition."

"Come on then," she said.

Keith got up off the curb and walked slightly behind the girl as she led the way. It struck him that the pretty face could be part of the group that was after him. But that didn't seem to matter. He did what any single guy would do when a cute girl offered help.

Denise got to the driver side door and opened it. She leaned on the hood and looked at the boy across from her. "So, serial killer man, what's you're name?"

"I'm Keith," he said.

"Keith, it is nice to meet you. I'm Denise."

"Nice to meet you." And it was, he thought.

"Now Keith, don't get any ideas or try anything cute. I've already broken one nose today and I'm just warming up."

Keith smiled and got into the car.

What should have been a relaxing day for Tommy was turning into one that was grating on his nerves. First the kid gets away, then James turns up dead after capping an innocent bystander. And in all of that, he still didn't have the tape.

At least the FBI was no closer to the truth. That he was sure of. The videotape had shocked the country and people in law enforcement and the government were acting irrationally. Congress was in the midst of passing tough anti-terrorism legislation. Irish communities were at each other, the pro-IRA factions being questioned by the more moderate majority. Sein Finn continued to deny involvement but no one was buying it. Danny Sullivan prayed for his own release.

And in the midst of this very carefully orchestrated confusion was a loose end in the form of a twenty-something party boy that had been all luck and no brains. But the kid had slipped up and it was just a matter of time.

"So, what is a pretty girl like you doing all the way out here," Keith said trying to break the ice with his new friend. She seemed nervous, edgy.

"Well, I was doing some graduate work at the juvenile detention center," Denise answered.

"Psych major, huh?" Keith said.

"You got it."

"I was accounting. Pretty boring stuff."

"You were?" She paused and looked over at him. "I thought you said you were in school?"

"Oh, sorry. I've been out for six years, but every time I get this close I feel like I never left. I wish I never left," he said.

"Then what are you doing in Lewisburg?" Her worst fears were starting to play out in her mind. Maybe this guy was a serial killer, she thought.

"Do you really want to know?" Keith asked.

"Yes, or I am pulling over and you can walk," Denise said with a tinge of anger.

"Okay, okay. Just don't break my nose."

"Funny."

"Okay. It all started with this girl and ended with me losing my job..." Keith went on to weave his country and western song reality (car stolen, lost girl, lost job), leaving out the events of the past day. That might freak her out. It freaked him out.

"So, I was handed this really big check today and figured I'd take a little vacation, get away from the city, get back to my roots. You know?" he finished.

"What about the hair?" she questioned.

"What about it?"

"Well, I don't think your cuffs and collar match."

"That's rather personal. But if you must know, I had it done today. I've always wanted to be a blonde. How did you know?" Keith said as he looked over her profile.

"Looks like some peroxide ran on your shirt," she said pointing to a discolored mark on his shoulder.

This girl was very sharp, Keith thought. Smart and getting prettier by the minute. Her profile was nice to look at. She wasn't classic, high cheekbone beautiful, but her small pixie nose, long neck and blue eyes were a great combination.

The radio played at a nice volume, not loud enough to make conversation difficult, but loud enough to fill in the gaps.

"So, how does the football team look this spring?" Keith asked.

Denise shook her head.

"What?" he asked.

"It just amazes me," she said shaking her head.

"What?"

"How everything for guys comes back to football. A guy could be talking about life on other planets and the conversation would drift to football."

"That is a gross generalization," Keith said, mock-offended.

"Oh, really? The 'life on other planets' conversation would break down to how teams would handle zero gravity and if there would have to be asterisks next to the records. Am I right?"

Keith smiled. Man, was she pretty. "No. Wrong again. Obviously they would have to play in domes with some sort of gravity stabilization technology. Duh."

Denise looked over at him and smiled. "By the way, they looked pretty good in the Blue/White game. They have a really good freshman running back from Cinnaminson that might get some playing time."

"You went to the game?" He was jealous.

"Sure. Where do you think I got my great tan?"

The reality of Keith's last twenty-four hours melted away as the car hummed along rural Route 45, the back way into State College. The trees and farms were in considerable contrast to his city existence.

They talked some more, on and off, during the ride. They covered a variety of topics and Keith felt an ease with her that he had never felt with Cindy or even Shannon. It was weird and pleasant all at the same time.

About three miles from town Keith stopped in mid-sentence to listen to a radio promo.

"Hey, collegers and collegettes, it's Crazy Lenny Williams and I'll be back tonight in the midnight to five spot. Tonight, we'll see how long it takes us to get fined by the FCC. Should be interesting." Keith recognized the voice. Then the trailer: "Crazy Lenny from twelve to five tonight and every week night, right here on Quick Rock."

Denise noticed Keith staring at the radio. "What is it?"

"Oh, nothing. Sorry. It's just that I did some college radio stuff at WPSU and knew a guy named Len Williams. I wonder if it's the same guy?"

"It could be. I've listened to him a couple of times and he's mentioned he's a bona fide Penn State grad," Denise added.

"Huh. Maybe I'll look him up," Keith said, his mind churning.

For the last couple of miles into town, the two were quiet, both wishing that the ride would last a while longer.

When they got to the edge of town, Denise broke the silence. "Is there anywhere in particular I can drop you off?"

Keith paused. It was over. He would get out of the car and never see this perfect girl again. "Uh, um. Why don't you let me off along Beaver Ave."

"Do you know where you are staying?" she said concerned.

"Actually, I was just thinking along those lines. I was kind of rushed today and really didn't plan this out too well. But I am sure I can find something," he said looking into the distance.

An awkward silence ensued. Denise felt like asking him to stay with her, but she realized that she didn't really know this guy too well and she was not that easy.

The station wagon pulled over across the street from the Phyrst, a bar tour favorite. "This is my stop," Keith said as he pulled his bag up off the floor and opened his door. He got out and closed it, then leaned in the open window.

"Listen, Denise. I can't thank you enough for helping me out. You saved me a long wait."

"Oh, it was nothing. I hate doing that drive alone and you were great company for a serial killer."

They both laughed.

"Look, I'll understand if you say no, but I would really like to take you to dinner to thank you for the ride," he said smoothly, surprising himself.

Denise's cheeks went flush and her eyes lit up, but she wanted to play it cool. "Well, I am kind of busy tonight..."

"I understand."

"But I can clear my schedule." Did she really say that?

"Great. I'll meet you at the Allen Room in an hour?" Keith checked his watch. It was just before seven.

Denise paused. She was constantly hit on by undergrads with poor lines and bad manners and this boy was a change from that. Keith was not them. "Sounds like a date."

"See you then," Keith said as he stood up from the window. He tapped her roof as she pulled away down Beaver Avenue. He knew full well that there was a chance that she would not show, that she was just being polite. But it was worth the chance.

He started to walk south back toward Atherton Street to find himself a place to stay.

chapter 28

Jacob had lost his charm very quickly for Alex. She was still bored and still horny and the endless hours of watching the television for developments was mind numbing. She needed a new diversion.

"Get in there, you smell," Alex barked at Stephenson. She prodded the senator into the bathroom as Jacob watched them both, keeping a gun on the senator. Jacob saw no use in putting the man in the shower, they just planned to kill him; it was an unnecessary risk. But he knew not to argue with her.

The senator's hands were cuffed behind him as he shuffled his feet along the tiled floor like a beaten man on a death march. His captors no longer wore masks. Bad.

Stephenson had only been awake a few hours a day. They woke him up, fed him, then drugged him again. He was as awake now as he was at any point since the videotape. How long had he been drugged? What day was it? His confusion was unnerving and the whole situation made him nauseous. In the past he had been physically beat up on the football field to the point of being sick with exhaustion, but this was different.

"What day is it?" he mumbled.

"It's shower day," she answered.

Jacob sat on the closed toilet seat while Alex uncuffed Stephenson and helped him take off the clothes he had gone to bed in almost a week before. Alex was like a patient mother helping the man strip. Jacob thought she was enjoying it.

"Get in," she ordered.

The senator lifted one leg and put it in the tub then the other. Alex cuffed his right hand to a water knob that was about chest high. She wanted him to remember that he was a prisoner.

She turned the cold water knob first. The showerhead spit water on the man and he cringed. She then added some hot water until the stream was warm. She backed away and leaned up against the sink, watching water pour over the very handsome and very fit senator.

"Why don't you get something to eat," she said to Jacob. "I can handle him."

Jacob left the room as ordered.

The water felt good on the senator's body, though he continued to shiver.

"Too cold?" she asked.

He shook his head no as he lifted his face to the showerhead. It was helping to clear his mind, wake him up.

After a minute or so of silence, the senator noticed that the girl was watching him and that she was smiling, enjoying herself. He felt embarrassed.

"Here," Alex said as she reached across and handed him a bar of soap. He began to lather himself awkwardly with his free hand.

"I must say, Phil, you have kept yourself in very good shape. How old are you anyway?" she said with a wink.

Stephenson didn't answer. He was getting angry now, he did not like being humiliated. What was this girl's game?

She continued, "Why, I would have to say that you are in better shape than Mitch. He didn't have near the muscle definition that you have. And I have got to be honest, you are much better hung than he was."

Stephenson turned to face her and hurled the bar of soap at her, missing her and hitting the door with a thud. She laughed.

Jacob knocked on the door. "Is everything okay in there?"

"Everything is fine. Phil dropped the soap."

Stephenson rinsed the soap off his body as Alex watched his every move, smiling. He turned the water off himself when he was done. He felt refreshed, maybe strong enough to take a swing at the psycho woman.

Alex opened the door and asked Jacob to get a towel. He returned with a towel and his gun. Jacob sat back on his perch.

Alex put the towel on the sink, went over to the senator and uncuffed his hand, then re-cuffed his hands behind his back. She guided him out of the tub and onto a tubmat. She took the towel and began to dry him off starting with his shoulders.

"Better than a sponge bath, huh?" she said, rubbing him seductively. "The only problem is you are getting me all wet."

She put the towel down and took off her sweatshirt. She was not wearing a bra and her breasts got both men's attention.

She got the towel and started once again to dry him off. She rubbed her bare breasts against him repeatedly as she moved the towel over his body. By the time she got to his hips, he had an erection.

"Looks like the little senator is ready to vote."

Stephenson turned his head away, unable to control his lower region. Thinking baseball didn't work.

When she was finished she put her sweatshirt back on, patted the senator's bare ass, and helped him back into his grungy clothes.

At least he felt a little bit more human, physically.

Denise sat at the upstairs bar of the Allen Room nursing a diet soda. She wore her favorite jeans, snug on her legs and butt but loose around her thin waist and a short sleeve denim shirt. Her blondish hair, usually in a ponytail, was down to her shoulders. She had even put a little make up on, though she really didn't need it.

It was just after eight o'clock and she had already convinced herself that Keith would not show up. In a way, she was hoping he wouldn't come. She didn't need to get involved with a stranger; she needed to concentrate on school.

"Can I get you a refill?" the bartender asked.

"No thanks. I'm okay."

The bartender smiled. He didn't mind paying some extra attention to the girl.

Denise looked down to the other end of the bar where a couple was having a heated discussion. They were it. A slow night in State College.

She looked at her watch again and wondered what she was doing there. She straightened her back and took a deep breath. She felt a hand on her back and turned.

"Hi," Keith said.

"Oh, hi," she returned.

"You looked surprised to see me."

"Well, no, um..." Denise looked away.

He sat down at the stool next to her. "It's okay. I didn't know for sure if you would come either. Though I must say that I am happy you did."

She smiled. "Did you find a place to stay?"

"Yeah. I'm at the very well appointed Beaver Motel out on Atherton."

"Sounds awful," she said with a chuckle.

"Well, the Nittany Lion Inn was booked, so I had to go down a notch." Keith waved the bartender down and ordered a beer. "So, do you like my new clothes?" Keith got up and did a twirl for her.

Keith had gone to the bookstore and loaded up on college wear. He was in a solid blue polo shirt with a PSU crest and blue and white striped shorts.

Denise watched, liking what she saw, then said, "Is there anything that doesn't say Penn State on it?"

"Nope. Not even my underwear."

"I'll take your word for it."

Keith sat back down. "You look great. I like your hair down like that."

"Thanks." She was shocked that he noticed.

Keith sipped his beer and left a five on the bar. "Are you hungry?"

"Very. The hostess said we could sit anywhere. As you can see they are not exactly packed," she replied.

"Great. Can we sit by the window?"

"Sure. Lead the way." She reached for his hand.

The two got up from their stools and navigated through the dining room of empty tables. They settled on a table that faced College Avenue. As they sat down, a waitress greeted them with menus.

"Can I get you two a drink?" she said.

"Diet soda, please," Denise answered.

"I'm fine," Keith added.

Keith looked out the window as the waitress walked away. From the second floor he could see the campus across the street. Cars eased by on the street below. Branches from a large tree across the street almost touched the window. Keith wondered if there was someone out there waiting for him.

Denise politely cleared her throat.

"Oh, sorry. I just spaced," Keith admitted.

"That's okay. It's a nice view. Do you want to split an appetizer?" she said over the menu.

"Sure. You pick."

"How about nachos supreme?"

"You know, you get prettier and prettier every time you speak," he said cheerfully.

"Well, you're growing on me, too."

The waitress came back and took their order. Keith switched over to diet soda.

A group of tan, pretty girls in shorts and tanks came in and sat down near them. Denise gave them a look. At least two of the three had to be cheerleaders or aerobics instructors. Keith did not look over at the table once and Denise noticed.

"So, what are you going to do?" Denise asked.

"I'm sorry, what?" Keith said surprised.

"So, what are you going to do with yourself? I mean this is like a vacation for you, right? What happens when vacation is over?" she clarified.

"Well, I've got this idea for a book," Keith said.

"Really? What kind of book?"

Keith went on to explain the concept of his book, how he had been riding mass transportation ever since his car had been stolen, recording conversations and writing commentary.

"Why didn't you mention this before?" she asked.

"I don't know. I'm kind of shy about my writing."

"Well. You shouldn't be. It sounds like a great idea. Do you have any of it with you?"

"No, sorry, I don't. But I would love for you to read it."

"I'd like that, too."

Their dinner came, a chicken sandwich and fries for Keith and a big salad for Denise. Keith looked out the window from time to time while they ate. The sun was setting and the overhanging trees blocked much of the light. The waitress came over and lit the candle on their table.

The cheerleaders had gone and Denise was relieved. Keith and Denise were alone. The waitress dimmed the lights.

"Can I ask you a question?" Keith said.

Denise smiled. "Sure."

"How old are you?"

"Oh, Keith, you were doing so well."

"Don't take it the wrong way. You just seem to be a lot more mature than the college girls I remember. Forget I asked," he said, hands up in surrender.

"I'm only kidding. It was fine to ask. I am twenty-five," she said confidently.

"Wow. You look much younger than that, but you seem older."

"Well, I was in the army for two years. The G.I. Bill is how I am getting through college."

"I never would have guessed that."

"Well, I don't wear a uniform anymore."

Keith smiled.

"What?" she said, squinting at him.

"I just had a flash of you in camo's and face paint."

"And?"

Keith leaned closer. "Very sexy."

"Well, thanks. I think."

The two finished what was left of their dinner. They skipped desert and Keith paid the bill.

"So, how would you grade our first date?" Keith asked, hoping for the best.

"I'd give it an incomplete."

"Really? Is that good or bad?"

Denise leaned forward and put her hand on Keith's. "It's good. It's very good."

Youngman was beginning to hate the gray room, especially when he was in it at eleven at night. He had to get special permission to see his famous client this late, but Danny was frantic and he hoped it was worth it.

Danny had seen plenty of visitors in the past few days, all of them from the FBI. But Danny knew nothing of the kidnapping plot and even though he was offered clemency, he stuck to his guns.

Danny came into the room with a guard and sat on his end of the glass.

"What took you so long?" Danny asked impatiently.

"Me? I was doing nothing as usual. I figured I would string you along and get you pissed and then come and see you. What do you think I was doing?" Youngman countered.

Danny put his head down.

"What's the matter?" Yougman asked.

"I heard a rumor that they are going to take me off of death row and put me in the general population."

"I haven't heard anything like that. Who did you hear it from?"

"I hear things, okay? Now the cons in the general population are pissed that some Mics kidnapped a US Senator. They are getting all patriotic. The word is if I go into the main stream, I won't last the afternoon."

Youngman smiled inwardly at the irony. Here he was trying to get his client off of death row and then when it happens, his life is in more immediate danger than it ever was.

"Danny, I will talk to the warden. I am sure it is just a rumor. They need to keep you alive to keep Stephenson alive," he assured the convict.

"Maybe. Maybe not."

"Trust me. I'll fix it."

Danny smiled. Everything Youngman had ever told him had come true.

"Do you think I will actually get out of here?" Danny asked seriously.

"At this point, Danny, anything is possible."

chapter 29

Small stacks of paper sat in neat piles on Tommy's hotel bed. Three rows of two. They helped create the road map that would doom a powerful man, a man that was just one piece of Tommy's revenge.

Tommy sat on the edge of the bed as the morning light just started to creep into his room. He leafed through the closest pile to him, a pile of newspaper clippings. The square cut outs were old and faded and turning yellow. Some clippings in the pile were twenty years old and Tommy had carried them with him for that long.

The first newspaper square was from the *New York Daily News*. It detailed a botched mid-town robbery attempt that had left two men dead. But that was only half of the real story; a third man died. Behind that article was a series of business section articles from the *Wall Street Journal* and *The New York Times*. The articles announced Charles Jones was succeeding Stanley Jorgensen as CEO and Chairman of National Merchandising. Jorgensen had died in the robbery attempt. More articles detailed Jones' rise to wealth and power.

The last square was the obituary for one Antonio DePasquale of Brooklyn.

Tommy's hands shook with anger and he exhaled forcefully. He got up and walked around the room and then sat back down. After all these years it still affected him.

Next he lifted up a pile of hand written notes. This was a bonus. The brunette had found them in the senator's study on the night of the kidnapping. It was the final draft of the Stephenson-Wrightman Act, a bill that would tie China's human rights performance to their trade status. Something not many people in business or politics wanted.

Lastly he checked the short stack with the cassette tape on top. The pages were transcripts of the tape. The tape was of the two planning meetings he had prior to the kidnapping. One was with Tarman, the other with Jones. It detailed the whole plan to eliminate the senator.

Tommy paper clipped each set of papers and put them carefully into a large manila envelope. He had decided to send the whole story from Jorgensen to Stephenson to that reporter who broke the kidnapping story, but he was having second thoughts. He had someone else in mind.

"Crazy" Leonard Williams stood stoically in front of the Sparks Building on campus. The lanky, freckle faced red head did not look like what he sounded like on the radio. In short, he had a face for radio, but his voice and ability to do impressions carried him on the airwaves. He actually looked like a typical student; jeans, sweatshirt and sunglasses. He was not that far removed from the experience.

Lenny looked around and enjoyed the lack of activity on campus. It was summer session and it was before eight, so not a lot was going on as not many students were in town.

He sipped the coffee that he had picked up at a convenience store on Atherton Street. He glanced at his watch: 7:57 A.M.

When Keith had called him during his shift last night, he had nearly fallen over. When he found out Keith was in town he was psyched. It would be fun getting together with an old radio buddy, someone who had helped him get where he was. And when Keith said he needed help the answer was "no problema."

"Hey man," a voice came from behind him.

Lenny turned and looked at the large double doors of the Sparks Building. It took a second for him to recognize Keith with the blonde hair, but it was him.

"Hey, how are you?" he said as he moved toward his old friend.

The two shook hands and went inside.

"Well, I've been better. But I think you can help me." He held up the tape player.

Lenny looked at it. "I will do what I can."

The two went up the stairs toward the studios that were WPSU, the college funded and student run radio station.

"We have the run of the place this morning. No one is in the studio. They have some PSA's at noon, but that's it," Lenny assured.

"This shouldn't take long."

"By the way. What's with the hair? Mid-life crisis?"

"Something like that," Keith replied.

"Looks good."

Lenny unlocked the doors to the production studio; he still had keys. The studio was down the hall from the record library and the broadcast studio. Lenny turned the lights on and the two sat down in chairs. Just like old times.

"So, what's on the tape?" Lenny asked.

"Well, I am not sure what I have here. Some of the words are overlaid with noise. I need some help getting the distortion stripped out. You know, get it cleaned up."

"Dude, no problem. So, what do you think is on the tape?"

"It's a conversation between two men," Keith said.

"And?" Lenny said, waiting for the punchline.

Keith gave a condensed version of his book concept and why he carried a tape recorder. He explained how the recorder had been left on inadvertently.

"Now here is the tricky part, which I really don't want to let you in on."

Lenny sat forward. "Dude, you can tell me anything."

"Lenny, believe me when I say this. What is on this tape could get us both killed."

"Come on."

"I'm more than serious. I am hiding out. That's why I dyed my hair. I am trying to get lost while I figure all this out."

"Okay. Let's say I believe you, which I do. Let me work with the tape and if I don't like the way it is going, I'll stop," Lenny reasoned.

"If you hear it you will be involved."

"Then you sitting here telling me involves me whether I hear the tape or not."

Keith paused. He was right.

Lenny continued: "Look, give me the tape, let me get it into a format I can work with and then let's talk."

"You sure?"

"Yes."

Keith handed him the tape.

"Keith, why don't you let me be for awhile. There is a soda machine downstairs. Why don't you take a walk and go get us some caffeine, okay?"

Keith nodded and left the room. If anything happened to Lenny because of him he would never forgive himself.

Lenny converted the tape to reel to reel and then began to play with it, stripping out the bass and the noise as best he could on the old equipment.

Keith took his time down the stairs, reliving some old times. Thursday night recordings and Sunday night live shows helped get his writing skills going in the right direction. It was a great experience.

After about ten minutes of wandering, he walked back into the room with sodas as Lenny took off his headphones.

"I was able to get just about everything cleaned up. This is a joke, right?" Lenny said as he took a soda from Keith and opened it.

"No joke," Keith replied.

Lenny paused. "It's all there. These are the guys who kidnapped Stephenson or am I missing something?"

"No, you are right on."

"Shit. Well, this has to go to the police, like now."

Keith shook his head. "Look, Lenny. Some bad men have already abducted me. I got lucky and escaped. Then they came to my apartment and tried to kill me. I got lucky again. So now I am suppose to waltz into that police station, where I still have outstanding parking tickets, hand them this tape and ask them to protect me? Come on."

"Dude, this is out of hand. All that happened to you, for real?"

"For real," Keith said emphatically.

Lenny contemplated the events, "So then what?"

"Well, give me the headphones and let me listen to the whole thing."

Sammy had not gone to college, not a surprise coming from his "family", so the impromptu trip to State College was something special. His large, black, four door, sedan sped down route 322, the last leg of his trip from Pittsburgh. It was a little after eight in the morning and all he could do was think about sleeping again. Wise guys were not accustomed to getting up at the crack of dawn.

Sammy was an 'electrician', at least that is what it said on his tax returns. But that was far from what he did for a living. And this was a job, just like any other.

The car ate up the road on the single lane highway just twenty miles outside State College. Sammy had come prepared with plenty of information and it was time to use it. He had a picture of the guy he was looking for that came over the internet. More importantly he had a list of lodgings and phone numbers that were printed off the State College web site.

He took the list of hotel phone numbers, held it in the hand he was steering with and dialed the first number on his cell phone with his free hand. First on the list was the Atherton Hotel. He knew that if the kid had any brains he would have registered under an assumed name. Sammy looked at the picture again. "You never know."

"Good morning, this is the Atherton Hotel. How may I direct your call?" a cheerful man answered.

"Can you connect me to Keith Garrity's room?"

"Hold please."

Sammy heard some tapping on the other end consistent with the use of a keyboard. "I am sorry, we do not have a Keith Garrity listed here. Are you sure you have the right hotel?"

Sammy hung up and dialed the next number. There were twenty-six hotels and motels on the list. He'd be done in less than 20 minutes. If he didn't hit on this, he'd have to go one place at a time with the picture.

Sammy looked down at the pile of papers on the passenger seat. The picture was on top. There was a note on the bottom: 'may have blonde hair'. Sammy smiled. The kid looked like a pushover. This was going to be easy.

"What the hell is a Potemkin Village?" Keith asked Lenny right after the tape stopped.

"Got me," Lenny responded.

"Sounds familiar. But I don't know."

"Sounds like the key to the whole thing. What do we do now?"

Keith thought for a second. He would have to do some research later. But now it was time to get Lenny out of this.

"Okay. Can you make two cassette copies off the reel-to-reel?" Keith asked.

"No problem." Lenny leaned over to a file cabinet, pulled two old tapes out and quickly recorded over them.

"Now, splice off the reel-to-reel," Keith directed.

Lenny took his razor blade and cut at the beginning and on the end and then spliced the master back together. He handed the brown tape to Keith. Keith went over to a wallet sized black box called a demagnetizer. He put the tape on top of the box, pressed the red button on the side and the box hummed. It also erased anything on the tape. Keith took the tape and put it in a trashcan.

"Okay. Now what?" Lenny said as he took off the headphones.

"Now, you go home and pretend that you never saw me."

"Come on. You heard the tape. They plan to kill the senator. We have to let someone know. We can't just sit on this kind of information."

"Listen. Forget you saw me, okay? I've already gotten one person killed in this and I don't want anyone else to get hurt. I have to figure this out, but I promise you I will do the right thing."

"But..."

"Lenny, you heard the man. 'No loose ends'. I am a loose end now and I have to get out of this by myself."

Lenny put his head down and thought for a second. He brought his head back up and extended his hand. "Good luck, man."

Keith shook his hand. "Do not mention this to anyone. I was never here. Right?"

"Right."

Keith was out the door of the studio and took the stairs two at a time as he made his way out of the building. The phrase 'Potemkin Village' played in his head. He was unclear what exactly the two men meant, but he was getting the feeling that the FBI was looking in the wrong place. He had some research to do to make sure.

Sammy got to the city limits of State College then cruised until he saw his first hotel. He pulled the car into the parking lot of the Ramada Inn on 322. None of the calls produced a Keith Garrity, though there was one Marla Garrity at the Days Inn.

Sammy walked confidently into the lobby which was littered with burgundy fabric sofas and matching chairs. A large atrium in the middle of the space let the morning sun in. There was a bar to the left, closed, and to the right a dining area with a breakfast buffet in place. The check-in desk was to his immediate left. The food made his stomach grumble.

"May I help you?" the young girl from behind the desk asked as he approached. Sammy looked her over. She was definitely a college student. Her long, auburn hair was at odds with her brown uniform, but she filled it out pretty well, he thought. Her nametag announced "LAURA".

"Hi. I need your help," he said gravely.

"Oh, yes, what can I do?" she offered.

"It's sad, really, Laura," he said as he leaned on the counter. "I'm a retired police officer that does some investigative work, you know, on the side."

"Like a P.I.?"

"Yeah, just like that. Anyway, I know this couple, old friends of mine. They have a son in college up here, he's a, uh, art major," Sammy oozed, displaying his graduate degree in the art of bull shitting.

"Okay."

"Anyway, their son, Keith, has had a drug problem off and on since high school. Every now and again he gets depressed and checks out, if you know what I mean."

"I know what you mean. The pressure of school can be killer," she said knowingly.

"That's what I hear. Anyway, the parents haven't heard from him in a week and his roommates don't know where he is. They even called a couple professors and he hasn't been to class."

"Did they call the police?" Laura asked.

"Well, Laura, since the kid is on probation they don't want to get the police involved. So..."

"They called you?" she guessed.

"Yeah, they called me." Sammy liked this girl, she was being very helpful. "Anyway, I have a picture here of him. Could you maybe take a look and see if you recognize him?"

The girl looked troubled. "I don't know. They have pretty strict rules about keeping guests names and stuff confidential."

"I understand. I am not asking you to tell me what room he's in, just if you've seen him. Okay?"

She paused and looked in both directions. "Okay."

Sammy pulled out the picture and slid it across the counter.

The girl took it and looked at it for a few seconds then handed it back. "Nope. I haven't seen him."

"Sure?" Sammy said with a disarming smile.

"Totally. I would remember a young guy. Most guests here are in for conferences or in on business. All older guys. You know, you might want to check the motels around here. Some have really cheap rates during the week."

"You know Laura, that is a real good idea. Thanks for the advice." He smiled and she smiled back. "Thanks again."

"Anytime," she said with a big, perky, smile.

Sammy turned and exited the lobby, giving the buffet one last look. He was back in the car and off to the next place.

The Pattee Library, the largest of the six on campus libraries, had changed a lot since Keith had been a student. Located about a hundred yards from the Sparks Building, the grand stone structure seemed as good a place as any to look for answers.

Keith strolled around and was struck by the number of computer terminals. Students sat at them and pointed and clicked and took notes. "Beats trying to find a book," he muttered to himself.

He sat at an empty terminal and started to browse. He searched the word 'Potemkin' first and got one hit. He clicked on it: 'Grigori Alecksondrovich Potemkin'. The screen pulled up a black and white sketch of the man. Keith read through his bio. A Russian prince of sorts during the reign of Catherine the Great, Potemkin was considered the most powerful man in Russia for nearly twenty years. He was Catherine's favorite, and was eventually given a southern territory to manage, the Ukraine. When Catherine came to visit, Potemkin was so intent on impressing her that he constructed false façades in front of dilapidated buildings to hide the true state of affairs. The tour was successful due to Potemkin's deceit and the term 'Potemkin Village' was born.

"That was easy," he said to himself.

Keith scrolled down the screen, reading and re-reading, making sure he had it right. He leaned back in his chair and stared at the screen.

"You've created a real Potemkin Village. That's what the man said," Keith whispered to himself. No one paid him attention. "A real Potemkin Village, right? You created a facade. A misdirection? Yeah, a misdirection."

Keith took a deep breath and stood up from his stool. He walked out the way he came in, past the stacks and rows of books, into the main lobby, through the turnstile and onto the stairs outside.

He stood and looked out over the campus. He could see down to College Avenue through the trees. "That's the answer. The IRA is a diversion. They kidnapped the senator and plan to kill him. They always planned to kill him. And they're going to make it look like something else. What is the best way to get rid of someone and not get caught? Make it look like someone else did it."

Keith started to walk, talking to himself. "So if it isn't the IRA, then who? Who would go to all this trouble?" Keith scanned his memory for any current events regarding Stephenson, but could remember very little, except for the visit to China.

"I wonder if he's dead already?" That stopped Keith in his tracks. "But what if he is still alive? How long will that last?"

He didn't have all the answers. Hell, what he had was very sketchy, but maybe it could steer the investigation in the right direction. But maybe not. Would anyone believe him? If he went to the authorities and they dismissed him, he was as good as dead. It wasn't so easy after all.

He checked his watch and smiled. He had one stop to make, then he would figure out what to do, if anything.

chapter 30

Denise had fallen. And she had fallen for a guy she had picked up hitchhiking. She was sure there was a cliché in there somewhere.

She sat at her kitchen table sipping coffee, scanning the *Centre Daily Times*, seeing the words and pictures but not reading. She was distracted. Keith had left abruptly in the morning and she felt he was trying to get away, nail a college girl and then move on. But he had promised her he'd be back by nine. She wasn't sure what to believe.

Whether he showed or not, she was going to aerobics class and was dressed for it. Her lycra top fit snugly over her upper body, her hair was up in a ponytail and she had a sweatshirt tied around her waist. She looked up at the clock in the kitchen: almost nine.

Denise shook her head. She had spent the better part of her social life turning guys down that hit on her. She had not had a serious boyfriend since before the army and certainly did not sleep with a guy on the first night. But all that was out the window and as the clock moved ahead, the worse she felt about it. She was sure he got back on a bus and was headed back to wherever he had come from.

"Stupid, stupid, stupid," she said out loud as she put her coffee mug in the sink. She untied the sweatshirt from around her waist and slipped it over her head. It was now a minute after nine. Class was in twenty minutes. She figured she'd get there early.

She grabbed her keys off the kitchen counter and took a water bottle out of the refrigerator. She went to the front door and opened it to leave. She ran right into him.

Keith grabbed a hold of her to keep them both from falling. "Whoa, hold on. What's the rush?"

Denise held on to him tightly and looked up at him and he smiled. "I'm not late, am I?"

"Well, a couple of minutes, I guess," she said as she let go.

"Looks like you're headed out. I can come back."

"No. Don't be silly. Come on in."

Denise went through the door and Keith followed. They stood in the middle of the undersized living room. Downtown apartments were very small.

"Do you want something to drink?" she said heading for the kitchen, not looking at him.

"No. I'm okay." Keith felt some tension between them.

"How is you friend? Lenny, right?"

"He is exactly the same, right down to the freckle," Keith said, trying to read her.

Denise rummaged in the refrigerator, forgetting that Keith didn't want anything.

"Is something wrong?" he asked.

Denise closed the door and looked up. "No, um..."

"Denise, if you want me to leave, I'll go."

She walked toward him. "No. That's the last thing I want. I mean, I wasn't sure..."

Keith finished her sentence: "Wasn't sure I would come back?"

She nodded affirmatively.

Keith walked over to her and put his arms around her. "Denise, the one thing about me you have to know is that I do what I say. If I promise something, I do it."

"I'm sorry."

"Don't be. I understand."

They embraced and then kissed. Denise took his hand and noticed the time on his watch. "Oh my God, I'm going to be late," she said.

"For what?"

"Aerobics. But, I guess I can skip it."

"Not on my account. Go ahead and we can talk later. I have some things to do back at the motel."

"Okay. I'll go if you promise me one thing."

"Name it," Keith shot back eagerly.

"Promise me that you will be here when I get back. Stay here with me. Don't go back to that motel."

Keith considered that for a second. "Are you sure?"

"Very sure. You can stay as long as you want, as long as you are honest with me about everything."

Keith paused, "Everything?"

"Yes, everything."

"Deal."

Denise got her keys and headed for the door. "Feel free to shower. If you need to write or anything like that, my computer is on the desk in the bedroom. Fridge is stocked."

"You are being too nice to me," he admitted.

"Well, just stay on my good side and everything will work out. I'll be back by 11:00." She smiled and was out the door.

Keith sat on the sofa. Had he told her everything? Not really, but she hadn't asked the right questions. It was a loophole that he was willing to accept.

He turned on the TV and clicked until he found CNN. He put his backpack on the coffee table in front of him and took out the two cassette copies and his tape recorder. He watched the screen, the anchors talking about the kidnapping and there he sat with the key to the whole thing right in front of him. Very weird.

He took one of the cassettes and popped it into the tape player next to Denise's TV. He turned it on and listened as the sound came through the speakers loud and clear. Lenny had done nice work.

Keith played it a few times, looking to catch something that he hadn't heard before, but it was what it was. He rewound the tape to the beginning and sat back down. The TV screen was on a commercial and when it came back it flashed a Stephenson tip line on the bottom of the screen. He memorized the number.

Someone or something was telling him to make the call.

Hunger had finally gotten the best of Sammy. He had shown the kid's picture eight places with no luck. He spotted the College Diner on his way to the Atherton, pulled over, parked on the street and went in.

"So, what's a sticky?" Sammy said to the waitress.

"It's a cinnamon bun that we are kind of famous for," she replied in a chirpy voice.

"Famous for, huh? Well, if that's the case, I'll have one of those and two eggs over easy."

The waitress scribbled down the order. "It'll be just a few minutes. More coffee?"

"Yeah, sure."

Sammy watched as the young thing walked away. Whoever thought to put these girls in shorts was a genius. "Gotta love college."

He laughed to himself. He knew he stood out, dressed in almost all black, close to fifty, looking like a mobster. But the kids in the other booths didn't look, stare, anything like that. They minded their own business.

The girl came back and refilled his cup. She was all smiles. Sammy picked the menu back up. It cracked him up. All the specials were named in college terms: "The Graduate", "The Undergrad", "The Cuma Sum" something or other.

Not a bad place to hide out, he thought. And all these kids being so nice and helpful. If they only knew what he did for a living.

The tide was high and water skiers zigged and zagged across the bay shooting walls of water into the air as they made their cuts. Donna watched them from the deck of The Marina restaurant back on the bay in Avalon. She had switched over to water after her sixth cup of coffee. It was just past nine.

She had spent the morning doing a piece about the yellow ribbons that now adorned every telephone and electrical pole on the island. And there were a lot of them as there were no underground cables to speak of. She finished the piece on the street in front of the Stephenson compound where flowers and "Come Home Safe" signs littered the curb.

Donna turned her attention back to her plate when a little girl in a yellow foam life vest waddled up to her table holding a pen and paper.

"Hi there," Donna said.

"Hi. Miss Venice, can I ,um, I mean, can I please have your biography?" the little girl said thrusting the pen and paper at her and then looking back at her parents who were at a table on the other side of the deck.

Donna took the pen and paper and smiled. "I would be happy to. And what is your name?"

"I'm Margie and I'm five." She held up her hand and wiggled her fingers. "Five."

Donna smiled again and signed the paper as the girl swayed back and forth, index finger in her mouth.

"Here you go, Margie," Donna said with a smile.

"Thank you berry much, Ms. Venice."

The girl ran back to her parents, waving the piece of paper. She nearly tripped. The couple waved to Donna and she back at them.

It was only a matter of time before the networks called.

Her phone rang and she fished it out of her handbag.

"This is Donna."

"You certainly are," the male voice said.

"Is this my special agent?" she said like a teenager.

"Yes ma'am," Thompson said.

"Is this call business or pleasure?"

"All business," the agent said.

"Well, I guess I will have to take what I can get. What's up?"

"They've moved Sullivan to solitary confinement."

"Solitary confinement? Why?"

"Seems that some of the other inmates have not taken kindly to the fact that a United States Senator has been kidnapped to free an Irish cop killer. They seem to think the way he got his stay was un-American."

"Wow. He's not in any danger is he?" Donna asked.

"Not much. They can't get to him in solitary. At least that is what the warden says," Thompson replied.

"Man, if anything happens to him, then Stephenson is dead for sure."

"Right on the mark, Ms. Van Ness. That is why they are taking the extra precaution. Death row is safe enough, but you never know."

"Well that is interesting news Agent Thompson. And I am assuming it still would be news?" Donna hoped.

"I bet if you could get on the air in the next ten minutes, you'd be the first," he said confidently.

"You're the best."

"I try."

"So, when do I get to repay you for this?"

"It's hard to say. I'll be in touch."
"Don't keep me waiting, Agent Thompson."
"I'll do my best. Gotta go."
"Bye." Donna ended the connection then hit a speed dial number.
"Jim, it's Donna. Got another hot item. Have Scooter meet me over at the compound. I'll be there in five."

Sammy stood at the register as his waitress came up front to ring him up.
"How was everything?" she said, looking him in the eye.
"I have to tell you, that was one hell of a meal."
"That's $5.75," she said as the register drawer opened.
"And cheap, too." He handed her a twenty, then looked down at the pastry selection behind the glass.
"Do you sell those stickies in bulk?" Sammy blurted.
"You mean, like in dozens." She handed him the change back.
"Yeah, whatever," he said, eyeing the pastry.
"Sure do. We actually fill orders from alumni all over the world," she said proudly.
"Is that right?" Sammy handed her back the money. "Give me a dozen."
Sammy left the diner with his pastry box and got into his sedan. Time to get back to work.

Keith dialed the number on the screen from his cell phone. He assumed that even tip lines could be traced.
"Stephenson tip line," a voice answered.
"Hi. I'd like to speak to the agent in charge."
"Do you have information regarding the senator's kidnapping?" the voice on the other side was no-nonsense.
"Yes I do and I would like to speak to the agent in charge," Keith responded nervously.
"Okay. But first, why don't you tell me and I'll pass it along?"
"Why don't you get me the agent in charge."
Agent Kittridge kept his cool. He had heard it all in the last three days. "As you can imagine, he is very busy. If you tell me and we can verify what you say is true, then you can speak with the director himself."
Keith paused. He wasn't going to get anywhere. This agent was the gate keeper, the filter and must have gotten a million fake calls, pranks, Prince Albert in a can kind of stuff.
"Okay. I have a tape recorded conversation between two men I think are involved in the kidnapping. Hold on."
Keith moved to the stereo and hit the *play* button and held his phone to one of the speakers.
When the conversation was over, he got back on the line.

"Where did you record this, sir?" the agent asked.

"I'd like to speak with the agent in charge, please," Keith said, feeling he had an edge.

"I'm sorry. I have no way of telling if it is authentic."

"Do you know what a Potemkin Village is?"

"No, I don't."

"Well I do and I would like to speak to the agent in charge," Keith almost demanded.

"Hold please."

Sammy spotted a motel called the Beaver something on his way to the upscale Atherton and decided to stop.

The kid at the desk tapped loudly on his laptop behind the counter. He didn't look up once while Sammy gave him the sob story and held the picture up in front of him.

The kid stopped tapping and looked up at the picture. "Yeah. I've seem him," he said matter of factly. "Checked in last night. Haven't seen him since."

"What room?" Sammy insisted.

"I can't do that. Leave a message and I'll give it to him when he comes back."

"Look," Sammy said using every bit of self control to stop himself from pulling the computer out from under the kid's fingers and throwing it out the window, "he could be in the room right now OD'ing. If I could just make sure he was alright."

The kid looked up. "Drug problem, huh?"

"Like I said, a bad one. He's been in and out of rehab since high school. His parents are really worried. You have parents, don't you kid?"

"Yeah," the clerk answered.

Sammy continued, "What if they couldn't find you? Don't you think that would drive them nuts?"

"Yeah."

The kid gave a pained look. He turned back and pulled one of the many keys hanging on the wall. "Okay. We'll go together. If there is anything going down we call the cops, okay?"

"Whatever you say," Sammy said with a wide grin.

Sammy followed the kid, who was very tall and too thin, to room 134 on the first level. The kid knocked and got no answer. He turned to Sammy and shrugged. Sammy returned a concerned look. The clerk put the key in the lock and opened the door. Sammy went in first, quickly scanned the main room and then went into the bathroom. He came out and shook his head.

"He's not here?" the clerk asked.

"Nope." Sammy took in all the details. Bed was not slept in. The only sign that someone had been here were some dirty clothes on the floor.

Sammy was out of the room and the clerk locked it behind them. "Thanks, kid." Sammy handed him a card with his cell phone number on it, behind it a folded hundred dollar bill. "If he comes back, please give me a call, okay?"

The clerk nodded.

Agent Thompson picked up the receiver at his make shift desk in the command center. "Thompson."

"Agent Thompson, this is Agent Kittridge on the tip line. I have a man that you may want to talk to."

"Put him on." He waited for the click, then said, "This is Agent Thompson, how may I help you?"

"Are you the agent in charge?" Keith asked.

"At the moment, I am second in command. The agent you are looking for is in a meeting."

"Then you'll have to do."

"Okay. What would you like to talk about?" Thompson said coolly.

"I have a tape to play you, a conversation that I recorded accidentally."

Thompson's pulse jumped a bit. "How does it pertain to the kidnapping?"

"You'll see." Keith repeated the process of playing the tape into the phone. When it was over he got back on the line.

"What is a Potemkin Village?" the agent asked.

"It's a term from Russian history that refers to a false facade, creating a diversion, a misdirection, take your pick," Keith responded.

Thompson's heart kicked into overdrive. Could he have been this lucky? "What are you suggesting?"

"I am suggesting that you at the FBI are looking in the wrong places. Whoever did kidnap the senator wants it to look like the IRA did it. It's a misdirection. The IRA has nothing to do with this. It's got to be another group or individual with a vested interest in having the senator go away."

"You sound pretty sure of yourself. How do you know the tape isn't a joke?" Thompson prodded.

"Because since I've recorded it I have been held hostage myself, shot at and chased down like a subway rat."

"Oh, really?"

"Yes, really. If you don't believe me, check with an Officer Jimenez of the NYPD. She and her partner found me on the floor of an apartment yesterday and cut me loose. Then check with the Hoboken police. My neighbor, a Ms. Osbourne, was shot and killed yesterday. It should have been me," Keith added.

Thompson scribbled notes down on a yellow pad. "Where are you now?"

"I am safe. I want you to confirm my story and call me back. I need your protection and I need you to believe me."

"Okay. I will check it out. Give me a number where I can reach you," Thompson said.

Keith gave the agent his cell phone number. "Then what?"

"We'll come and get you. Fly you back to New York, put you in protective custody, ask you some questions. What's your name son?"

"Keith."

"Okay, Keith. Give me about ten minutes and I will call you back either way. Okay?"

"Okay. I'll be waiting." Keith hung up.

Thompson didn't need to confirm the story, he knew it was Keith Garrity and he knew it was for real. He did need ten minutes to come up with a plan. He scribbled a few notes on his pad, then used his cell phone to make a call. It almost took the entire ten minutes.

Once done, he dialed the standard phone.

"Hello?"

"Keith, this is Agent Thompson. I'm sorry I took so long, but I had some arrangements to make after I confirmed your story."

"Now what?"

"A few things quickly and then we'll talk about how we get you back here," the agent said.

"Okay."

"Now, these men on the tape. Can you describe them?"

"I wish I could. But to be honest I was too drunk to remember either of them. They're dark blurs to me."

"That's okay. We may be able to help you with remembering. Have you told anyone else about the tape?"

"No. No one else. I have been too scared to do anything but run," Keith admitted.

"Okay, son. We want to get you in here and keep you safe. Where are you now?"

"I'm in State College, Pennsylvania, near Penn State's campus."

"Okay. We can have a man out there in a few hours. You picked a good place to hide, that's in the middle of nowhere. Do you feel safe now?"

"I'm good," Keith responded casually.

"Okay. Let's say I can get an agent to you by 1:00 P.M. It's a little after ten now."

Keith gave it a quick thought. "Make it 2:00 P.M."

"Okay. Two it is. Where can the agent pick you up?"

"Have the agent meet me at the lion near Rec Hall."

"The lion?" Thompson wrote that down and underlined it.

"Yeah. It's a statue. More like a shrine. Have the agent ask anyone in town for directions."

"Will do. The lion at 2:00. And Keith?"

"Yes."

"Based on what you have told me some very bad men are looking for you. Stay put until you absolutely have to move. Got me?"

"Yes, sir," he responded.

"Keep your cool, son, and this will all work out. We'll see you later today," Thompson finished.

"Okay. Bye." Keith disconnected and turned his phone off. He got up from the sofa, went into the bedroom and sat at Denise's desk. He turned on the PC and clicked on a word processing program. He couldn't just leave. He had to tell her something.

Thompson made another cell phone call and relayed all the updated information to his other employer. Once he was off the phone, he got up and went for some coffee.

Agent Kittridge was pouring himself some tea when Thompson entered the room.

"Agent Thompson. Did anything come out of that call?"

Thompson smiled. "Well, it started off promising enough with that tape. But then the guy started screaming that the aliens were coming for him and he needed to be protected from their mind sucking death ray."

"Oh, sorry to waste your time like that. I thought he sounded sane," Kittridge said apologetically.

"No problem. It gave me a much needed laugh."

Thompson patted the junior agent on the back and left the room.

Keith sat and typed his story into a blank worksheet. He explained what he thought had happened to him, the whole truth, and the reason he was leaving. She would be back before he left and he would tell her a lie, tell her anything so he could leave and meet the agent by 2:00 P.M.

Hopefully he would be able to make it up to her, come back into her life once this was all behind him.

He finished the page and saved it under "KEITH". She may find it right away, or maybe in a few weeks. He hoped that he could get everything cleared up before she got to it, but just in case things didn't work out, she would know the truth.

Keith shut the computer off and headed for the bathroom to take a shower. The water felt good and he wanted to shave, but he didn't have a razor and wasn't about to try Denise's. As he lathered up he thought of the best way to tell her that he was leaving, the best lie.

Through the pounding water he didn't hear the front door open nor did he hear the bathroom door open.

The shower curtain jerked open and he nearly fell over. Denise was standing there, stripped of her workout wear. "Mind if I join you?"

He smiled and nodded. She climbed in the shower and Keith had something to tell her but, for the life of him, he couldn't remember what it was.

chapter 31

It was just a matter of time now. Tommy walked calmly down 5th Avenue in Manhattan in his navy, double-breasted suit with a designer tie. In his right hand he carried a briefcase that contained a newspaper and a single cassette tape. The endless sea of people seemed to carry him along in their tide. It was lunchtime in mid-town.

The mass of human beings did the WALK/DON'T WALK Pavlovian shuffle at each street corner. He made his way south out of the lower fifties and into the forties. He was one speck of a man.

On 43rd Street he made a right at the New York Public Library and headed toward Sixth Avenue. The sun was strong and it seemed like summer had finally arrived. His forehead perspired slightly, just above his reflective, black framed sunglasses.

He crossed over Sixth and went into a yogurt shop at the end of the block. He stood in line patiently and when it was his turn, he ordered a large vanilla frozen yogurt. He went back across Sixth to Bryant Park and strode along a walkway.

In the late eighties and early nineties, the area known as Bryant Park was fenced off, under a constant state of construction. Located behind the library, the finished park took up almost half the city block and proved a very versatile space that hosted fashion shows and screening parties.

Tommy settled down on a wooden bench under a thick maple tree. He ate his yogurt slowly, watching all manner of people move by him. Businessmen and women, roller bladers, dog walkers, tourists, all going somewhere. The crowd, the sheer number of people, served his purposes well.

Halfway through his frozen lunch, Tommy opened his briefcase and pulled out a *USA Today*. He read the sports section between spoonfuls.

When he finished, he put the paper down and leaned back. A smartly dressed woman in a cream suit attacked a hot dog on the bench across from him. Behind him a radio played softly as a young girl and her dog rested on a blanket. More and more people cruised by him and no one gave him a second look.

He took the rest of his paper out of the briefcase and put it on his lap. The cassette tape was wedged in the pages of the business section. He then stood, paper in hand, walked a few feet to a trashcan and deposited his yogurt container, the paper and the tape.

He went back to the bench, closed his briefcase and sat back down, resuming his reclined position. He looked across the street to the ATM machine. The camera in the kiosk may be able to pick him up through the trees. He was sure the FBI would try it. No matter. He waited until two other people dropped refuse into the can and then got up.

Two minutes later, he was in Times Square. The giant news ticker above read: "KIDNAPPERS SILENT AS STEPHENSON'S FATE IN THE BALANCE." Tommy stopped under the marquee of a movie theatre and watched the jumbo TV as he took out his cell phone from his suit pocket. He dialed the FBI tip number.

"Stephenson tip line," a male voice answered.

"A tape with instructions for the release of Danny Sullivan is in a trashcan in the northeast corner of Bryant Park. Have a nice day."

Tommy reset the phone and called the same number at NBC he had called on Monday. He gave the same message to the person that answered. He called the other New York based networks. He was tempted to go back and watch network gophers and FBI agents all going for the same trashcan, comically smashing heads as they all lunged simultaneously.

Instead, he hailed a cab, and headed for New Jersey.

Denise didn't break his nose, but she was tempted. After a few hours of intimate pleasure, Keith dropped the bombshell that he had to leave for a few days. She did not respond well and Keith knew he had hurt her. She had stayed in bed while he dressed and left.

What had started out as a sunny day was quickly turning gray. *The weird weather patterns of central Pennsylvania*, Keith thought. He had a lot of time to think as he walked the half-mile from Denise's apartment to Rec Hall and the lion statue. When he got to the bronze colored symbol of Penn State, he sat on the curb, and put his head in his hands.

The life-sized, stone lion was situated on a knee high, stone base. The statue seemed to stare at him. Keith was a little early.

A few minutes later, a Winnebago pulled into the Rec Hall parking lot. An older man and his wife got out and walked, holding hands, to the lion. Their vehicle had a variety of bumper stickers plastered on it boasting such locations as the Statue of Liberty and the Calgary Stampede.

The woman got to the lion first and the man snapped some pictures of her in various poses around the lion. Then they switched places. Keith imagined the couple traveling the country and stopping off at any and every point of interest like the huge ball of twine and the UFO museum. Now, maybe they had seen it all.

He watched as they went through a roll of film. Shots of the lion, the woman and the lion, the man and the lion. He wondered if he would ever find someone to spend his life with, to travel the country with when they got old. He thought of Denise.

He had used a job interview as an excuse to leave. He had said he called his machine and a big five accounting firm liked what they saw on his résumé and wanted to bring him in. It was better than the truth. He tried to convince her he would be back, but she shut down and 'yes'ed him as he dressed.

The man came over Keith's way, breaking his depressing recollection. "Would you mind taking a few pictures of my wife and I in front of the lion?" he asked.

Keith smiled as he got up. "Not at all."

The man handed him his camera and scampered back to his wife who was standing on the wood chips that surrounded the statue. Keith got right in front of them and inspected the camera to make sure he could work it.

"The button is right there on top," the man said as he put his frail arm around his wife. They both had on Yellowstone Park tee-shirts and baseball caps.

"Okay. Say Nittany Lion." The couple did and Keith snapped their picture. "Let me get one more." The couple reset and Keith said, "Say, Business Logistics." The couple looked confused, then said it in unison.

The couple waddled over to Keith and he handed the man the camera. "What's Business Logistics?" the woman questioned.

Keith went on to explain. "Penn State is the country's leading Business Logistics school and the faculty is renowned in business circles for their teachings in supply chain management." They hung on his every word like he had just given them all the answers to life.

They thanked him and waddled over to their Winnebago and were gone. It was two minutes to two and it started to rain.

Keith went back and sat at the base of the lion as the rain started to get heavier and stared down Fraser Street. His guess was that the FBI agent would come this way rather than navigate the intricate campus streets. The rain didn't bother him.

In the distance he saw a large, black car make a right off of College Avenue onto Fraser Street. The car kicked into gear as it headed up the hilly, tree-lined street, passing the Dieke Building on the right and fraternity houses on the left. Rain began to pelt the windshield and the driver turned on his wipers.

At the next intersection the car paused as the driver looked both ways at the four way stop sign and then eased through the intersection.

The car passed some more frat houses to the right and left as the road began to curve right. The Winnebago came toward the car in the opposite lane and was quickly it.

Keith watched nervously as the black sedan slowly pulled into the lot at Rec Hall and he stood. The driver looked lost. *Could it be the FBI?*, he thought The driver saw him and directed the car over. Keith stepped off the curb and into the street. The car stopped in front of him and the window came down.

"Keith?" the driver asked.

"Who are you?" Keith asked back.

"I'm Special Agent Walker," Sammy said in perfect, unaccented English.

"Who sent you?" Keith said.

"Come on, get in the car and you can ask me all the questions you want?"

"Who sent you?"

Sammy shrugged. "Special Agent Thompson. I got off the phone with him a few hours ago. I'm from the Harrisburg regional office of the Federal Bureau of Investigation. Want to see my badge?"

"What did Thompson tell you?"

"He didn't go into details. Just said that I should pick up a Keith at the lion statue in State College at 2:00, take him to the airport and a plane would be waiting for him. Said to make sure you had the tape. That was it."

"Anything else?"

"No. Now, maybe you want to get into the car before you get totally soaked," Sammy pleaded.

Keith gave in, satisfied that this was the guy. He knew the names and the plan. He walked around the car and got into the passenger side.

"Are you okay?" Sammy asked.

"Yeah, fine. Just a little wet. That's all."

"Thompson said I should take you right to the airport and wait for the plane the bureau was sending. How does that sound?"

"Sounds like a plan," Keith responded.

"Do you have the tape?" Sammy asked.

Keith went into his bag and pulled out one of the copies. The other was wedged inside his pants and pinched his leg when he sat. The original was hidden even better.

"Great. Hold on to that." Sammy spoke slowly, making sure his accent did not slip through.

The car pulled out as the rain pounded the earth.

Youngman was once again on the other side of the glass from his client. "I just got off the phone with the FBI."

"Now there is something new. How are they today? I kind of miss them."

"They've received instructions from the kidnappers."

Danny suddenly sat up straight in his chair. He had been waiting since Monday for word of his fate. "Don't just sit there, tell me!"

Youngman gave a dramatic pause designed to reinforce to Danny who the boss was. "You are to be driven to an airfield in Northeast Philadelphia by 6:00 P.M. tomorrow evening. All flights are to be diverted. A plane will land between 6:30 and 7:00 P.M. You will get on it."

"Where is it going?" Sullivan asked impatiently.

"No idea. They have made it clear that if they are interfered with before they get to their final destination, Stephenson will be executed."

"Holy shit. I can't believe it. I am gonna get out of here."

"As it stands now Danny, you look to be in better shape than you were last week." He knew his client would never set down a free man, if he got onto the plane at all. The United States government would not set this kind of precedent, not with a terrorist organization. But he was tired of cautioning Danny. Let him believe what he wanted.

The rain continued as Keith sat alone in the large sedan. The agent had gone into the small airport to check on the flight status. They had been sitting in the parking lot for almost an hour. The rain blurred everything.

Agent Walker hadn't said much, not even light conversation. Maybe he wasn't a talker, but he didn't ask Keith anything about the tape, no questions at all. In fact he acted like he was having trouble staying awake. Some protection.

The door opened and the agent plopped into the seat. "The traffic guy said the plane is about an hour from landing. Bad whether and 'dat.'"

Keith went pale. Where did that accent come from? He straightened up and looked over. The man didn't seem like an FBI agent. He was a little old and a little heavy. Not to mention, what was with the car? It was a boat, not what he thought a standard issue FBI car would be.

That expression: 'an 'dat.' That was a Pittsburgh-ism, he knew from his years rooming with guys from Pittsburgh. How could he ever forget it? The agent said he was from Harrisburg.

But, the agent knew the whole deal. He had spoken to Thompson. Only Thompson knew the details. Only Thompson knew he would be at the lion at 2:00 P.M.

Sammy tapped his fingers on the steering wheel trying to make time go faster. The navy suit was a little tight as the tailor did a rush job while he waited. He even bought a pair of sunglasses to complete the look, but was bummed out because it was raining and he couldn't wear them.

"Keith, if you're hungry, I have some sticky buns in the back," Sammy offered. "I had one for breakfast. Outstanding."

Keith was hungry and leaned over the seat to grab one. He brought the box forward and put it on his lap. There was a problem. The box was from the diner in town. How could he have had them for breakfast in State College if he didn't get to State College until 2:00 P.M? Unless he was already looking for him. "Shit."

The doors locked automatically and Keith felt the cold steel of the revolver against his temple, then down into his ribs.

"I was doin' real well, ya know? But these damn stickies, they are all I could think about since this morning. Stickies on the brain. And I know what you were thinkin'. How could I be in Harrisburg and have breakfast in State College? Nope, can't be done. Tripped up by a pastry."

"I don't know what you are talking about, Agent Walker."

"Hey, kid, nice try, I might be dumb, but I'm not stupid. I saw your face, you figured me out. And it was just a matter of time before I screwed up, ya know? But I thought

I did pretty well considering. If the damn plane was on time, I win an award for best performance by a wise guy. Had you fooled good, didn't I?"

Keith felt sick. He thought to scream, but no one would hear him with the windows shut and the rain pounding like a relentless drum solo. He'd run out of lives. The gun pressed against him. He could struggle with him, but that would be over before it started.

"Oh, where are my manners? My name is Sammy, nice to meet you. How 'bout one of those stickies?"

chapter 32

The last piece of the plan, the illusion, was left optional and since Tommy was having so much fun he decided to go for it. With the kid under control and the FBI chasing its tail, it was too good to pass up.

A white van with phone company markings pulled up to a telephone on the service road outside the prison where Danny Sullivan had been for the last decade. The prison was within sight, a good quarter mile away.

The brunette got out of the van dressed as a telephone repair person.

She was up the pole, digging one cleated boot at a time into the wood. Once at the service box, she fiddled with her belt and pulled out a blue phone and began to feign checking connections. Her biggest advantage was that she could see any potential trouble from her perch. There was none that she could see.

After a few minutes of the telephone pantomime, she pulled out a small metal box the size of a TV remote control from her utility belt. She attached the magnetic side of the box to the underside of the box on the pole. She descended carefully and once she was down, she gave it a quick look. What she left looked as if it belonged right where it was. She got into the van and pulled away.

The rental truck exited off of Interstate 78 near Harrisburg, then pulled into a self storage center a few miles from the exit. Jacob got out of the truck and unlocked the cyclone fence that surrounded the four hundred plus storage units. He drove the truck to row #3 where the largest units resided.

The truck stopped in front of unit 45-D which was roughly the size of a two-car garage. It was one in a series of units all connected in a row as far as Jacob could see. Jacob unlocked the storage unit and rolled the door up. Cool air rushed out at him.

Jacob got back in the truck and pulled it into the unit, snugly fitting it next to the blue van that was already in there. He didn't bother to wipe his prints off of the wheel or the door.

He then got into the blue van and it took two tries to start, but when it did he pulled it out. He got out of the van and looked up and down the row. No one. The only noise was the 'whoosh' of the cars passing along Interstate 78. Jacob closed the door three quarters of the way and then slid under it. He went into the rental truck and pulled out a bag. He took the wires out first and connected them to the track that the door ran on. Then he connected the explosives to the wires and secured it. He slipped back out of the door and closed it, locking it as well. He got back into the van and drove off.

The Gulfstream began its descent toward Teterboro Airfield as the sun started to fade from the New Jersey sky. Keith sat quietly in his leather seat; he had no choice, he was gagged. The two men that had taken him from Sammy in State College played cards across from him.

The Gulfstream was a state of the art plane priced in the twenty million-dollar range. It was able to fly from Moscow to Los Angeles without refueling. This particular plane was part of the Interjet fleet, a company that leased the plane in a time-share arrangement with several businesses.

Tommy Fortune leased the jet through Chesapeake Environmental Services, a company that he was a majority but silent partner in. It had been a great asset.

When Keith got on the plane, Sammy had told the two men that the tape was in his bag and they had gone through his things, claiming what they thought was the only copy. Once that was out of the way, they cuffed him to his seat and taped his mouth shut. Then they sat down and played gin rummy.

Keith still had a copy and the original but he was wondering what good that would do him. He had stared at the two as they played cards through the whole flight. The conversation was worthy of being recorded. One of the men was heavy set, maybe in his mid forties with an incredibly bad toupee. His black silk suit and collarless shirt added to the look. The other guy was much younger and had all his hair. His wide collared purple shirt, which opened to expose his abundance of gold chains and chest hair, was eye catching. Keith felt like he was at a casting call for a mob movie.

Keith had escaped death twice and by the looks of things, a third escape would be a miracle. His mind wandered. Maybe they would let him go since they had the tape? Right. And maybe they would let him date their daughter. Maybe he could talk his way out? Convince them that there were other copies of the tape and if anything happened to him, the authorities would be sent the copy? *That was the oldest bluff in the book,* he thought, and as dumb as these two looked, he doubted they would fall for that one.

Suddenly and without fanfare, the plane dipped, angled and descended. It seemed to pop out of the clouds and drop onto the runway. Parallel parking in Hoboken seemed more difficult.

The jet taxied to a private hangar and rolled right in. Keith was uncuffed and led out of the plane at gunpoint, backpack in hand, as the plane engines whined down. The gag stayed in place.

"Hey, kid, you like baseball?" the older one said with a slimy smile. "We're gonna give you the best seat in the house." Of course, he couldn't answer.

Keith was put face down in the back of a mini-van with heavily tinted windows. They cuffed his hands behind him. He was more comfortable in the plane.

The fat one got behind the wheel and the other one, they could be brothers, got into the passenger seat. The van pulled out of the hangar, onto the tarmac, then off airport grounds onto Teterboro Road. They were headed for East Rutherford.

"I wonder where the dynamic duo is taking us now," Cauley mused from the driver's seat.

"I hope somewhere where they actually do something illegal. These two can't just drive around and hang out all day," Harper responded.

Agents Harper and Cauley also turned onto Teterboro Road and kept a safe distance between their van and the Manna brothers. The agents were fairly new to the Organized Crime Task Force and were assigned to tail the Manna brothers. The Mannas were soldiers in New Jersey's organized crime 'family'. Frankie, thirty-nine, had done little jail time despite being a career criminal. His younger brother, Paulie, had stayed out of jail altogether.

The Mannas had been under surveillance for close to two weeks after an informant had leaked that the two were involved in bringing a large shipment of heroin into the country. But so far, the Mannas did little else but drive around and hang out.

Cauley and Harper were sure something was going to go down at the airport, but they saw nothing that gave them probable cause. A couple of wise guys hanging out at the airport didn't constitute a crime, but they were intent on seeing where this led. They were convinced that the Mannas had picked up something, drugs probably, from one of the planes. But despite their best efforts, they didn't have the whole picture.

The Mannas van cruised at the speed limit down Route 17 until it turned off onto Paterson Plank Road, a road that ran behind the New Jersey Meadowlands Sports Complex.

After about a half mile on that road, they turned off onto a dirt access road meant for construction vehicles, past a small sign that read: "Welcome to the future home of the Yankees."

From the floor, Keith could tell the change in road surface and surmised that a dirt road could not be good.

The van rumbled, jerking and swaying, through an open 18-foot high chain link fence and into the enormous shell that would someday be the new Yankee Stadium. The construction site was roughly a half-mile from the rest of the Meadowlands Complex that included Giants Stadium, the Meadowlands Racetrack and Continental Arena. Construction crews had recently finished the stadium's shell; everything from the cement spiral walkways that would bring in the 52,000 fans to the dugouts to the foundations for the seats. From the inside of the stadium it looked as if it had been robbed; no seats, scoreboard, bases.

The new stadium, which had been debated in the papers and on the sports talk shows for the better part of two years, was a large triangle, open at the base, with rounded edges. The open end faced Manhattan and a batter at home plate would easily be able to make out the Manhattan skyline less than ten miles away. A taste of New York in the Jersey swamps.

The mini-van rolled into the stadium from the right field entrance. Frankie navigated them through the dormant construction equipment that was scattered across what would be the field. He stopped the van in a clear dirt area where second base would eventually be.

One of the mobsters turned to Keith and said, "So, where would you like to sit for the games? Along the first or third base line." He let out a twisted chuckle.

Keith's stomach came up to his throat and then dropped down to his groin. Four words popped into his head: "Jimmy Hoffa, Giants Stadium."

Paulie got out first and opened the sliding rear door. Keith rolled out onto the ground, then struggled to get to his feet, but the handcuffs were too much for him to get his balance. Paulie planted his foot into Keith's back and dropped him. Flat on his stomach with Paulie standing over, Keith had nowhere to run.

Paulie leaned down and pressed a gun to Keith's temple. *Not again*, Keith thought to himself. "Now why would you want to run away from a coupla good guys like me and Frankie, huh? We just want to talk, that's all."

Frankie came over to join his brother. He leaned down and unlocked the cuffs and ripped the tape from Keith's mouth. Keith let out a yell.

"Yell all you want, you yuppie asshole. No one will hear you," Frankie said.

Paulie went to the van and pulled out a shovel and Keith's backpack. He threw the shovel and then the bag at his head. Both missed. "Get up and start digging," Paulie yelled. "You try anything funny and I'll end it right here."

Keith got to his feet as Frankie and Paulie watched. He picked up his bag and the shovel and started to walk away from them, half expecting to feel bullets hit his back and head.

"That's good. Right there. Face us and start digging," Paulie instructed.

Keith turned to face them. Frankie was now sitting on the edge of the van frame at the sliding door opening. The van looked to be slumping in his direction from the weight. Paulie stood between him and the van, arms crossed, gun in hand. Keith started to dig and tried to remember how the different TV and movie heroes got out of this kind of situation. But Keith was coming up short in the escape department.

The sun was now gone and the night was lit by the racetrack lights. Paulie came a little closer, a few feet from him. He lifted the gun, "Pick up the pace, Frankie and me want to catch the Sixth race over at the track." Paulie laughed at his own joke and turned to Frankie who almost fell over laughing. The mobsters showed a low tolerance for humor.

Keith did not laugh and while the chucklefest went on, he judged the distance between him and Paulie to be about shovel length. He whispered to himself, "I am going to drop you like a bag of dirt." He went back to digging. If he could knock the young one senseless, he could outrun the fat one. With all the construction vehicles and the cloudy night, he was sure he could get lost quickly.

Frankie continued to chuckle lightly, then his laugh turned into a full-fledged smoker's black-lung hacking fit.

"These two must be fun at parties," he muttered.

Frankie then added to his brother's joke, "Yeah, hurry up. Paulie and I have a sure thing in the sixth." Another seizure, this time at his own joke.

Paulie turned to laugh with Frankie, but quickly turned the other way, toward the gate and the headlights.

Keith turned as well as a dark van sped into the stadium, but it was going too fast, popped a tire, jerked out of control and railed into a dumpster, stopping it dead.

As Paulie started to turn back to him, Keith's shovel was already halfway through its sideways arc. The flat part of the shovel connected with the side of Paulie's head and Keith felt and heard a crunch. Paulie fell motionless to the ground.

Frankie opened fire on the van. Agent Cauley quickly disentangled himself from the van's airbag and rolled out of the van, taking a position behind the metal dumpster. He returned fire while Harper struggled to get out of the van, sending Frankie running for cover. "Where is that damn helicopter?" Cauley said to no one in particular.

Keith grabbed his bag and took off into the night. Frankie paid him no attention. He looked back at Paulie, who had not moved. He wondered if he had killed him.

The FBI helicopter came up over them from out of nowhere and hovered, spraying a searchlight over the field. Keith watched as the light hit Frankie. "This is the FBI, put down your weapon!"

Frankie responded with several shots at the chopper. The chopper returned fire, then lurched and circled. Smoke was coming from its tail. Frankie got lucky and hit the helicopter.

Keith did not want to see how the gunfight ended and he turned and ran. The FBI was not an organization he trusted at this point. That Agent Thompson had set him up. He had to have, there was no other explanation. So, then, who could he trust?

He moved quickly in the shadows, ducking behind construction vehicles until he got out to the left field entrance. Gunfire continued behind him. He made a break for the ramp that led out of the stadium and made it easily. He felt along the cyclone fence, looking for a hole to climb through. He found a spot where the ground had been dug out and the fence had been pulled up, probably by some kids wanting a peek at the new stadium. He slipped under the fence leaving his new friends behind him.

The area surrounding the stadium was marsh, in some places more solid than in others. The sound of traffic from Routes 3 and 17 became louder.

Keith moved quickly and quietly, keeping his head low, below the grass line of the marsh. He could see the lights in the distance and headed toward them. Every few steps he looked back to see if someone was following him. Nothing.

The path to the racetrack was not an easy travail. At one point, just before he got to the edge of the parking lot, he waded through a river that came up to his chin. He held his backpack over his head the whole time, keeping it and its contents dry.

Once out of the river, totally soaked, he heard the sirens for the first time. He couldn't tell where they were coming from or where they were headed. But there were a lot of them and he needed to hurry.

He got to the far parking lot of Giants Stadium, the outskirts of the Meadowlands complex. The racetrack was still a few hundred yards away and he was now visible without the marsh to hide him. He stepped out of the grass and onto the macadam of the lot. He bent down onto one knee and tried to catch his breath. Then there were more sirens and they were getting closer. He could see flashing lights heading into the complex from the Route 3 entrance. He had to hurry.

He stood and sprinted across the vacant lot, the overhead motion activated lights came on as he passed each one, tracing his run. His legs cramped slightly and the damp air burned his lungs. He felt like he had run a four minute mile as he crossed the vacant lot, then the street in between it and the first occupied lot.

He now saw the flashing lights coming his way and ducked between two parked cars. He sat up against a red sports car and leaned back on it gently, not wanting to set off the car alarm. He was having trouble catching his breath and his chest expanded and contracted violently. He was cold and wet and tired.

Keith opened his bag to see if there was a way out in there. He fished out his phone. Maybe if he could play the tape for the right FBI guy, he could get out of this. Then he remembered the good copy of the tape was in his pants and soaked. "Shit." He went back in his bag, through all his clothes, and grabbed his deodorant. He took the top off and slid out his recorder and the original. It just fit.

"Forget it," he said. "No more cops."

He dialed the only number he could remember.

"Hello," the female voice answered.

"Cindy, it's Keith."

"Keith? Where have you been? The police are looking for you. Are you okay?"

"Yeah, Cin, I'm fine. Listen, I need your apartment for a couple of hours. I can't go back to my place."

"Derek is picking me up in like five minutes. When are you coming? I can blow him off," she volunteered.

"No. Go with Derek, I'll be fine. I just need a place to think for a few hours. Then I am going to the police," Keith assured.

"Are you sure? I can stay."

"No. I am sure. I just need to shower and lay down."

"Hey, that sounds better than going to the movies with Derek," she said playfully.

Keith didn't laugh. "Listen, just leave a spare key under your doormat. I'll lock up when I go."

"Okay. Do you remember the code to get into the building? It's 1257," she said.

"Thanks. I almost forgot about that." Keith heard a buzzer go off on the line.

"That's Derek. I can't go with him. I'll just wait for you here, okay?"

"Come on, Cin, I'll be fine. I'll tell you all about it tomorrow."

"Promise?"

"I promise," he said.

"Okay. I'll leave the key under the mat. I'll see you tomorrow?"

"Sure thing. I gotta go. Tell Derek I said 'hi.'"

She laughed. "I will. Bye, Keith. Be careful."

"I will. See ya."

chapter 33

The red lights continued to flash as police cars criss-crossed their way up and down the lanes of the Meadowlands parking lots. Several thoughts went through Keith's head in rapid succession, but the synapses responsible for "what do I do now" had failed to fire. He leaned against the red car clutching his cell phone. The fetal position felt like a good idea to him at that moment.

Then the lights were on top of him and he quickly got on all fours and crawled to the next parking space where a huge SUV was parked. Its high clearance allowed Keith to roll under with no problem, backpack and all.

He watched as the slow roll of the police car wheels passed by him, his heart pounding against his chest and the cold black top.

He thought this was a perfect place to hide for all eternity. He closed his eyes and tried to come up with a way to get to Cindy's apartment without getting caught.

Then there were voices, a man and a woman. They moved closer. The tone of their conversation was that of the hushed anger that married couples seemed to perfect shortly after taking their vows; forceful but audible just above a whisper.

Then the truck doors opened and slammed. The engine started above him and the huge wheels began to move. Keith rolled to the passenger side, just missing the oncoming rear wheel which was the diameter of a hula hoop.

The truck was out of the spot when he saw the brake lights flash red. He crawled quickly behind the nearest car. The brake lights went dead and the truck moved on.

Then, sanctuary: a porta john. Keith stood and surveyed his new world of rowed, parked cars. The police light show had moved to an adjoining lot, methodically going down all the rows. Keith calmly walked into the portable toilet and ducked in.

It was dark inside and smelled, but it beat the undercarriage of a moving sport utility vehicle. Keith changed out of his wet clothes and into a tee shirt and shorts. It was all he had. He stuffed the wet clothes into the toilet hole. He ran his fingers through his hair, unsure of what it looked like.

"Hey, you almost done in there?" a slurred voice demanded with a loud bang against the molded plastic door.

"Be right out."

Keith opened the door and came face to face with a drunk, gum chewing, high hair, Jersey girl. "It's all yours."

"What-ev-er," the girl chomped.

The door shut behind him. Keith took out his cell phone and pretended to talk on it, moving his arms wildly as he made his way to the main entrance.

When he got there, an older man in a security guard uniform stood near the door. "What race just went off?" Keith asked.

"That was the seventh."

"Great. I have a tip on a horse in the eighth."

"Better hurry," the guard encouraged.

Keith did just that. The admission booths were closed this late into the night so he made his way up the escalator. Once at the top, he went to the left to the betting windows.

The scene in and around the windows was what he expected. He had spent many a night in his misspent youth at the Atlantic City track. Same scene, different players.

He sat down in one of the powder blue bucket seats indigenous to all racetracks he had been to. A crowd of men stood in front of one of the high mounted TV screens watching a simulcast of a race somewhere where it was still light out. Losing tickets littered the floor. The man two seats from Keith smoked non-stop, lighting a new cigarette as the old one died down. He was overweight, with a big bushy black mustache and big-lensed, frameless glasses.

Keith turned to the smoking man. "Who looks good in the eighth?" He knew he would get an answer, everyone at the track had an opinion.

"Not betting on the eighth," he said with a puff. "Too busy keeping track of Holiday Park."

"Oh, okay. That's cool."

The man then turned back to Keith. "But if I was betting it, I'd look at Eponymous." The man handed Keith a worn tip sheet. He began to read about the horse, but found it unnecessary as the man recited the write up verbatim.

"Now, this horse has been hurt, out about three weeks. Saw him run at Monmouth before the injury. Won by four lengths. Word is that he's ready."

Keith glanced at the odds. "Why is he 10 to 1?"

"It's early. The odds'll come down once the real bettors get into the action," the man puffed.

Keith handed the card back to the man. "Thanks for the tip."

Keith got up and went over to a vacant window manned by an older woman with a beehive hairdo. Her nametag said Bernadette.

"Hi, Bernadette," Keith said with a smile.

"Hi. How can I help you, sir?"

"I'd like ten to win on five in the eighth."

She punched the keyboard in front of her as she spoke. The ticket squirted out of the machine and she handed it to him. "Anything else?"

"Uh, yeah. My buddy over there has had too much to drink tonight," Keith moved out of the way so she could see the smoking man. "Anyway, I'd like to get him a cab or a car ride home. Do you have the number of a car service?"

"No problem." She opened a drawer beneath her machine and pulled out a business card. "These guys will come out here. They're good, but not so cheap."

Keith smiled as he took the card. "Thanks. You've been a great help."

Keith went over to a phone stall and dialed the 800 number for the limousine service. They said they could be out to the track in thirty to forty minutes. Keith told the dispatcher to call his cell phone number once the car was out front. The last person he had given his number to was Agent Thompson. Keith had trouble believing the FBI had sold him out. But there was no other explanation.

The eighth race went off at about 10:45. Eponymous was consistent, he started at the back and stayed there the whole race. Keith looked over at the smoking man as the race ended. He shrugged and went back to his *Racing Forum*.

A half hour or so later the ninth race was ending when his phone rang. It was one of two people.

"Hello," Keith said.

"Mr. Smith."

"Yes." He had used an assumed name.

"This is Josh from the limo service. I'm outside the main entrance, car 154."

"Great. I'll be just a minute."

Keith wedged himself into the middle of the crowd that was leaving the track. Once he was near the end of the escalator, he could see his car and the '154' in the car's passenger side window. He also saw that three police officers looking over the crowd as they passed, each checking a piece of paper against the male faces that passed. The two men in the navy blue suits didn't escape his attention. Could one be his friend Thompson? Keith stopped at the bottom of the escalator and left the crowd, ducking behind an admission booth.

He tried to concentrate, come up with a way out, but the oncoming noise was a little much. A group of half a dozen girls, a little tipsy and a lot loud, came barreling down the escalator.

"What are you waiting for, a bus or something," one of the girls said to him as they regrouped right in front of him.

"No," he said shyly.

"You're too cute to be alone. Where's your girlfriend?" The girl was close to his own height, a little heavy, but very cute.

"She dumped me, here at the track," Keith said.

"What a bitch." The girl turned, "Hey girls, can you believe that this guy's girlfriend dumped him at the track?" The other five girls giggled their way over to him to see what their friend caught. A chorus of 'no ways' and 'you've got to be kiddin' me's' erupted.

"Do you want to go home with us, lonely man?" the girl said.

"I'd love to, but I have a flight to catch."

"Blow it off," a red head from the group blurted and the other girls giggled.

"I'd love to, really. How about we meet halfway?"

"We usually don't settle for less than all the way," the first girl said. "Do we girls?" They all laughed.

Keith smiled and pointed. "See that limo. That's my ride to the airport. But I would be happy to give you girls a ride to your car."

"Is there booze in the limo?" another one said.

"There is only one way to find out," Keith replied.

The six girls all looked at each other and then agreed. They each grabbed a piece of Keith, an arm, his back, his ass, anything. The group walked right out front, the girls laughing and screeching like they had just caught a rock star. Keith kept his head down, right by the law.

They all piled into the limo. Keith watched from behind smoked glass as the police continued to look for him.

"Where to?" the driver asked.

"What spot are you in, girls?" Keith asked.

"Hey, there's no booze in here," the red head announced. She was the drunkest.

"We're in W-3, a white SUV, Mr. Lonely Man," the first girl said as she rubbed Keith's leg.

"Hey, there is nothing to drink in this stinkin' car!"

"Take a pill, Janice," another girl said.

The limo cruised the lot until the driver found the while SUV. Janice bitched the whole way while her friends told her to shut up already.

Once they were out of the car, Janice leaned over and threw up. The others helped her into the back of the SUV. As they drove away, the other five girls waved and blew kisses. The driver looked at Keith in the rearview mirror.

"Don't ask," Keith said shaking his head.

"Where to now?" the driver asked.

"Hoboken."

The ride took thirty minutes to cover about ten miles. They got stuck in the traffic coming out of the Meadowlands as well as the construction near the Lincoln Tunnel, even though they didn't use the tunnel.

The car dropped him off at the PATH station, not at Cindy's apartment. He was not quite ready to settle in for the night. He paid the driver in cash and tipped him excessively. He walked down the street as the car pulled away. Thursday night and the bar scene was wild once again. A long line formed outside Texas/Arizona, the bar across the street. He walked two blocks to his gym, Hudson Health and Fitness.

The health and fitness industry in Hoboken was highly competitive. With the high number of young urban transients in the city, there was a high demand for work out facilities. Because of the demand and needs of the working young, some gyms stayed open twenty-four hours a day. Keith's gym was one of those.

Keith entered the lobby and handed his membership card to the girl at the front desk. She scanned it without looking up. All paid up and able to pass through. She handed the card back to him.

Keith made his way past the treadmills and stair climbers that dominated the first floor. There was a young woman on a treadmill and a man on a stair climber. Each of them talked into a headset connected to their cell phones. He walked past them and down a flight of stairs to the locker rooms.

He stopped at the bulletin board located on the wall just outside the locker rooms. The board was cluttered with homemade ads, the kind with the tear off phone numbers on the bottom, that sold exercise equipment or solicited a roommate. But not tonight. All the ads were pushed to the edge to make room for an article from the *Hoboken Observer*: LOCAL MAN SOUGHT IN MURDER. There was an old college yearbook picture of Keith in the middle of the print. Someone had drawn a mustache on him. "Nice," he said.

Keith went into the locker room and sat on a wooden bench in front of his locker. He leaned over and dialed his combination, left, right, then left again. He kept a fresh set of clothes there in case he couldn't get into his apartment. He took the towel out, placed it next to him on the bench and began to undress. He needed a shower badly after his jaunt through the Meadowlands. He smelled like old clothes.

He did his best thinking in the shower, he thought to himself. Too bad, since he only spent about five minutes a day in the shower. But he stayed in the hot steam and pelting water for a good twenty minutes. He went over every detail he could remember, from the time he left Moran's to the time he walked into the gym. It was eerie, like something that had happened to someone else. But it had happened to him and he wondered when it would end. Would it ever end?

He ended the shower and dried off and got dressed. He looked at his watch and it was a little after midnight. He thought about going back to his apartment, but that didn't seem wise. He hated to use Cindy's place, but he was out of options. He looked at his watch again and wondered if Stephenson was still alive. Maybe he was, maybe he wasn't. Either way, Keith wasn't sure he could help. One thing he was sure was that he needed a beer.

Alex broke her stare at the darkness and pulled out the map from the glove compartment. They were getting the chance to see most of Eastern Pennsylvania the hard way, by traveling on little roads marked by tiny lines on the map.

From the safe house, they had taken the big purple line, Interstate 80, east to Stroudsburg, then hopped on a thin gray line, Route 191, until they got on a red line, 611 south. A few miles later and they were back on a slightly thinner red line, Route 32, that ran along the Delaware River on the Pennsylvania side. That's where they were.

The road was rural and dark and one lane in each direction. They would cross into New Jersey just south of Trenton.

The clock on the dashboard red 12:23 A.M. in an eerie blue/green LED readout as they crossed the state line between Pennsylvania and New Jersey.

Their cover story this time was that of employees of the Chesapeake Environmental Services Company. They had supposedly just picked up two crates of spare parts needed to repair a damaged dredge boat in Townsend's Inlet. In the one box was the drugged senator, in the other enough explosives to punch a nice sized hole in the hull of a large ship. They even had identification cards from the company. Jacob was a laborer, Alex a mechanical engineer.

The van traveled at the posted speed limit of forty- five. It handled well for a van, Jacob thought, even with all the added weight.

Alex was noticeably quiet and was keeping a close eye out for any law enforcement. They were so close to the big payday.

"It'll take us an extra two hours taking these roads. Why can't we get on a highway and get moving?" Alex said, showing her first signs of stress. Her nerves of steel were fraying. She wanted this to be over and to be with Tommy. Jacob had helped take the edge off, but he was a boy.

"I know what you mean. I looked it over again this morning. But you know the plan. Besides, we'll be on the parkway soon enough," Jacob reassured her.

"Well, the plan seems to be working. We haven't seen another car for twenty minutes."

Jacob nodded. He was ready for this to be over as much as his beautiful companion.

It was late in Manhattan, but not for a man who typically put in eighteen hours a day. The last thing on Jones' list was to proof a speech he was to give at the "Retailers of America" breakfast in eight hours. He was the keynote speaker, their "Man of the Year." He was considered an innovator and a visionary in the industry. His buying philosophies, store merchandising approach and knack for turning a profit in any economic climate were the stuff of business legend. And now his downsizing was seen as a bold move, the wave of the future in retail.

It was ironic, he thought, that his greatest accomplishment could not be shared with his peers. In a few short hours, with the death of Stephenson, the fate of US-China trade relations would be cemented in business' favor. No revocation of MFN, no sanctions, no more pesky senator.

He stood in front of his desk and started to rehearse. "They say that the department stores are the dinosaurs of retail, headed for certain extinction while others do things better, cheaper and faster. But I disagree, and if I didn't, I wouldn't be here today. There are no dinosaurs. The consumer does not care what segment you are classified in—department store, category killer, discounter, catalog or internet. It simply does not matter to them and I believe it never has."

He paused and scribbled "and never will" at the end of the sentence. He continued: "Our customers are complex, yet driven by simple things. They want compelling product at fair prices and want to be treated like human beings. It's that simple. And if you can provide that mix, execute it with passion, then it won't matter if you are a department store, a category killer or a guy opening his own store. The customer cannot be fooled. They know the real thing when they see it and feel it."

He rehearsed a pause, then went on. "So, now, since I have given away the secret of retail, we're finished right? Sell all my stock and pack it in? Hardly. Because as easy as it is to say the words, it is as hard to execute that strategy.

"So, who will be successful in this new millenium? It won't be a category of retailer, that I am sure of. It will be the best retailer in each of the categories. It will be the retailer who can execute simple but meaningful principles. The retailer that finds the next great item, the next best way to service their customers, that is who will win out. It is a time for taking chances like never before. We are all pushing each other to greatness and the risk taker, the innovators, the committed will survive. There are no dinosaurs, only those who think like cavemen."

He stopped and sat at his desk. He made some notes in red pen. He was certainly practicing what he was preaching.

If they only knew.

chapter 34

He had stopped at a little hole in the wall Irish bar halfway between the gym and Cindy's. Oddly enough it was a bar that Keith had passed many times, yet had never been in. Keith had been in most Hoboken bars, not an easy feat as there almost as many bars as people. The bar had few lights on and the deep brown wood made it all the darker. A good place to hide.

"What'll you have?" the bartender asked. He had a thick brogue and Keith pegged him as a real honest to goodness Irish national. Locals called them "off the boat Irish." Keith wasn't sure if that was derogatory or not.

Keith ordered, "Black and tan, please."

"Right," the bartender answered and was off.

The bartender came back with a pint. Keith slipped a ten on the bar which the red haired bartender took and rung up on a depression-era cash register. Keith tipped him a dollar out of his change.

The beer tasted great, more heavy and substantial than the light beer he had been drinking the last few months. He felt oddly at home.

The first beer went down without a fight and he ordered another. His mind was running too quick and needed to be slowed. So many questions. What to do next? Was this all real? He missed Denise. Cindy going to the movies with Derek? That asshole Thompson. Did he kill that mobster? Add that to the list of problems.

The second beer got him to a nice little buzz and the third made things all the more clear. Bravery in a beer bottle. He had decided to call the FBI from Cindy's.

He paid up and left the bar. He walked the five blocks to Cindy's without incident, *a refreshing change*, he thought. He punched in the security code, and the door buzzed and he entered the vestibule. He punched the code into another box and that door put him in the lobby. He took the elevator to the third floor, mapping out a mental strategy the whole way. He got to 3-B, bent down and got the key from under the mat, unlocked and opened the door. He was now ready to make the call.

The apartment was dark. He closed the door behind him and before he could find the light switch, a light went on. "Not again," Keith moaned.

"So, you must be the great Keith Garrity," Tommy Fortune said. He was sitting in Cindy's antique wooden rocking chair, one gloved hand on the lamp he had just turned on and the other on what looked to be the largest handgun in the world.

Keith slumped back against the door and lowered his head, shaking it in disbelief. "You guys just don't give up, do you?"

"No. But neither have you. You've been a royal pain in the ass the last few days. I must say, though, you have been a challenge," Tommy admitted.

"Well, then, that makes it all worth it now, doesn't it?" Keith said sharply.

"Perhaps."

Keith picked up on a slight accent. He knew the voice.

"How did you find me this time?" Keith asked.

"We tapped the girl's phone. She's very pretty."

"Where is she? You haven't done anything to her?"

"No. She must be out with that boyfriend of hers. Derek is his name, am I right?" Tommy said.

The voice, Keith thought. *The tape. It was him.*

"Yeah. How'd you know I'd call her?" Keith questioned.

"I have learned a great deal about you in the last few days. You're twenty-eight, a Scorpio, father left when you were nine, raised by your mother with your younger brother and sister. You are the first person in your family to graduate from college. Congratulations. Had a good job until recently. You're trying your hand at writing a book. Your mom gave that information readily." Tommy smiled.

"What did you do to her?" Keith said moving closer.

"A phone interview. I said I was from a job search firm and I was checking references. Very nice lady." He waved his gun toward the sofa for Keith to sit down. "But the big news is that you have the missing piece to the Stephenson kidnapping."

"I have the tape, the voices, but not the faces. See, I was too drunk to make out who did the talking."

"I'm not surprised, but I could not have assumed that," Tommy responded.

"So, you were on the bus. Who was the other guy?"

"That is what I want to talk to you about."

Keith looked confused. "Really?"

Tommy uncrossed his legs and leaned forward on the rocker. "Really. I actually feel kind of bad about the last few days. You were not part of the plan and I hate collateral damage."

"Well then, all is forgiven." Sarcasm in a bottle.

Tommy smiled. "See that? Keeping your sense of humor in dire circumstances is a very admirable trait."

"I'm flattered," Keith said sarcastically.

Tommy laughed lightly. He pointed to the manila envelope that was on the coffee table that separated them. "Pick it up. Open it."

Keith leaned over and opened it. He looked through the articles and the handwritten speech. It made no sense to him.

Tommy interrupted, "All the answers to all the questions the world has about the kidnapping are in that envelope. It's yours."

"What? What am I supposed to do with this?"

"Use it for your book. It would be a best seller."

"Oh, I get it. You got tired of trying to kill me, so now you're my friggin' agent. No thanks." Keith put the material down on the coffee table.

"Okay. Someone will get it regardless. And if it's not you, I will have to kill you. Sorry."

Keith leaned over quickly and picked the envelope back up. "I don't know what I am looking at here."

"There is a narrative to go with it. Do you have your little tape recorder?" Tommy queried.

Keith patted his bag. "Always."

"Well then. We have a deal?" Tommy said.

"Do I have a choice?" Keith said rhetorically.

"No, not really."

"So, if you're my agent, do I get to know your name?" Keith questioned.

"Sure. It's Tommy Fortune."

"You made that up, right?" Keith let out a slight smile.

"In a way. Are you ready to take a trip?"

"Where to?" Keith said, playing along, not knowing what to make of the man across from him.

"The beach. We're going to see the senator."

"He's still alive?" Keith's pulse quickened.

"For now, but not for long."

Keith contemplated that. He had no better move to help the senator than to be brought to him. But then what? Maybe, just maybe, he could contact the FBI then.

"Read through the material. Figure out what you want to ask me," Tommy instructed. "I'll give you five minutes, then we're gone."

Keith spread the clipped piles out on the coffee table. He read through each while Tommy got up and got a beer out of the refrigerator. It was all confusing. Sure, things were grouped together, but they made little sense in relationship to each other. Little sense, until he got to the transcript of the tape. That tied a lot of it together.

"Time's up." Tommy stood and Keith began to put the paper back in the envelope. "Let's get moving then," Tommy said. "And don't forget to leave the key under the mat."

She had to be dreaming. Her alarm clock said 2:34 A.M. That could not have been her doorbell. There it was again.

Donna rolled out of bed and slipped a robe over her naked body. "Just a second," she said into the air, annoyed. "This better be good." As she made her way to the front door, she did the math in her head. She had to be up at 4:00 A.M., only an hour and twenty-six minutes to sleep.

She got to the door, eyes closed. "Who is it?"

"Thompson."

She instantly opened her eyes and ran her fingers through her hair. "My special agent?"

"One and the same," he whispered through the door.

She cracked the door and peeked out behind the chain lock. "What makes you think I'm alone?"

"I took a chance. But if it's a bad time..."

"It's not that bad." She closed the door, undid the chain, opened the door and let him in.

"I know I should have called, but this was kind of last minute," he said apologetically.

"Well, you can make it up to me." She slid her robe off her shoulder and it dropped to the floor. Thompson could make out her curves even in the dark.

The two came together. Thompson kissed her neck, then shoulders and gently moved her against the wall. He kissed his way down—cleavage, breasts, stomach.

Donna played with the agent's hair as he moved down. She leaned her head back against the wall and picked a spot in the darkness to concentrate on. Her breathing got heavier, her mouth dry and she closed her eyes. "This will do just fine."

The explosion was small and barely audible, but had its desired effect. The top of the telephone pole blew off, taking telephone and electrical wires down with it. Every alarm clock, light and phone would be out in the immediate area, including the ones in the prison that held Danny Sullivan.

The blue van was right on schedule, taking the Sea Isle exit off the Garden State Parkway right at 2:45. Once over the bridge that led to the island, Jacob made a right onto Landis and headed down toward Townsend's Inlet, where their boat was docked at a marina off 85th Street.

Ten minutes later, Jacob pulled the van into the small marina parking lot. The early risers were a couple hours away and the restaurant wouldn't be open for a while.

Alex was first out of the van and opened the back door. She had the dolly pulled out and on the ground as Jacob met her. In the darkness and in silence they slid the heavier of the two boxes out, the one with the senator in it. They positioned the six-foot crate on the dolly, standing it up. Alex left Jacob and went to the boat slip to uncover and start the boat. Jacob leaned the crate back, taking the weight, and began to pull the dolly across the gravel parking lot. He walked backward and arched his neck to see where the parking lot ended and the dock began.

Alex started the boat and broke down its covering. The engine was distinctive against the quiet night, but no lights came on from the surrounding homes.

Jacob struggled with the crate. The gravel was giving way and the ground beneath was moist. The weight of the wheels dug into the gravel making it difficult to pull, like he was in quicksand. By the time he got to the ramp, he was winded and his back killed him. He paused and arched his back slightly to stretch it. The dolly straightened only a few degrees, but the inertia from the shifting of the senator's weight sent it over.

Jacob could only watch as the crate hit the ground with an ugly thud. Alex jumped out of the boat and ran over.

"What the hell happened?" Alex demanded.

Jacob shrugged. "It slipped." They both inspected the crate and it had not split anywhere. They both worked quickly to get it back on the dolly.

Alex collected herself. She could kill him now, but she needed him. She calmed down and joked, "Good thing it wasn't the other crate."

Jacob smiled weakly. He leaned back and had the dolly moving across the planks of the dock. They both loaded the crate into the back of the boat. Jacob went back for the other crate while Alex waited. The second crate was on the boat and Jacob went back to park the van on the street.

The boat pulled out of the slip with Alex at the helm. She was truly multi-talented. The boat glided through the black water of the back bay, then into the rougher inlet. From the inlet they could see the lights of a dredge boat straight ahead. There would be a lone watchman on the boat who was told that parts to fix the hydraulic pump would be delivered between 3:00 and 3:30 A.M. As per Tommy's instructions, the boat was to be shut down under the guise of a mechanical failure.

Alex looked off to the left and saw the condo that she and Tommy were to meet. *Finally*, she thought, *so close*. They would make love and then watch the show.

And then collect the money.

chapter 35

This was not how Keith had envisioned his summer. He had expected to get shot down by beautiful girls, not shot at by angry men.

The car sat at a traffic light, waited for it to change to green, then proceeded into the intersection. Keith judged the car to be a mid-nineties model, if that new. The seats were worn and the odometer had over 90,000 miles on it.

The car traveled the speed limit along Route 9 with Keith at the wheel, Tommy in the passenger seat and Keith's tape recorder between the two of them. Keith had been instructed to take the "long way" down to the parkway, bypassing the New Jersey Turnpike and its toll takers.

Tommy had laid out all the ground rules as they left Hoboken. First, no questions until they were on the parkway. Second, if Keith were to do anything that resembled calling attention to the car, Tommy promised he would be shot in the leg first so he would feel the pain and then in the head. He had emphasized this by pressing the gun to Keith's temple during the explanation. But that was nothing new to Keith.

Keith spotted a police car parked at a convenience store about a hundred yards ahead. He eased up on the gas.

Tommy jabbed his leg with the gun. "Slowing down could be construed as trying to catch someone's attention. Get it back to the limit."

"Sorry. Old habit."

With that tested, Keith got the car back up to the posted forty-five.

"What are you doing?" Jacob asked nervously.

Alex throttled the boat down and the engine stopped. "Let's do it here," she said, moving to him.

"What?"

"Come on. Job done, time to celebrate. Let's do it here," she said as she lifted her shirt over her head.

Jacob wondered if she knew what a bra was as he watched in disbelief.

Alex walked back to his position at the back of the boat. "Come one. One last time."

"Why not?" Jacob said, giving in.

Alex pressed her body against him as they worked on each other's pants. She gently pushed him to the floor of the boat, his pants around his ankles. Jacob closed his eyes. His head spun as the stress of the week finally dissolved. He was relaxed enough to notice the boat's rocking matching their own. Alex leaned forward, touching her breasts to his chest.

She whispered in his ear, "Goodnight Jacob."

He opened his eyes, but it was too late.

The car began a slow climb up the north side of the Driscoll Bridge. The Garden State Parkway was on the other side.

"Here," Tommy said handing Keith a roll of tokens.

"Stay away from the toll takers."

Keith took the roll from him. No toll takers meant no contact with others. Tommy was a smart man.

The car approached the first booth and Keith tossed a token in the basket. The green light flashed 'Thank you' and he proceeded.

Keith leaned over and clicked the *record* button on his recorder. "How did you find me in State College?"

"No screwing around with you, huh? How do you think?"

"It had to be Agent Thompson, right?" Keith guessed.

"We knew you were there before that. The whole bus ticket buying thing was very clever," Tommy replied.

"I got it from a book," he admitted.

"I'm sure. One problem though. You assumed we would only check credit card records. You didn't think we would talk to the ticket agents, did you?"

"I'll remember that for next time."

"That is how we knew you bought the ticket in cash. Then we almost had you in Lewisburg."

Keith was surprised. "Really?"

"Yeah. Got there a half-hour after you got off the bus. The bus driver was very helpful. He recognized your face but told us you had blonde hair."

"Blondes have more fun," Keith said.

"I'm partial to red hair myself."

Keith paused. "What about the mobster?"

"Now that was Thompson. He led me to you."

"He's on your payroll?"

"The FBI doesn't pay real well and Thompson likes the ladies. Don't you recognize his name from the articles?" Tommy questioned.

Keith recounted as best he could. But he had only five minutes with them. Then it clicked. "He was the agent that shot that Westie. Let me guess, the dead guy was a friend of yours."

"Yeah. A good friend," Tommy said and then looked away.

"So you didn't choose Thompson at random," Keith continued as some of the puzzle came together.

"I don't do anything randomly."

Keith filed that. "So, you plan to get Thompson back? How?"

"I had a couple ways, but I think the best will be to have you expose him and his involvement in the kidnapping. I couldn't have done it without him," Tommy revealed.

Keith sat silent, the cruise control pegged at fifty-five. They'd be in Avalon around 5:30 A.M., just as the sun came up. He thought of bad things happening to the agent and pulled back. Is that what he really wanted?

"Seems like you need some time to think," Tommy said. "I have a call to make to our mutual friend."

Donna laid in bed in the dark resting, but wide awake. She had to get in the shower soon and was exhausted. Thompson slept next to her.

Thompson's cell phone rang and he grabbed it off the nightstand. "Yeah." He listened and sat up. "You are kidding me?" Thompson got up and went into the bathroom. He closed the door halfway. Donna was curious and could hear every word.

"Morrison, how does a guy get dead in solitary confinement? What riot? Shit. I'll be there in an hour and a half," Thompson said in a hushed but audible voice.

Donna closed her eyes and pretended to be asleep. Thompson came to her side and shook her. "Hey darling, I have to go. Big trouble. I'll call you later."

"Okay. Anything I should know about?" she said innocently.

"I'll let you in on it the first chance I get."

Thompson dressed quickly and raced out the door. Donna sat up and listened as his car started and then trailed off.

Donna's mind went to work. Sullivan is dead? *Now that was a story*, she thought. But did she hear it right? News of his death would doom Stephenson. Could it be? It had to be. It would be a huge story. But what if she was wrong? What if Thompson had it wrong? Then the senator would die and she would be responsible? No thanks. A network job was so close she could taste it. She picked up the phone and dialed a friend at Channel 10 in Philadelphia.

"Mark, it's Donna. I need a favor. Has anything come over the wire about a riot at the prison where Danny Sullivan is being held?" she paused. "I'll hold."

Donna waited as her old college friend, who worked the graveyard shift at the news desk, checked.

Mark came back on the line and Donna repeated back to him the important details. "No riot, huh? Just a power outage. And the phones are down. No, I have no idea what is going on. Call me if you hear anything. And Mark, thanks a million."

She hung up the phone and got out of bed. Opportunity missed? Maybe. Then the phone rang. "Hello, Mark?"

"No, this is Jim."

"Oh, what's up?" Donna responded.

"We have a floater up on the Inlet beach. Pants down at his ankles, hole in his head. I know it is small potatoes for you, but it is news."

"Give me twenty minutes to put may face on and I'll be there," she assured.

"I'll have Scooter meet you," Jim replied.

"No problem." She hurried into the bathroom not sure if she had missed a story or saved her career.

The car with Tommy and Keith continued to cruise down the near empty parkway.

"What was that all about?" Keith asked. Tommy had dialed the phone, held it to his ear for a second, then turned it off.

"A signal to Thompson to get the ball rolling."

"What ball?" Keith asked.

"He will leak a story to the press that Danny Sullivan has been killed in his cell. The power and phones are down at the prison, no one will be able to readily confirm or deny the report. It will all be very confusing."

Keith thought for a second. "Then that gives you your fictitious reason to kill the senator? The would-be kidnappers see a report that Sullivan is dead and then they go ahead and kill the senator in return, right?" Keith guessed.

"You are catching on." Tommy was impressed.

"That sucks. You suck."

Tommy turned to Keith, "Look, some people throw stones and never know where they hit, never understand the damage, like Thompson. Others sharpen stones and make spears and are deadly accurate. They throw with intent. I have a keen sense of what my actions bring and take responsibility for them. Do you?"

Keith sat silent. He reached over and clicked the recorder off. "I need a break."

They sat in silence as night began to give way to day. They passed exit after exit, toll booth after toll booth, past Tom's River and Long Beach Island. Time went quickly for Keith as he wrestled with what to do next. There was only one solution. He reached down and turned the recorder on.

"Okay. Where is the senator going to be killed?" Keith said insistently.

Tommy turned to him. "He's in a crate on the dredger that is anchored in Townsend's Inlet."

"He's been there the whole time?"

"No." Tommy went on in great detail about the safe houses, the cover stories, the landfill. It was an elaborate plan to say the least. And Keith was getting it all on tape.

"So, how do you plan to kill him?"

"There is a second crate on the boat. It is an explosive. Ka-boom," Tommy said, accentuating the effect with a hand gesture.

"How will anyone know that the senator was on it?"

"The bomb is rigged to blow down with all its force. It will blow a whole in the bottom of the boat. It won't necessarily blow the senator to bits. In fact, my guess is he drowns," Tommy said with little emotion either way.

Keith took it all in. He needed the details and Tommy was accommodating. "What time?"

"What time what?"

"What time does the bomb go off?" Keith was pressing.

"We will have a spectacular view of it right about 6:00 A.M."

"You're going to watch it?"

"Yeah. So are you," Tommy informed him.

"You're a sick bastard."

"Watch the language, or I'll change my mind and you'll be fish food," Tommy warned.

Keith looked at the road ahead. He had been up for what seemed like forever, but did not feel the least bit tired.

"Okay. What is the deal with the CEO. Jones."

Tommy smiled. "I think you can figure that one out."

Keith thought for a second. "He's the other man on my tape. He wants the senator dead?"

"Right on both accounts. He hired me to stop the senator from causing trouble with China's trade status."

"Come again?"

"Have you heard of Most Favored Nation trade status?" Tommy said as he adjusted his position in the seat.

"Sounds familiar," Keith said, searching his memory.

"It more or less means that a nation with MFN status has normalized trade relations with the U.S. Nations without MFN status are charged prohibitive duties and tariffs."

"So?"

"Stephenson was going to introduce a bill that would tie China's human rights record to trade status. That would remove MFN and jack up the price of everything made in China that was imported into the States." Tommy picked up the recorder and flipped it over. "Made in China. Jones' company imports about four billion a year from China. His profitability would hit rock bottom without those cheap imports. Could put him out of business."

It clicked for Keith. "I get it. The senator's speech in the packet. So why not just kill him?"

"Bad theatre. That's what Jones wanted, but it would have raised too many questions, and you Americans love a good conspiracy. Speculation 'why' would have raged for years. My way had a built-in conspiracy; a start, a middle and an end. No questions as to who did it."

Keith noticed the sign for Sea Isle City. He was four miles from the Avalon exit. He needed a plan.

"So what's with the Jorgensen guy?" Keith said, trying to keep Tommy busy.

"That's part of my revenge on Jones. Almost twenty years ago my friend Tony and I took a contract to have Jorgensen killed. Jones paid for the hit. He wasn't moving up the corporate ladder fast enough. This was a big stone to throw.

"It was supposed to look like a robbery. And we capped him all right, easy. But his driver was packing, a detail Jones had left out. Tony took a shot to the chest, killed him right there on the street. I killed the driver and got Tony home so he couldn't be tied to the murder. His family has been grateful ever since."

"So, you want me to take Jones down for you, too?" Keith reasoned as his mind worked overtime.

"My little friend, I have already taken him down. A dead senator will carry the death penalty. Game, set, match," Tommy said smugly.

Tommy wriggled in his seat and rubbed his leg. He moved his seat back and undid his seat belt. He stretched the leg out the best he could. Keith looked over at him. He looked at the glove box and the dash above it and it hit him. He looked at the steering wheel.

Keith clicked the recorder off as they came up on the exit. He slipped it back in his bag as Tommy continued his contortions.

"Leg hurt?" Keith asked.

"It's stiff. Old army injury," Tommy replied.

"Too bad."

Keith eased the car onto the exit, he knew it well. It snaked to the right then back to the left before it intersected with the access road.

He checked the speedometer, he was right at forty and then gunned the engine into the first curve.

"What the..." Tommy grabbed for his gun. Too late.

Keith kept the wheel straight and drove through the turn, planting the car into a telephone pole.

Keith was overcome with the whiteness of the airbag and the jolt of the impact. His body rushed forward then was repelled back all in an instant.

Tommy didn't fare as well. No airbag deployed on his side and he hit the dash hard before crashing through the windshield. Game, set, match.

The airbag slowly deflated as Keith shook off the impact. He reached for his bag and found it. He had some trouble opening the door as the metal frame was bent. He was finally out.

Tommy had been thrown clear from the wreck and Keith walked over to him. There was no movement, his face was bloody and he did not look like he was breathing. He considered feeling for a pulse or calling an ambulance, but every minute he wasted on Tommy was a minute less he had for the senator.

He made his choice.

chapter 36

Alex had watched the events unfold from the balcony of the condo that overlooked Townsend's Inlet. She could see everything on both the Avalon and Sea Isle sides. She and Tommy would have a front row seat for the fireworks.

She had watched with some curiosity as the police and press had discovered Jacob's body. He had washed up on the Sea Isle side. She hadn't bothered to weigh the body down. She wanted the police to be busy when the dredger blew. The more confusion, the better.

The June morning air was cold coming off the ocean and the sun had yet to take command of the day. She rubbed her legs in an attempt to warm up. She held her coffee mug close to her chest.

She checked her watch and it was twenty minutes to fireworks. Tommy would be there any minute and she knew he wouldn't miss this for the world.

Keith ran as fast as his legs would take him down the access road that led into Avalon. He was a half-mile from the accident when he got an idea. He made a left onto the dirt road that led to the building with the satellite dish and TV 39 sign on its side. He only had about twenty minutes.

Once at the building, he burst through the door and found himself in a lobby that reminded him of a doctor's waiting room. The room was complete with outdated magazines, water cooler, seashell wallpaper and dime a dozen sunset art.

He was greeted by the station manager, Jim.

"May I help you?" Jim said.

Keith was bent over, panting and sweating. "I need to see Donna Van Ness."

"Ms. Van Ness is on assignment. Can I help you?"

"I know where Senator Stephenson is," Keith blurted.

"Is that so? And I suppose you were on the grassy knoll in '63?" Jim thought that was clever.

Keith got upright and was a full head taller than the man. He gave him a nasty glare and went to the water cooler for a drink and to calm down.

Jim folded his arms and tapped the floor with his foot. "We get lunatics in here all the time claiming all sorts of things. People down here spend too much time in the sun, if you ask me. If you say you know where he is, then prove it."

Keith dug in his backpack and pulled out his recorder. It had not been damaged in the crash. He rewound the tape a bit and then handed it to the man. "Listen."

Keith had found the point where Tommy was going through how they planned to load the senator on the dredger. After about thirty seconds, Keith grabbed the recorder out of the man's hand.

"It's all here. Everything. The bad guy is sitting at exit 13 in a pool of blood. I may have killed two people this week and may make it three if you don't get me in a car and to the bay."

Jim considered what he had heard.

Keith then pulled out the manila envelope. "I have more details in here. It's your story if you get me to my boat."

For an instant Jim didn't know what to do. Then, in a flash, he was inspired. "Let's go. I'll call Donna from the car."

The old bronze car kicked up dirt as Jim floored it out to the access road. Keith was in the passenger seat and took out his phone. He dialed his shore house and got the machine. "Come on Eddie, I know you're there." He dialed again, and got the machine again. On the third try, someone picked up.

"Who the hell is this?" a groggy voice answered.

"Eddie, it's Keith."

"Go away, man. I'm sleeping," Ed responded.

"Eddie, I need you to get up and get the boat started."

"No way. It's too early to ski."

"Eddie, listen to me closely. You know the senator that was kidnapped? I know where he is. He is on the dredger in the inlet. I want to go get him. Understand?"

"That's bullshit. You can do better than that."

"Okay, Ed. I have known you for fifteen years. Would I try to get you out of bed before noon if it wasn't important?" Keith asked.

Silence. "Wow. You're serious."

"Very," Keith insisted.

"Alright, man. I'll get the boat going. Where are you?" Ed said, clearing the cobwebs.

"Just hit Ocean Drive. Be there in two minutes."

Jim was on the phone with the Coast Guard and they were explaining to him how they didn't appreciate hoaxes. Jim hung up and called Donna. He told her to get down to the inlet right away. He told her to look for a boat going toward the dredger. She argued with him and he hung up.

The car sped over the bridge that led back to the bay and was at Keith's summer rental seconds later. Keith jumped out and headed around back to the boat. As promised,

Ed was behind the twenty-two footer and the engine was going, kicking up smoke and water. Keith untied the rope on the dock and jumped in the back.

The boat pulled back and then forward into the bay. Keith went to the front. "Thanks, man."

Ed looked over at him with bloodshot eyes. "Let's make it happen, captain," he said with a salute.

Monty Little had had a dozen jobs since getting out of prison, but this was his favorite. He liked the little beach towns and working on the water. He was one of the crew that assembled the pipes on the beach used for transporting the pumped sand. It was honest work and kept him out of trouble long enough to get his SCUBA certification. He wanted to someday do underwater welding. It was dangerous, but the pay was great.

He had positioned himself on the northeast corner of the dredger and watched the scene on the beach. Cops, reporters, dead guy. The reporters had gone and now all that was left were the cops and the dead guy. It was almost as exciting as the late night delivery of the machine parts that he had stowed down below. The woman that drove that boat caught his attention. It was like seeing a mermaid.

The dredger had been down for a day, mechanical failure was the prognosis. He had volunteered to take the night watch, like anyone was going to steal this boat, he reasoned. The extra pay would buy him some more beers in town. He'd be off at noon and ready to go.

On the beach the coroner was now taking the body away. *Poor guy*, Monty thought. He had called it in, spotting the body in the darkness. At first he thought it was a drunk who fell asleep on the beach, but when it didn't move as the tide came in, he figured it couldn't hurt to let someone know.

It had been a busy morning. Donna and Scooter pulled up in the van and parked near the bridge. Back to the inlet. They had covered the floater and then were called to cover a Coast Guard rescue at the south end of Stone Harbor. They had made good time back.

Scooter hoisted the gear onto his shoulder and followed Donna over the sea wall and onto the beach. "What is Jim talking about?" she said as she looked the inlet over.

"Over there." Scooter pointed to a boat with two men in it. It was on the west side of the bridge but was heading toward the dredger. Scooter angled for a better shot and zoomed in. There was a tall blonde guy driving the boat and a light haired guy in a wet suit in the back.

"This better be good," Donna said as she checked her appearance in her compact.

The ride from 21st Street out to the inlet took less time than normal as Ed ignored the NO WAKE signs. Keith had taken the time to explain what he thought he knew to Ed.

He told him about the explosives. Somehow, he knew Ed wasn't getting the gravity of the situation.

Keith had changed into a wet suit, an 8MM shorty he used for water skiing in the cold bay. He had a feeling he would be spending some time in the water.

Alex had been given one instruction if things went wrong: make sure Stephenson does not get off that boat alive. And it looked like things were going bad.

Alex had watched as the news crew pulled up and climbed the sea wall. They were filming a boat headed for the dredger. Through the scope of her high powered rifle she saw the reporter point to the boat as it got closer.

On top of that, Tommy was late. He was never late.

She stood just inside the sliding door that separated the living area from the balcony. She focused her scope on the boat that was on its way to the dredger. The boat disappeared behind the bridge for a few seconds and she looked up to get a better overall view. Then the boat popped out on the other side and she went back to the scope.

"Calm, calm," she whispered to herself. She took a deep breath and moved onto the balcony. She knelt on one knee and used the rail to steady her aim.

Her focus was back on the boat. She focused on the driver. It was obvious where they were heading. She had a small window of opportunity before the boat would slide behind the dredger. She began to sweat in the cool air. The driver bobbed up and down with the choppy water.

There. She had the shot. Clean. Finger on the trigger, but then he bobbed again and the shot was gone.

Ed pointed to the news crews on the beach and waved playfully. He had only been up for ten minutes and his blood alcohol was still way above the legal limit.

Behind him, Keith worked on tying the water ski rope around the large, over-inflated inner tube. He didn't have much of a plan, but what he had come up with included getting Ed as far away from the explosion as possible.

He tied a SCUBA weight belt to the rope where the it met the inner tube with the hope that the weight would keep it steady, stop it from drifting. Keith had had visions of doing wreck dives over the summer. He was hoping he didn't become one.

The boat rocked violently, the swells were aggressive, as Ed navigated to the side of the dredge boat.

"Okay, Eddie, here's the plan. I am going to drop the inner tube close to the ladder of the dredger. I want you to pull out as far as you can without pulling the tube any farther. Got it?" he said.

Ed nodded. The reality of the situation was starting to sink in. Keith tossed the tube in the water and dove in after it. The water was freezing.

Monty had watched as the amateur boaters had fiddled around the side of the boat. *They really shouldn't be getting this close*, he thought. Then a guy in a wet suit popped up on his deck.

"Hey, what the hell do you think you are doing?" the crewman demanded.

"Where are the two crates that were delivered this morning?" Keith shot back, staring the man down.

"I said what the hell are you doing?"

Keith looked through him. "And I asked you where the crates were."

Keith won the battle of wills.

"Yeah, two crates, delivered around three. Machine parts for the busted pump. Why?" Monty asked.

Keith ignored the question. "Senator Stephenson is in one of those crates."

"Who's in the other one, Jimmy Hoffa?" Monty responded.

"No. Enough explosives to blow this thing to Atlantic City."

"Bullshit!"

"Are you willing to find out?" Keith pressed

Monty considered that.

"Where are the damn crates?!" Keith yelled.

Monty stood for a second and scratched the tattoo on his left bicep. "One crate is in the engine room."

"The other?!"

"Down in storage, the hold where we keep the pipes."

Keith had to make an educated guess. Explosives would do more damage in the engine room. And Tommy had said the senator would probably drown. "Which one was heavier?"

"The one in the hold," Monty guessed.

"Take me there," Keith demanded.

"What if that's the wrong one?" Monty asked as he led the way.

"If it's the wrong one, it won't matter. We only have a few minutes."

"Shit!" Alex yelled. Being calm went out the window. She could only see a portion of what was happening on the deck of the boat as the control house and crane obstructed her view.

She was also aware that Tommy was now very late and knew something had happened to him. The next person she saw on that deck was going down.

"There it is," Monty pointed with the crow bar he had picked up off the deck. They had climbed down into the hold.

Keith checked his watch. There was not much time. He began to sweat. He went to the crate and listened. No sound. No time to waste. Keith took the crow bar from Monty and wedged it between the box frame and lid. The sound of nails squeaking against wood beat the sound of an explosion. He wedged the crow bar in another spot and pushed down. The lid popped up some more. Monty grabbed the side that had popped up and worked it with his hands, Keith went to the top short side of the box and pried again. This time the lid popped off, sending Monty to the metal floor.

And there he was. United States Senator Phillip J. Stephenson.

"Grab his legs!" Keith yelled against the sound of his internal clock.

The two lifted him out of the box and put him on the floor. Monty checked for and found a pulse. "He's alive."

Keith looked over at the ladder that led to the deck. "Any ideas?"

"Get him on my back," Monty grunted.

Keith helped get the senator up on Monty's shoulders. Monty was very compact and muscular. He carried the senator across his shoulders.

"Once we get up there, you got a plan?" Monty said.

"As a matter of fact, I do," Keith replied.

"Great. You go up first and when I get close to the top, lean over and help me get him up. Got it?"

"Got it," Keith nodded.

Keith was up the ten-foot ladder attached to the wall of the hold while Monty hunched, then decided to put the senator over his right shoulder. The weight shifted awkwardly. Monty started up the ladder and made it more than halfway pretty quickly, but seemed to stall. "Shit."

Keith leaned over and grabbed the senator's arms and pulled. It took some of the weight off of Monty and he moved quickly again and was up on the deck.

Then they heard and felt the thud. The metal hull whined and creaked and the boat leaned to the Sea isle side.

They both bent down and picked the senator up, this time they wedged their shoulders under his armpits and carried him. "Into the water. There is an inner tube we can float him on," Keith yelled.

The senator began to make noise as a secondary explosion rocked the boat and sent a fire plume into the air.

Keith and Monty got to the edge of the boat with the senator. Monty could see the tube and the boat it was attached to. "On three. One, two,..."

At three Keith felt a sharp, hot, piercing pain in his free shoulder. It knocked him to his knees as Monty and the senator went airborne, headed toward the inner tube. He felt his shoulder. The wetsuit was torn, he felt blood. He looked over. The pain was unreal. He had been shot. He fell forward, hit his head on the metal deck and rolled into the water.

The impact and the temperature of the water woke the senator up some, enough for him to help Monty get him into the inner tube. The senator sat across the tube looking like a man who fell asleep in his pool floatee.

Monty looked back for Keith and saw him floating face down. He swam through the swells over to him and flipped him over. Keith was out and bleeding.

Monty swam to the tube with Keith under one arm. When he got to the tube he locked his free arm around the tube as best he could and held to Keith with the other.

Ed saw all three on the tube and gunned the engines. The rope went tight and the propeller churned water. The tube began to move and pick up some speed, but they were a heavy load.

The dredger behind them listed to one side and was on fire.

Monty struggled to hold onto Keith and the tube. Keith was bleeding from the shoulder and head. They were no more than twenty yards when yet another explosion sent flames into the air.

"Now that's something," Scooter said from behind the camera.

"I hope you got all that," Donna said fixing her hair.

"I got it all."

"Hello, national news," she said with a smile.

Alex threw the rifle across the room. After the first shot, a hit, it had jammed.

This was the worst case scenario and she was losing her cool. She had to get out of there and out of town. She had to find out what had happened to Tommy.

In the cold water of the inlet, Monty's strength gave out and let go of the tube. Without their weight, the boat and tube picked up tremendous speed.

Ed intentionally beached the boat right in front of Donna and the camera. He was a safe two hundred yards from the smoldering and sinking vessel. He went to pull the rope in and realized he was two bodies short.

Monty lost Keith momentarily in the choppy water, then got him back and flipped him over. Keith was not breathing. Monty locked his arm around Keith's good one and began to give him in-water mouth-to-mouth. He had been trained to perform this maneuver in SCUBA classes and was required to know it to work on the boat. The idea was to keep water out of the mouth and lungs while resuscitating the victim. Getting to shore was secondary.

On the beach, Ed pulled the senator off the tube and made sure he was breathing. Then Ed pushed the boat back into the water and he went for his friend.

"He's not breathing," Monty yelled as Ed pulled beside them. Ed leaned over the side of the boat and lifted Keith in with Monty pushing up from beneath.

Ed tried to clear Keith's airway, but was not a hundred percent sure what to do. He gave way to Monty once he climbed in the boat. Monty put pressure on the shoulder wound first, then went back to CPR. Ed gunned the engine and headed for the beach.

"Anything?" Ed yelled back.

"Not yet," Monty screamed in between breaths. Keith was not responding. The smoky dredger creaked and whined behind them. The Avalon emergency siren wailed.

Ed beached the boat again and he and Monty got Keith onto the beach. EMT's had shown up and Ed and Monty let them do their work. Keith was put on a stretcher and loaded into an ambulance while they looked on.

Scooter filmed the events while Donna gave shocked commentary.

The ambulance pulled away in a flash of light and cry of the siren.

Ed used Monty to balance himself and dropped to one knee. He watched the dredger catch fire and burn, then turned to watch the ambulance speed across the bridge.

Ed looked up at Monty. "What just happened?"

chapter 37

Donna sat calmly in front of the camera. Her delivery had been perfect throughout the hour and though she knew it was the end of the summer and that the real anchors would come back next week and that only a third of the regular audience was watching the news magazine show, she couldn't help but think that this would lead to something big.

The red light went on and she was back. "Finally tonight, some closure on the Stephenson kidnapping case. As we approach the end of a summer that started with the senator from Pennsylvania being abducted and held hostage for seven days, we end with news on some of the men involved.

"First, Danny 'Mad Dog' Sullivan lost his appeal today for a stay of execution based on his lawyer's claim that the nervous breakdown that Sullivan suffered when he was not released from prison has left him mentally incompetent. A date for Sullivan's execution has not yet been set.

"Next, the man accused of paying to have Stephenson killed, former CEO of National Merchandising, Charles Jones, has avoided the death penalty by pleading down to a life sentence with no parole for his involvement in the kidnapping plot. He is also under indictment in New York for the murder for hire of his predecessor, Stanley Jorgensen. New York is awaiting extradition.

"And this week, the senator himself was not able to garner enough votes for his bill that would restrict trade with China. The vote went 57-43 against. Stephenson says he plans to continue the fight.

"And finally, some good news. Keith Garrity, the young man who saved the senator's life in a daring rescue and then spent the next two weeks in a coma fighting for his life, has signed a book deal. The book which is due out this Christmas deals with his involvement in the kidnapping as well as other social issues."

Donna smiled. She had nailed it. "Well, that is all we have this evening. I hope you enjoy your holiday weekend. This is Donna Van Ness and this has been *Headlines*."

Only a few people in the Princeton Bar and Grill had paid attention to the broadcast. After all, it was the Thursday night before Labor Day weekend and it was the last karoake Thursday of the summer. The bartender switched the set over to the Phillies game.

Keith sat at the far bar, the one closest to the package goods area. On stage he watched in horror as Ed and Howard butchered "Paradise by the Dashboard Light." It was particularly funny, because they couldn't decide who would sing the male and/or female parts.

He sipped on his first beer since what he and his friends referred to as 'the incident' and scanned the crowd. He was finally off the pain pills and though he would never be able to throw a 90 MPH fastball, his shoulder was almost back to normal. The only permanent scar was a one half-inch red line right below his hairline on his right forehead. And the blonde hair had almost grown completely out.

His housemates had all come down a day early to celebrate his re-entry into society, but he kept them at arms length, at least he would for another half hour. The stool next to him was empty and judging by the time, she wasn't going to show. Donna did not report on that part of the story.

Donna had not been so forthcoming about her relationship with Agent Thompson. Thompson was going to trial for his role in the kidnapping as well as for trying to suffocate Keith as he laid in a coma in his hospital bed. Thompson had believed that Keith was the only link to him and the kidnapping. He hadn't known about the documentation that Tommy had collected.

Keith still had nightmares about the last moments with Tommy. The crash, the blood. Tommy had died so that Keith could save the man he was trying to kill. While it seemed like a fair trade, it still troubled Keith.

"Paradise" was mercifully over and the crowd clapped and hollered, but Ed stayed on stage. He had become a local hero in Avalon. He was the guy that drove the boat, the guy that waved the whole time, the guy on camera. Rumor had it that he hadn't bought a beer all summer, that his money was no good in this town.

"I'd like to dedicate this one to my boyfriend, Keith," Ed said seriously. Karen, his girlfriend, screamed at him to sit down. The bar roared.

Keith smiled and noticed that a beautiful young lady from across the bar had been staring at him on and off. She was a knock out. They made eye contact and she smiled.

Ed was in rare form and was cheered wildly. Keith clapped and yelled and Ed blew him a kiss.

Keith then watched as the girl made her way over to him. She stood next to him and asked, "Is this seat taken?"

There was no clever reply, she was gorgeous. "No, it's not."

She sat and put her beer on the bar. She was tall and lean and put curves in the dress she was wearing that the fabric seemed ill equipped to deal with.

The bartender came over to her. "Can I get you another?" he said to the girl.

"Sure, another light beer and him?" she replied.

The bartender stared at Keith and he shrugged. "I'll get the beer, but you are on your own with him."

Keith spun to face her. "Do I know you from somewhere?"

"I don't think so," she answered.

"Do you know me?"

"Not really. But I think you're cute."

"Really?" Keith was pleasantly surprised.

"Well, not cute. Sexy is better," she said.

Keith took a long gulp from his beer. This was too good to be true.

"Listen. I am not usually this forward. But, my friends are having a little party, house on the beach, the whole deal. Problem is they are all couples and I need a date."

"So I'm a charity case?" Keith replied.

She leaned over and kissed him, moving her hands down his chest to his groin. He surrendered.

"Does that feel like charity?" she whispered into his ear.

"None that I give to."

"So, my car is out back. What do you say?" she said as she moved closer.

Keith drank the last of his beer. "Nothing holding me here. I just have to visit the men's room and I'll be right back."

Keith got up and walked quickly to the men's room. He returned a few minutes later. Ed was back on stage killing another classic.

Keith sat back down and turned to the girl. "Would you mind if I watched him finish? He's a friend of mine."

"Oh, no problem. Hey, isn't he that guy that drove the boat on that videotape of that rescue?" she asked.

"That's him," Keith said with authority.

"Wow. I was glued to my set that whole week. Watched the news non-stop."

"Yeah, that week was kind of a blur for me."

The two sat as Ed finished. Keith hopped down off the stool and put his hand out for the girl. They walked out the back and she led him by the hand to a secluded spot between the bar and the adjoining restaurant.

"I know who you are," she said as she draped her arms over him and started to kiss his neck.

"Who's that?" Keith said, playing along.

"You were the other guy in the boat. The one who got shot." She moved one hand to the button on his shorts.

"That would be me."

"I remember that day," she continued to kiss him and his neck, then his lips, then back to his neck. Her free hand worked on his shorts. "I lost my boyfriend that day."

"Oh, shit. I'm so sorry. Car accidents are such an awful way to go. I should have been more careful," Keith said, now completely sure who she was.

She stopped kissing him and jumped back. "How did you know?"

"Come on, Alex. It's Alex, isn't it? I'm not this stupid or this easy," he said coldly.

"Go to hell." She reached under her dress to her thigh and pulled out a stiletto. Her eyes lit up and she lunged at him.

Keith blocked her lunge forearm to forearm, knocking the knife from her hand, coming face to face with her. She head butted him and knocked him back to the wall.

Her foot came from nowhere and just missed his chin. The momentum from the missed kick put her off balance. Keith gave her a sidekick to the stomach and dropped her to her knees.

Though he was fighting for his life, it flashed to him that he was hitting a girl. That pause resulted in a fist to the groin that dropped him to the ground, reeling in pain, down on all fours.

Alex felt for her knife on the ground, found it and got to her feet. She straddled Keith like a horse, grabbed a hand full of hair and pulled his head back. She pressed the blade against his neck. "Goodnight, Keith."

"Freeze!" Agent Jackson yelled and Alex turned to look at the man with the gun. Keith swung his elbow up violently, catching her in the ribs. She fell backward off of him, whacking her head on the cement. She was knocked cold.

"Where were you?" Keith gasped, struggling to get up.

"Got here as fast as I could. The Windrift is not exactly around the corner. Anyway, I could hardly make out what you were saying. What was that in the background? Sounded like a stuck pig," Jackson commented.

Jackson moved over to the woman and kicked the knife out of her hand. He had wanted to keep a close eye on Keith once he got back into real life. He had a feeling that Tommy's girl would come after him based on the senator's description of her behavior.

"I called from the pay phone near the bathroom. And that squealing was Ed. Karoake night," Keith explained.

"Well, I'm just glad I got here when I did."

"Come on. I had her," Keith said.

"Bullshit."

"Look, can you handle this from here, big man? I have some friends to see."

"Go. Go before I have to bail you out again," Jackson replied.

Keith shook the agent's hand and walked back to the bar as Jackson cuffed Alex and called for back up.

Keith was back at his stool alone, not because he wanted to be, but because everyone he knew was on stage.

"Sorry I'm late," a voice came from behind him.

Keith swiveled to see Denise standing there looking so beautiful.

"I didn't think you were going to show," he said.

"Neither did I. It took you long enough to call me," Denise said calmly.

"I know. But the FBI thought I could still be in danger. I didn't want to get you involved until this was all cleared up."

"Honest?" she asked.

"Yes, honest. I thought about you everyday. Well, everyday that I was conscious," Keith explained

"I was worried about you, you know. When your name was mentioned on the news, I knew you hadn't told me everything." Her eyes met his.

Keith looked for the right words and settled on the truth. It was what he was best at.

"I know. I just couldn't do it," he admitted.

"But you did. The other day I found the file you left on my computer. You wanted to tell me the truth, but I know now you couldn't."

"I'm sorry, Denise."

"Oh just shut up and kiss me."

The two locked in a kiss and the bartender did a double take. They moved back from each other and sat in a comfortable silence.

"My book is going to be published. The last conversation with Tommy was the clincher," Keith said in a modest tone.

"You're kidding? That's great. I am so proud of you."

Keith smiled and reached down for her hand.

"Hey, how about we get out of here. Maybe take a walk on the beach?" Keith said as he held her hand tightly.

"I would settle for the parking lot."

Keith laughed inwardly and smiled. "How about we start with the beach?"

THE END